COLOSSUS

A SCI-FI POLICE PROCEDURAL NOVEL

SIU BOOK 1

TOBY NEIGHBORS

Colossus: A Sci-Fi Police Procedural Novel

Copyright © 2025 by Toby Neighbors

ISBN: 978-1-968189-17-4 eBook

978-1-968189-18-1 Print

Mythic Adventure Publishing, LLC

Idaho, USA

"Honesty" is such a lonely word
    Everyone is so untrue
    Honesty is hardly ever heard
    And mostly what I need from you

HONESTY - BILLY JOEL

CHAPTER 1

SERGEANT SAWYER FLINT had been in the Metro Police Department for twenty-two years and, in all that time, he had never wanted to kill a man more than he did as he sat in the civil court proceeding and listened to the lies his ex-wife's lawyer made about him. Flint was no saint, and he worked a high-stress job that often times took a toll on his personal life. But he was not the monster his ex-wife and her lawyer were making him out to be.

When the hearing ended, Flint walked out of the courthouse a very poor man. He had just been ordered to pay his wife half of his salary and to sign over to her half of his pension. But it was not his first trip down the alimony highway. He was, what his friends in the police force called, a two-time loser. On the other hand, as long as he could afford to make his rent and feed himself, he would be okay. His entire life was policing and he loved the job. Some cops retired after twenty, although Flint would work until they kicked him out of the building and took away his badge.

He settled into his hovercar, a standard-issue government vehicle that was parked in the courthouse parking complex. It lifted off the ground at the touch of a button and a woman's voice asked him for the destination.

"Precinct 31," he said.

"Determining route. Do you have a preference?" the woman's voice said as a hologram map of the Upper Eastern Megalopolis appeared. There were three route options lit across the map in different colors.

"Let's do yellow," he said.

"Very good, Sergeant. Beginning route to Metro Police Precinct 31 on Wabash Avenue," the car's computerized navigation and control system replied.

Flint leaned back in his seat and pulled out his phone. There were always messages, memos or emails to reply to and he needed something for his hands to do. The temptation to pull out a vape pen was hard to resist when he wasn't busy. It helped to have something else in his hands. He had quit smoking four times and started smoking five times. He didn't like having bad habits, but he worked long, sometimes grueling hours, lots of nights, subsisting on bad coffee and fast food. When he did have a moment of relative peace and quiet, a smoke helped him settle down and live in the moment, as the shrinks liked to say.

He had the usual number of service-related announcements. There were always BOLOs going out and suspects that law enforcement officers were to be aware of. A third of all arrests were made while suspects were breaking a different law, only for it to be discovered that they were wanted in connection with another crime. Flint took his time with each such announcement. They didn't stay in his brain more than a single shift, but at the start of every workday, and sometimes in between calls, he checked the memos.

There were emails, too. Most were simple requests or reminders to take care of some administrative task that was also part of his job. There was always busywork, and Flint understood that in every police force, there were two kinds of cops. The first loved the streets. They wanted to be out, on patrol, looking for suspects and stopping crimes in progress. It didn't matter the call or the danger; they were men and women of action who merely tolerated the administrative burdens of being a police officer. The second kind of cop was the opposite of the first; they loved the idea of being a law enforcement official, but they found a way to stay behind a desk most days. They were the cogs in the bureaucratic machine, moving files along the electronic pathways, reinforcing rules onto other cops and creating tasks that kept them busy off the streets. Flint knew some of those kinds of people were needed, yet he would have bet his badge they could be reduced by two-thirds and still the force would go on, perhaps even more smoothly than before.

When he reached the station, he congratulated himself on having left his vape pen in the hidden interior pocket of his coat and got out of his hovercar less than a block from the police station. There were parts of the metropolis that spanned the East Coast of North America that rarely saw improvements. Anywhere near a police precinct was rarely ever clean or modern. No one wanted to live in the shadow of the law and there were always people in need crowding the sidewalks. Next to Precinct 31 was a homeless shelter, an old church that hadn't been in use for over a decade and a community center. The rest of the block was filled with storefront bail bondsmen. Flint knew career criminals who had utilized every single bond establishment.

"Flint!" a loud voice greeted him as he entered the busy precinct. "Loudin wants to see you. ASAP," the desk sergeant said.

"Thanks, Charlie," Flint replied as his shoulders sagged a little. Loudin was a lieutenant whose main job was staffing. He hired all the administrative people and put on recruiting fairs in communities, high schools and college campuses. Flint didn't want to get sucked into that world. Not that there was anything wrong with recruiting new police, it was a vital task. The Metro force had over a hundred thousand officers, with cops retiring every single day. Keeping their numbers up and crime down was always a priority.

Flint bypassed the hall that led to his section of the station. He had been a major crimes investigator for over ten years. It was all he ever wanted to be. When he walked into a crime scene, the other officers stepped back and deferred to his experience. Flint didn't need people to bow and scrape. He didn't care about accolades or medals. Rank was merely an indication of experience and proficiency in his opinion. And while most cops his age had either taken the early retirement option or taken the lieutenant's exam, Flint preferred to work the streets.

He climbed the stairs up to the third floor and found Lieutenant Bradley Loudin's office. The door was open and Flint leaned against the jamb until Loudin looked up and waved him to a seat.

"Hey, thanks for coming up," the lieutenant said. "How'd it go in court?"

"I didn't kill anyone, but I thought about it long and hard."

"That bad?"

"Truth and justice are not to be found in the civil courts," Flint said. "The judge ordered me to fork over half my salary and pension to my ex-wife. Can you believe it? She cheats on me, runs off and I get stuck with the bill."

"It's a hell of a thing, man, I'm sorry," Loudin said, leaning back in his chair and smiling bigger than he should have. Flint suddenly felt like he had walked straight into a trap. "What would you say if I could change all of that?"

"I'd say we better be careful that we don't say anything that can be used against us in a court of law."

Loudin laughed. It was loud, and maybe a little obnoxious, but Flint smiled at his own joke.

"Look, I just got a request for a special unit, and I'm looking for someone like yourself to head it up. Compensation is what you're making now, but it includes housing and meal vouchers. Plus, you can retire outside of this jurisdiction and avoid all the hassle of paying your ex."

"How's that legal?" Flint asked.

"Let's just say it's way, way, outside our jurisdiction."

CHAPTER 2

SECUNDO WAS the first fertile world that humanity had discovered. It was six light-years away from Earth, and while no life had been found on Secundo, humanity had begun to seed that world. Everything flourished on Secundo, including the people who were living there. And a massive ship had been built to transport people to the new world. A few thousand wasn't enough. An international group had spent a decade building a ship that could accommodate half a million people, including passengers and crew. There was no shortage of people eager to make the trip. Every nation on Earth was given a set number of passenger slots. The first ten percent of cabins were sold to wealthy individuals who would travel in a more posh section of the ship. The next fifteen percent was earmarked for specialized craftsmen and those considered experts in their fields. The other seventy-five percent were dolled out via lottery.

Flint hadn't bothered to apply for the lottery. Everyone he knew, if they were being honest, wanted to go to Secundo. Earth had become an exclusionist nightmare. Governments all over the world had seized all the land and relegated humanity to fifteen-minute cities. Flint, being a law enforcement professional, was one of the few people with privileges to travel anywhere within the megapolis that spanned the entire east coast of North America. But most people lived in huge high-rise apartment complexes with grocery stores, home goods, dining and entertainment on the lower levels of their buildings. Most worked from home. Flint knew people who were born, lived their entire lives and died in the same apartment complex. The idea of an open world where you could travel wherever you wanted, do what you wanted, work how you wanted and be with whoever you wanted was a dream for most people. Billions of people applied for the lottery. Only three hundred thousand were chosen. The other seventy-five thousand people would be workers on the enormous vessel, which would need everything from maintenance crews to service industry professionals ... and even security officers. Plenty of good police had applied for a minuscule shot at getting on board, but Flint was not a believer in luck and he wasn't looking for an escape. Maybe one day, when he was too old to work in law enforcement and he had at least dipped his toe into the private sector of security work, he might try. But by then, he would almost certainly be too old. There were strict age limits and health requirements for getting on board.

The ship's name was *Colossus* and she was all of that. In fact, the ship was essentially a city in space. It had taken ten years of continuous construction, and another two of safety testing and upgrades, but it was almost ready to start taking passengers on board. The crew and workers had already been shuttled up.

"You know Ben Heath," Lieutenant Loudin asked.

"He's good police," Flint said.

"He is. He won the lottery and was assigned to lead an elite team of officers in a special investigation unit."

"SIU," Flint said. "Heard of that too."

"Did you hear their shuttle had an issue. They tried to abort, but the shuttle crashed. Ben was killed, two members of his SIU team as well. The other two were hurt in the crash. They'll need extensive medical treatment. And that leaves me with a problem and you with an opportunity."

"What are you getting at, Lieutenant?"

"I've met with the Commissioner. We put together a short list of replacement candidates. You're at the top of that list, Sergeant. We want you to take Ben Heath's place, select a team, and serve on the Colossus."

Flint leaned back in his chair. He wasn't taken completely by surprise very often and he had never seriously considered leaving Earth. Like everyone else, he had seen the videos and documentaries about Secundo. It wasn't hard to imagine what life could be like on a world where a person could roam through forests and wade into rivers. It seemed like paradise, but there had to be a catch. There was always a catch.

"You want me?" Flint asked.

"You've got the experience we need. No family to leave behind. Hell, Flint, you're even between partners."

It was true. His last partner had taken early retirement and he was flying solo. In fact, he only had two open cases and he could easily pass them off. It was also exciting to think about leading his own team. Special Investigation teams had full authority to step in and take charge of any scene, any crime. They had oversight but also autonomy. It was something he had always hoped he might be able to do one day.

"And what's the catch?" Flint asked.

"No catch. We need someone ASAP. You just passed your annual physical last month. We'll need you to read up on spacecraft regulations for security personnel and select a team. We need to get you on that ship as soon as we possibly can."

"I pick my team?"

"Each one has to be cleared, but ... yeah. You pick 'em and then get on a shuttle."

"I don't know if I can get my belongings sorted in time," Flint said. "Vanessa still has stuff in my apartment."

"This is a special assignment, Sawyer. You basically take one bag of clothes and one suitcase's worth of belongings that will be stowed for you during the trip. You get that on the other side. Everything else is provided for you. You'll have a private berth, meal vouchers and plenty of work to keep you busy. It takes two years to reach Secundo. Once you're there, you can decide if you want to stay or come back for another tour on the Colossus."

"And my ex?"

"Once you sign on, the department will offer her a settlement."

"She might not agree."

"She will," he said. "We can be very persuasive when we need to be."

"I keep my salary?"

"It'll be directly deposited into your account on the ship, just the same as normal. You'll need to sign a form to move your money from your local bank account to a shipboard account, but it's as easy as that."

"And my pension?"

"Will follow you. There is nothing to lose in the situation. The only question is, do you want to go?"

He knew the answer immediately, but still felt a bit leery. Nothing had ever come easy to him. But, after a moment's reflection, he realized he didn't care. He didn't care about the money or what he was leaving behind. The chance to lead his own Special Investigation team was worth whatever he had to give up.

"I'm your man," Flint said.

A grin of relief nearly split Loudin's face. "Oh, man, you had me worried for a minute, detective."

"How much time do I have?"

"Shuttle leaves tomorrow night at twenty-one hundred hours. Here's a list of everything you need to do. Anything else is up to you."

"How big will my team be?"

"You and four others," Loudin said. "And one should be a K-9 specialist."

"Got it," Flint said, already thinking of a few people he wanted to approach. "Any restrictions on who I can bring along?"

"You've got candidates in mind?"

"A few."

"Give me their names, and I'll clear them. Not everyone's eligible, you know. There's no spare room for families. They need to be single, in good health, with no open IAD investigations."

"Got it," Flint said. "Let's start with Becky Nash."

CHAPTER 3

BECKY NASH HAD DONE the work — long hours sifting through Delmont Finnegan's social media. Del was wanted for robbery, assault and possession of an unregistered firearm. There was also a bench warrant for failure to appear before a circuit court judge. He had been on the run for over a year, somehow evading the authorities at every turn. She had no doubt the people around Del were helping him. Some were friends, some were family, but most were just people who thought resisting the authorities was a moral good.

Becky didn't blame them. She grew up with people who espoused such opinions. Many of her own family had disowned her when she joined the police academy. Although Becky had known from a very young age that she wanted to be a police officer. She had an inquisitive mind and a desire to help others. She was also a firm believer that justice would and could be served if the people dispensing it were good. To make a difference, one just had to get involved.

She had served as a patrol officer for six years before being called up to the Narco squad. A year of busting low-level dealers had led to her current job with the fugitive task force. There was something very satisfying to Becky about tracking down wanted fugitives. Most - like Delmont Finnegan - deserved to be in custody, not roaming the streets or terrorizing the innocent. That's why Becky had spent the last six hours in a laundromat washing and drying the same set of clothes while she watched the back alley across the street. It was the rear entrance and exit to the Piper's Club, where up-and-coming performers were known to hang out after gigs. Delmont was seen with a young rapper who went by the name Lect Trick, a fact Becky had learned by looking through a lot of old photos and videos on the internet and social media platforms. It seemed so many young criminals just couldn't help but share their secrets with the world online. After seeing Del with the rapper in several posts, she ran facial recognition on the man. His real name was Billy Evans and he had a short record. It was mostly petty crimes such as loitering after hours or criminal mischief, but it was enough of a file that his alias was listed. When she ran Lect Trick through social media, she discovered his act. It wasn't to her taste, but more importantly, she discovered that he was performing at the Piper that night, which was why she was at the laundromat watching the club.

Her phone rang and she checked it. It was Sawyer Flint. She had worked a case or two with him in her Narco days. She had helped him run down a thug who had murdered two rival gang members and then disappeared from the grid. In most places, there were cameras that recorded everyone and everything happening around them. That video was fed into the Metro Police AI, which was supposed to catalog and keep tabs on anyone breaking the law or anyone wanted by law enforcement. But while interfering with the surveillance equipment carried a heavy criminal penalty, ingenious ways had been discovered to thwart it. A device could be made with regular D batteries that sent enough current through a lamp post or street sign that would scramble the cameras. There were also easy-to-make signal jammers that could be carried on a person's body that created enough static on the video to thwart the AI program. Crews of city maintenance workers spent all day, every day, replacing the cameras only to have them ruined again, often within minutes of a new install. And so, many places never had their cameras replaced. It was a fine system in theory, if you could get past the invasion of privacy that came with knowing everything you did was recorded and observed by the government. But Becky knew automated systems would never replace good old-fashioned police work carried out by real cops.

She hit the button on her phone to send Sawyer to voicemail. Whatever he wanted from her, she felt certain it could wait. And almost as soon as she set the phone down, the rear exit to the Piper's Club opened, and out walked her suspect. He was surrounded by several associates, both men and women. Lect Trick came out too with an even bigger entourage. All Becky needed was a little backup and her day would end with a high-profile collar that would look stellar on her record.

When she picked up her phone, it rang before she could make the call. It was Sawyer again. He must really need something, she thought, but then sent him to voicemail again and called the nearest precinct. The groups from the club lingered in the alley. The far end was crowded with garbage and Becky was a patient hunter. Two patrol cars glided in from either side of the street, neither making any noise. Becky smiled, got to her feet, and went out to make the arrest.

"You Officer Nash?" one of the patrolmen asked.

"In the flesh," she said. "Spread out behind me. Watch for weapons. Delmont's known to carry. His friends might have weapons too."

"Where do you want us?" asked the other pair of patrol officers as they approached the alley.

"Visible," Becky said. "When I give the signal, hit your blue lights remotely. A little shock and awe never hurt in a situation like this."

She entered the alley with four patrol officers in uniform behind her. Becky drew her service weapon from the concealed carry holster that tucked into the front of her blue jeans at the waist. She didn't know if she would need it, but it never hurt to let a suspect see that she was armed and ready.

"Delmont Finnegan!" she shouted.

There was music throbbing from the club and nearly twenty people talking in the alley. Heads turned, conversations were cut short and eyes narrowed. A few people looked around, trying to find a fast way out of the alley, but there was none. The far end was blocked by two dumpsters and bags of trash. A person could run that way, but there was no guarantee they could get through. Going back into the club was a better option, but the rear door opened onto a narrow hallway. If more than a few people ran for it, those unfortunate enough not to reach it first would be left exposed.

Becky knew what that meant in the minds of most people living on the fringe of civilized society. She had rules of engagement and couldn't fire her weapon without cause or in a reckless manner where innocents were likely to get caught in her crossfire. But most people believed the lies about rogue cops who shot first and didn't care who died. Becky wasn't there to kill anyone and she wasn't interested in Delmont's associates. They might be wanted for all sorts of crimes, but she only wanted Del.

"Delmont, there's no place left to run," Becky said. "Get on your knees and place your hands on top of your head."

That got a reaction from the crowd. Becky was barking orders, but it was as if the onlookers had been physically assaulted.

"I'm not here for anyone else," Becky said. "Just Del. The rest of you can walk away right now."

"Ain't nobody going anywhere," Delmont shouted. "They's five of you and a lot more of us."

"That may be how it looks to you, Delmont, but the truth is we have people all around the club and both ends of the alley. Even if you run, you won't get far. And if you do something stupid..."

She had her weapon pointed just above Del's head. They were forty feet apart. His hands were on his hips.

"I can't get caught up in nothin', Del," Lect Trick said. "I got agents coming to the next show."

"Yeah, I feel ya, dog," Del said. "Go on back inside. I got this."

The rapper didn't hesitate. He hurried toward the club and his entourage followed. Even a few of the people who had come out into the alley with Del left him and went back inside.

"You're under arrest, Del," Becky said. "Don't make things worse than they need to be. Get down on your knees."

"For a fine shorty like you, I would be happy to, under different circumstances, baby."

"Hands on the top of your head."

"Can't do it," he said.

Had he run the other way, he might have escaped. Becky was fast, but chasing down a full-grown man on the run for his freedom was never easy. But Del didn't flee. Instead, he charged right at Becky. She could have shot him. The patrol officers would have agreed that Del was threatening her and she would have been justified in putting him down. Yet she didn't shoot. Not that she was hesitant to use her firearm when the need arose, but she wasn't afraid of Del Finnigan. Instead, she let him get close, then slid to the side and kicked his foot as he tried to run past her.

Del went down hard on the dirty pavement and a patrol officer pounced onto his back. The other people were watching, wide-eyed. A few had even pulled out their phones to film the arrest.

"Stop moving!" the patrol officer shouted. "Give me your hands! Give me your hands!"

Becky stepped close as the patrolman handcuffed her fugitive. "Delmont Finnigan, you are under arrest." She pulled out her Miranda card and read him his rights. She could have quoted them from memory, but the regulations said she had to read them to him. Which she did. "Do you understand these rights as I have read them to you?"

He didn't respond. The patrolmen pulled Del to his feet and he glared at her, but didn't resist. She took his silence as him practicing his right to avoid self-incrimination.

"Take him in and start booking him. I'll be there to sign off. Good work, officers."

The other cops smiled. One set led Del away, the other returned to the car, where they would radio in that they were no longer assisting Becky and back on regular patrol. Becky returned to the laundromat. She got her clothes from the dryer and checked her phone. She had missed two more calls from Sawyer Flint. Whatever he wanted had to be important, she decided to call him back on her way to the precinct.

CHAPTER 4

"IT'S about time you answered your phone," he said.

"I was in the middle of a bust," she explained. "What's so urgent?"

"I need to ask you some questions."

"Do I need my union rep?"

"No," Flint said. "You seeing anyone... romantically?"

"I don't date cops, Flint. You know this."

"I'm not hitting on you, Becky. Answer the question."

"I'm married to the job."

"That a no?"

"Correct. I am not seeing anyone romantically, as depressing as that is."

"You might change your mind," Flint told her.

"I'm flattered, Sawyer, but you're twice my age."

That wasn't exactly true, but he was too old to date a woman still in her twenties. Flint enjoyed the company of women, which is why he had been married twice. But he worked a lot, didn't make much money, and had trouble connecting with women outside of the physical. They always seemed to want a deeper, more intimate connection.

Deep down inside Sawyer Flint was a cage of horrors that he never let out, even when it cost him his marriages.

"I'm not hitting on you, Becky. I just got called up to work Special Investigations on the *Colossus*. And I'm looking to build my team."

Her mouth went dry. She knew she should say something, but there were no words. Becky Nash had applied for the lottery and put in for security on the massive transport vessel. She had been denied both times.

"I need people I trust, Beck. Good police, willing to do the work. You're at the top of my list, but we leave tomorrow night. You interested?"

She had to work her mouth to get some saliva going and swallowed the lump that was in her throat.

"Hell yeah," she said.

"Good. One down, three to go."

"Who else do you have in mind?"

"Dave Bannon is on board," Flint said. "I'm on my way to see a guy named Logan Keys. You heard of him?"

"No," Becky admitted.

"Meet me at the training center. We can talk to him together."

"On my way. Anyone else?"

"We need a K-9 specialist. Know anyone?"

"As a matter of fact, I do. Jeopardy Bess is like a dog whisperer. Her dog has more busts than anyone I know in Narco division."

"Call her," Flint said. "Find out if there's any reason she shouldn't go. Everyone needs a clean physical, no strikes on their personnel file, no open IAD beefs, that sort of thing. We're looking for single and ready to leave Earth without looking back. You understand?"

"Absolutely," Becky said. "I've got to book my fugitive, and call it in to Detective King in the two-nine. Then I'm hustling to the training center. How come we're in such a rush?"

"The squad assigned to the *Colossus* got taken off the board when their shuttle malfunctioned. They need a replacement team fast. That's us."

"I appreciate the invite, Sawyer. I wanted this all along."

"I remember you talking about it," Flint said. "That's one of the reasons I called."

"What's the other?"

"Trust," he said. "I want people who will have my back. Your friend, is she good police?"

"The best," Becky said. "Likes animals more than people, but she is loyal and extremely capable."

"Good. Call her. See you soon, Beck." The line went dead, and Becky held herself together until she was certain the connection had ended. Then she carefully put the phone in the mount on her dashboard and screamed. It was loud and strangely out of character for the straight-laced policewoman. Once she calmed down, her mind began making a list of things she needed to do. There were more questions than answers, but the only thing that really mattered was that she was leaving Earth.

Becky was not the type of person who hated the government or who rebelled at the idea of those in charge caring more about the planet than the people on it. But, like most people who grew up in a tiny apartment watching her parents struggle to make ends meet, seeing crime run rampant all around them, and most of her friends falling prey to the temptations that perpetuated a broken system. Her friends from school were mostly either addicts, gang bangers, single mothers dependent on social services or dead. So, few had made the ambitious choice to find a way out like she had. Not that Becky was special, in fact, most of the people she had known growing up wouldn't speak to her because she was a police officer. They felt she had betrayed her own family, which was absurd, but she had chosen a different path. The truth was, even with her own apartment, in a better complex than the one she had grown up in and a job she loved, her life was still pretty empty. Her parents had both passed away, her mother from cancer when Becky was nineteen and still in the police academy. Her father died a few years later from a drug overdose. He had never gotten over the loss of his wife and, while he didn't shun Becky, he wasn't happy about her vocation. It was like he was ashamed to have raised a daughter who would join the police force. He never said that, but she could see it in his eyes and in the way he acted whenever she came home to see him. His drug use had further alienated the two of them. She tried to get him help, but he refused. The rest of her family made excuses for him. And after he died, his cousins, aunts, and uncles had written her off. Some had even blamed her for his death, as if his shame at her decision to be a police officer had driven him to abuse drugs.

Secundo seemed like a dream come true. It was a place where the old ties to her past life could be truly severed. Maybe, on that world, she could find the time to slow down and even open herself up to someone special. She had dreamed of having a home, with a yard, perhaps a pet and, eventually, a family. Of course, there would be plenty of hard work to do. Building a life on a distant world wouldn't be easy, but it would be a fresh start in a place without all the pitfalls and social pressure to make bad choices. It seemed to her that a person could do something worthwhile in a vibrant new world and be part of something good rather than just repeating the mistakes that kept so many people tangled up in crime, poverty and unhappiness.

At the precinct, she went directly to her Captain's office. She still needed to sign off on her bust, but she was the type of person who believed in being up front and honest with others. That included her superiors on the police force. Her Captain was a lifer named Tom Goodman, and she thought his name reflected his nature quite well. He was a quiet, patient person, a good man in a hard, stressful job. She hated the fact that leaving would add to that stress, but she knew she couldn't pass up the opportunity.

"Thought I'd see you," he said when she knocked on the door to his office. "Come in."

"You got the call?"

"I did. Congratulations on the assignment. I hate to lose you, but who could say no to an offer like that?"

"Thank you, sir. I've enjoyed working for you."

"With me, you worked with me, Nash. And the pleasure has been all mine. I will miss you. But I'm proud of you, too. One of our own on the *Colossus*. That's something to be proud of. You go and represent us well, officer. That's all I ask. I've already begun reassigning your case load. Sanders is booking your perp. Nice recovery there, by the way. It's a good thing you didn't have to fire your weapon."

It was the first time Becky realized how close she had come to losing her spot in Sawyer Flint's Special Investigation squad on the *Colossus*. If she had shot Delmont Finnigan, the Internal Affairs Division would have opened a case and done a full investigation into the shooting. She would have been put on desk duty until she was cleared, which usually took a couple of weeks. A shiver of fear ran down her spine. She had been one bad decision away from missing the biggest opportunity of her life. And that scared her way more than a gun fight ever had.

"Yeah," Becky said. "I got lucky."

"Luck seems to happen for good people who do the right thing, officer. Keep that in mind. Now get out of here. Send us a note from the *Colossus* if you get the chance."

She shook his hand and left, thankful to have worked for a good supervisor. He had never judged her by her gender, or skin color, or even the neighborhood she came from. When he looked at Becky Nash, all Captain Goodman saw was blue.

Becky wasted no time cleaning out her locker. There wasn't much there anyway. She was already in street clothes and hadn't worn a uniform since joining fugitive recovery. Everything fit into her purse, which she slung over one shoulder before going out to catch a public transport to the training center. On the way, she made a call to her friend.

Jeopardy Bess was an interesting person. Her father was a college professor and her mother was a dancer with a professional theater troupe. Their love affair had been short-lived, but produced a child neither wanted. They named her Jeopardy and passed her back and forth between them until she was old enough to be sent off to school. Theirs was not a healthy relationship and Jeopardy had cut off contact with both of them shortly after turning eighteen. Her absence from their lives seemed not to affect either of them in the slightest. The deep void left by their loveless family bonds was part of what made her love animals. Dogs, she always said, were nothing if not loving.

Becky had become fast friends with the K-9 handler. They were specialists who weren't assigned to any one precinct but moved around depending on the need. They did their best to keep in touch, yet they were both busy people with jobs that required long hours. Still, they had a lot in common and Becky had no doubt that Jeopardy would jump at the chance to join her on the *Colossus*.

"Hey girl, you busy?" Becky said when Jeopardy answered her call.

"Actually, I am."

"Well, take a second because I'm about to change your life."

"I don't do blind dates," Jeopardy said. "... and since when did you decide that dating someone was life-changing?"

"I'm not talking about a man," Becky said. "I'm talking about the opportunity of a lifetime. Sergeant Sawyer Flint just got picked to lead Special Investigations on the *Colossus*. He offered me a slot."

"Are you serious?"

"I am."

"Becky, that's incredible news. Congratulations!"

"Hang on, it gets better. He needs a K-9 specialist, and I gave him your name."

"Get out of here."

"I'm serious."

"Don't play with me, Becky. That's cruel."

"I'm not playing. We're meeting at the training center right now. Drop everything and join us."

"I was planning to take Lucky to the park for some exercise," she said.

"It can wait, Jeopardy. This is a once-in-a-lifetime shot at getting off this planet. You have to take it."

"The training center? On Jefferson Avenue?"

"Yes, the police training center. Get a move on it. He wants to meet you."

"I've never met Sergeant Flint."

"He's good police. Sharp, fair, hard-working. We worked a few cases when I was in Narco and, since then, I helped him track down a fugitive he was chasing. I trust him, Jeopardy. And SI is a big step up for both of us. Plus Secundo, can you imagine that? Lucky would go crazy with that much space to run around in."

"Okay, I'm on my way," she said.

"You're clear, right? No open IAD beefs?"

"None," she replied.

"And no man?"

"Girl, if I had a man, you would know it."

"See you soon," Becky said. "Good luck."

"Thanks."

They ended the call. Becky had other friends she wished she could bring along, but space on the Colossus was very limited. And while she would miss her friends, she wasn't going to let anything keep her from grabbing onto the opportunity before her with both hands. A new world meant a new life and that was worth fighting for.

CHAPTER 5

DAVE BANNON WAS WAITING JUST inside the training center near the desk where officers scanned their IDs and got towels for the weight room. Flint came in fast and Dave felt his nerves ratchet up a notch. The offer Flint had called him about seemed too good to be true.

"Detective," Flint said, scanning his ID. "Good to see you."

"And you, Sergeant," Dave replied. "This isn't some elaborate prank, is it?"

"No," Flint said, before turning to the civilian working at the desk. She was busy folding clean towels. "Can you tell Officer Becky Nash that we're in the boxing gym?"

"Becky Nash," the woman said without looking up. "Boxing gym. Got it."

Flint turned to his friend and put a hand on Dave's shoulder. David Bannon was a good investigator with a great mind for details. What he wasn't so great at were people skills, especially dealing with conflict. Not that Dave was afraid to fight. He could go toe-to-toe with thugs on the street and was an excellent marksman. But one of the primary jobs of law enforcement is diffusing stressful situations using words and exuding a sense of calm. Dave struggled in that area and had learned that he worked best in partnership with officers who could handle conflict. That allowed him to use his talents in solving crimes and gathering reliable evidence. Flint knew that prosecutors loved Dave. He was an ideal witness who could recite the facts with clarity on command.

"Are you ready for this?" Flint asked.

"I'm with you one hundred percent," Dave replied. "Who are we here to see?"

"Lieutenant Loudin recommended this guy. His name is Logan Keys. You heard of him?"

"No," Dave admitted.

"Me either. They said I could pick my own team, but it only seemed right to give their guy a shot. They weren't pushing a lot of people, so..."

"Will this be my partner?"

"No," Flint said. "You'll work with Becky Nash. You know her?"

"Sure," Dave said. "We crossed paths when she was in Narco. I've seen her name on a lot of arrest records, too."

"She's good at finding people," Flint said. "Has a knack for human nature and works tirelessly. You'll make a good team."

"Alright," Dave said.

He wasn't picky about his partners, although they were sometimes picky about him. Dave had learned that most people didn't like to be corrected. It didn't matter if they were talking about a case or discussing something that happened in a movie they saw as a kid. Dave, on the other hand, had a compulsion to set the record straight. He liked exactness and correct information, which wasn't always shared by the officers he worked with. Everyone in the department had preferences when it came to partners and Dave did his best to fit in. But for some people, his idiosyncrasies drove them crazy. All he could do was hope that Flint had picked a good partner for him. It was certainly within Sawyer Flint's strengths: an eye for talent and a solid grasp of human nature.

They went into the boxing gym. The training center was a large complex with various areas for a wide range of interests. There was a room full of cardio equipment, as well as an elevated track that was exactly one-eighth of a mile. There was a room full of weight training equipment and another that had functional exercise equipment. There were rooms used for yoga, Pilates and a variety of martial arts classes. The Metro Police offered all types of combat training, from Krav Maga to Brazilian Jiu-Jitsu. But boxing was still the most popular combat/fitness technique. In the boxing gym, there were people working heavy bags, speed bags, hitting targets that swayed back and forth on springy stands to improve striking accuracy, or practicing their footwork. In the center of the large room was a traditional boxing ring. If cops had a beef with one another, they settled it in the ring.

Flint found Logan Keys waiting in one corner. He wasn't massive, just five feet ten inches tall, and all muscle. He had a scar under one eye and jet black hair. Across the ring was a bigger man, at least four inches taller than Logan, and probably forty pounds heavier. There were a few other officers standing around the ring watching. Flint and Dave Bannon joined them.

"Are you going to say something?" Dave said.

"Not until this is over," Flint said.

The bigger fighter was moving around, staying loose and warm. Logan looked bored. Another cop got into the ring and held up both his hands.

"You know the rules, gentlemen," he said. "You leave whatever issues you've got on the mat. You will fight a clean fight and obey my instructions. Three-minute rounds, started and stopped by my whistle. If you agree, shake hands and return to your corner."

Logan held out both of his gloves. The bigger man glared at him, then hit the extended hands much harder than was necessary. Logan didn't flinch or complain; he just moved back to his corner.

Flint stepped over to a cop he knew named Jackson.

"What's their beef?" Flint asked.

"LeSean and Keys were partners," Jackson said. "But LeSean stepped out on his wife, wanted Keys to back up his alibi. Keys refused to lie for his partner and LeSean's wife left him. That was nine months ago."

"Why wait so long to settle things?" Flint asked.

"They aren't fighting about that. LeSean's ex called Keys as a witness in their divorce proceeding."

Flint wasn't sure what to make of that. The police sought truth but were confronted constantly with lies. When it came to supporting one another, the tradition was clear. Blue backed blue, always, no exceptions. It wasn't necessarily moral, but it was useful in protecting the people who were putting their lives on the line to stand against lawlessness and injustice. Still, not lying for your partner wasn't a deal breaker for Flint. In fact, he felt some admiration for Keys, and yet, testifying against the man seemed one step too far. Flint had just gone through a painful divorce himself. He had sat quietly in court while his wife's lawyers spewed unfair and false allegations about him. Had one of his former partners joined in her case, Flint would have had more than words for that officer.

The whistle was blown and the boxing match began. Both men stepped forward, but LeSean charged ahead like a raging bull. He came with a flurry of punches, most were wild. Logan Keys never stopped moving. He swayed back and forth, bobbing and blocking punches with his own gloves as he circled around his opponent. Flint could see that Keys had skill. Flint had grown up watching the sport of boxing and got involved as a teenager, fighting in a few amateur tournaments before joining the force. He didn't have the talent to go pro, but he could see talent in others. There were times when he considered leaving the force to become a fight promoter and manager. He could have made a lot more money in boxing, but his heart was never in it.

Logan could have countered several times, but he didn't. Instead, he just kept bobbing and weaving while he circled around the ring. When he threw a punch, it was nothing more than a tap jab, just touching his opponent, the punch usually landing but causing no damage. It was as if Logan wanted his partner to know he could hurt him, yet wouldn't. LeSean, on the other hand, wasn't a skilled pugilist. He was a brawler. There was a call for that kind of raw aggression, even in the boxing ring. But Flint knew a skilled fighter could weather a brawl, which is exactly what Logan did. And before the first round ended, LeSean was running out of gas. When they were sent back to their corners, neither man had hurt the other, but LeSean was breathing heavy and sweating profusely. Logan seemed barely even bothered by the fight.

"It isn't a fair contest," Dave said.

"Real fights rarely are," Flint replied.

While they waited for the fight to resume, Becky Nash arrived. She brought along a woman Flint had not met, Officer Jeopardy Bass. Introductions were made, and then all the attention turned back to the ring. When the whistle sounded, both men moved forward. Logan had his hands up protecting his face, but Flint could see his mouth moving. He was talking to his opponent. Maybe warning him of what was coming, or perhaps taunting him, Flint couldn't be sure. Logan remained calm. LeSean was tired, but still angry. He continued throwing punches that either didn't land or were caught on Logan's gloves. And then Logan threw a real punch. It was a tight right hook that came in low under LeSean's elbow and caught the bigger man in the ribs. It staggered LeSean and Logan could have capitalized on the moment. Instead, he held his ground but lowered his gloves. When he spoke, Flint couldn't hear him, but he read the fighter's lips, *That's enough, man. We're square.*

LeSean's rage wasn't spent, even if his body was falling behind. He came at Logan with a haymaker that Logan Keys easily ducked under and followed up with a two-handed shove. LeSean fell into the ropes and bounced back, turning and throwing another wild punch. Keys swayed back, then surged forward with a series of hard jabs straight into LeSean's face. The bigger man's head bobbed backward and blood gushed from his nose, but Flint could tell that Keys was still holding back. He could have pressed in and gone for the knock-out, instead, he backed up. When LeSean came lumbering forward and threw a feeble punch, Keys dropped his gloves. The punch landed flush on Logan's jaw. His head whipped to the side and dropped to his knees, then onto his back.

"Yeah!" LeSean shouted. "That's what you get!"

He cursed his former partner, who didn't try to get up. The referee held LeSean back and Logan seemed stunned.

"It's over," the cop holding LeSean said. "It's all over."

Flint couldn't help but smile. He knew a fall when he saw one. There was no shortage of examples. And while Logan hadn't worked hard to sell his own defeat, he had been smart enough to wear LeSean down. The bigger man was gassed. Flint knew there wasn't much on the punch that took Logan down.

LeSean's friends helped him out of the ring. There was talk of beers and celebrations while Logan sat alone in the ring. The referee asked if he wanted help and he shook his head, waving the man away with one glove.

"Dave, have Logan meet us in the martial arts instruction room," Flint said.

"You got it," Dave replied.

Flint turned to the two women. "Let's talk. I know you've got questions."

"Only about a thousand," Becky said.

Flint led the way through the boxing gym and back out to one of the empty training rooms. There were mats on the center of the floor, although the edges were bare. There were chairs, too. Flint sat down and waved to the seat beside him.

"Have a seat, Officer Bass. Tell me about yourself."

Jeopardy sat down. She was clearly nervous, her body stiff. Her back didn't even touch the rest behind her.

"Academy class of eighty-one. Two years on foot patrol. Two years riding, then I moved over to K-9 services. That's where I've been ever since."

"Tell me how you feel about working cases," he said. "Without your service animal."

"I'm police," she said, "twenty-four seven. When my animal isn't needed, I still go out on patrol. Just filling in as needed. I've worked two homicides and more narco cases than I can count. I've drawn my weapon six times in the line of duty. I fired once. Was cleared in the shooting."

"Who'd you shoot?"

"A gang banger who refused to leave his vehicle. When the patrol officer I was assisting tried to physically remove him, he produced a weapon."

"Did the perp live?"

"No, sir," she said, her eyes never leaving his.

"How do you feel about that, Officer Bass?"

"I did my job. It's not a memory I linger on, but it's not something I'm ashamed of either. There's no doubt in my mind the offender intended to kill a cop. I will never hesitate to use whatever force is necessary in that situation."

"You've been working with narco-dogs, but my guess is you'll have a trained police dog on the *Colossus*. We'll have modified weapons too. How do you feel about leaving your partner behind?"

"That's not easy, sir, but Lucky's near retirement age. He'll enjoy his golden years, and I'll be moving on to a new partner anyway. This opportunity couldn't have come at a better time."

"And you're comfortable working with a dog for patrol and appre-hensions?"

"I'm more comfortable with animals than people, sir. I can handle any K-9 situation."

"Alright. You have a clear record?"

"I do, sir."

"I'll get your assignment approved through Lieutenant Loudin. Once he signs off, you're on the team. We leave at twenty-one hundred hours tomorrow."

"Not much time," Becky said.

"No, it isn't. Bring your money and pension transfer over. We can't take much, one police duffel with clothes, toiletries and personal items. All equipment will be provided, which means you turn in your service weapon, your uniforms, badges, everything."

"But we're still police?" Jeopardy asked.

"We'll be joining the *Colossus* crew as Law Enforcement Agents. Same job, new title. You'll get new shields, new unis, a private berth on the ship and meal vouchers. The journey takes two years, so the ship will provide banking. You'll have off time, maybe not a lot, but you'll be able to mix and mingle with the other passengers and take advantage of the recreational facilities."

As he finished explaining, Dave entered with Logan Keys. The latter was in police sweats and had his gym bag in one hand. Up close, Flint noticed Logan's hooded eyes. There was nothing cheerful about his face; the man was grim, almost dangerous-looking.

"Can you three give me a moment with Officer Keys?" Flint asked. "Nash, call Loudin. Have him clear Bass."

"On it," Becky said.

They all three shuffled back outside. Flint looked at Logan and smiled.

"Quite the performance out there," he said.

"Sir?"

"You took the fall well," Flint explained. "It's pretty clear your old partner bought it."

"It was a fair fight."

"We both know that isn't true. You could have really hurt him if you wanted to."

"Didn't want that."

"Good. Why'd you testify?"

"I was subpoenaed. I didn't have a choice."

"You could have backed your partner up."

"I had his back," Logan said. "You don't know the whole story."

"That's true," Flint said. "Give me the quick version."

"He has a son on the autism spectrum. The last thing LeSean

needed was to run around on his wife. I told him that. He wouldn't listen. I didn't rat him out, but he knew I wouldn't lie if she asked me what he was doing."

"Pretty strong convictions," Flint said. "Is everything that black and white for you, Officer Keys?"

"I wish it was, sir," he replied. "May I ask what this is about?"

"I'm putting together a Special Investigation team that will work the *Colossus* on the trip to Secundo."

Logan's eyes widened, but he didn't interrupt.

"Lieutenant Loudin recommended you. And I've got one slot left to fill. From what I've seen in that ring, you know how to handle yourself. Tell me about your service in Metro."

"I'm fourth generation," Logan said. "My great-grandfather was a detective back before the mega city merged together. He was Boston PD. I still have his badge."

"That's quite a legacy," Flint said. "Who's your father?"

"Antonio Keys. He was killed trying to stop a home invasion. Estranged husband broke into his wife's place and my Dad was first on the scene. Lieutenant Loudin was his partner back then. I was just a kid."

"Damn," Flint said. "I'm sorry, Logan."

"Thank you, sir. He died doing what we do, running toward danger. I've always been proud of that."

"You should be."

"My mother passed when I was a teenager. Lieutenant Loudin took me in, treated me right, and when I finished school, he sent me to college. Paid my way out of his own pocket."

"You're a college boy?"

"Associates degree in criminal justice," Logan said. "But I'm better on the street than in a classroom."

"You and me both," Flint said. "I barely made it out of high school. The Marines were my higher education."

"Thank you for your service, sir."

"Tell me, Officer Keys, are you even interested in the job?"

"Absolutely, sir. I applied for the lottery and a security gig on the *Colossus*."

"I'm guessing your record is clear?"

"Yes, sir."

"No open IAD investigations?"

"No, sir."

"What about relationships. You dating anyone, Keys?"

"Not at the moment, sir."

"Any other family that you're going to miss when you're ten million miles from Earth?"

"Lieutenant Loudin is about as close to family as I've got left, Sergeant. I guess if he recommended me for the job, he won't miss me too much when I'm gone."

"I concur. Go get the others. We've got a lot to cover and not much time left."

Logan stepped out into the hallway and beckoned the others. They shuffled in and Flint looked at his squad. Two faces he knew and trusted. Two, he didn't. He would watch them, and time would tell if they were worthy of his trust. There was a good chance that they would all be bored out of their minds on the voyage. But half a million people in a confined space was always cause for caution. Things could go south fast. Flint was excited about the opportunity and ready to get on board. They all had a lot to learn, and the sooner the better in his mind. The future was suddenly bright and exciting. He hadn't been so excited since his first solo patrol as a rookie. If nothing else, he was thankful for the opportunity to do something new and adventurous. And he could tell by the looks on the faces of his new squad, they felt exactly the same way.

CHAPTER 6

IT WAS Lieutenant Loudin who met them at the shuttle service. They were getting a direct flight to the space station where the *Colossus* was docked. Loudin took their badges and guns and gave them each new electronic tablets.

"These have the specs for the *Colossus*," he said. "You'll need to memorize the layout. It's an eighteen-decker ship. Different sections, lots of places for things to go off the rails."

"It's not a pleasure cruise?" Flint asked in mock horror.

"No, it's a work trip," Loudin said. "And to make things more difficult, you can't use real guns."

He opened a hard case container with a briefcase-type handle. It looked like the type of hard case someone would carry diamonds in on a movie, with a pair of handcuffs around the handle and their wrist. Inside were five pistols. They were stainless steel with black rubber pads on the grip.

"Farson semi-autos," Loudin said. "They fire rubber bullets using a frictionless slide thingy. I don't know, they aren't supposed to kill people or punch through the hull of a spaceship."

"Great," Flint said. "Toy weapons."

"We are the weapons," Logan said quietly.

"Plus, a K-9," Loudin said. "He's already up there."

"The passengers have all been vetted, I take it," Flint said.

"They have. But not every country is as stringent or organized as we are," Loudin said, which caused Dave to chuckle. Loudin looked up and frowned. "Needless to say, you should be ready for anything. Your uniforms and other gear will be up there on the *Colossus* already."

"Who's in charge?" Flint asked.

"Captain is a military man. His name is Walter Hastings, a Brit, I think. Your direct supervisor will be part of the police administration. The Commissioner is Monty Forrest. He's a good man. He'll have department heads, I'm sure. The main force is just patrol. Officers in uniforms making themselves visible around the ship, so people feel safe. But you'll be the main investigative squad. I want to wish you all well in your new lives. If any of you are crazy enough to come back, you can transfer back to Metro."

Flint stuck out his hand. "Thanks, Lieutenant. We appreciate this opportunity."

"Wish I was going with you," he said. "But duty calls."

He gave Logan a nod of encouragement, then headed away. Frank propped the hard case with their pistols on top of his rolling suitcase. A hover cart was waiting. They piled their luggage on and then found places for themselves. The automated cart trundled across a part of the airport that few people outside of the airport employees ever ventured. They passed several massive planes and eventually arrived at a small, sleek-looking aircraft. The co-pilot was waiting for them. He checked the weight of all their bags, then showed them where they could stow them in the belly of the vessel. Then the five police officers climbed the steps and got on board. An hour later, the shuttle broke out of the planet's atmosphere and into space. There was some laughing and joking as they experienced zero gravity for the first time. And two hours later, they docked with the International Space Station.

Artificial gravity had been a major breakthrough in space travel and even space living. There were four space stations in orbit around the sun. Two were high-end luxury vacation destinations. And two were scientific laboratories. The ability to stay in space for long periods of time was the result of artificial gravity. Flint didn't mind the feeling of weight again. The flight in zero gravity had made him feel sick to his stomach. Thankfully, he held himself together and didn't embarrass himself in front of his new squad.

There wasn't much to the space station. It was essentially a docking platform that allowed visitors to move from one ship to another. It was a long, modular vessel with big solar sails for power. At over seven hundred feet long, it was bigger than two football fields end to end, but it was absolutely dwarfed by the *Colossus*. Moving people to another star system was a long, expensive process. The VIPs who were making the trip had paid over a billion dollars each. Some with families had paid much more. Flint knew that, apart from the job, he could never have afforded the cost involved. Even before his marriages and their accompanying alimony, he still wouldn't have been able to afford it.

The *Colossus* was eight miles long and two miles wide. Oval in shape, she had eighteen decks, with a transparent dome over the top and an arch that spanned from starboard to port over the center and was covered with LEDs that acted like a sun. It looked like a humongous snow globe. On the bow was the command center and the offices for both the naval personnel and the administrators of the ship's nearly half a million people. The interior side of the C&C structure was completely flat, with interlocking display panels that formed a massive screen that was nearly half a mile wide and five hundred feet tall. It was visible from anywhere on the top deck, which was filled with streets, huge gardens, businesses, and recreational spaces. In the very center was a classic town square. Around the outside of the upper deck was the Tube, an enclosed public transportation train. It stopped at depots every two miles, where banks of elevators could take passengers down into the lower decks, where Staterooms, VIP cabins, and standard berths were located, along with massive warehouses of supplies for the trip and the destination.

Flint and the other officers had studied the layout on their tablets during the ride up. The ship was, in fact, a very well-organized city, with everything from workspace to recreational space, schools and all the necessities for people to live just as they had on earth. There were laundromats and tattoo parlors, parks with playground equipment, spas and the inevitable detention spaces. There was a court of law and assembly spaces for special occasions. No weapons were allowed on the ship other than those carried by law enforcement personnel. There was a hospital and pharmacies with drug delivery services. A funeral parlor. The trip would last for two years and it was inevitable that in that time, some people would meet their ultimate demise. The builders had spent many long weeks planning for everything they could think of.

"I can't believe this is really happening," Becky said as they went up a ramp that led into the *Colossus*.

"Nothing wrong with being excited," Flint said. "Just keep in mind, we've got a job to do as well."

"Sergeant Flint?" a big man in a police uniform said as they made their way into the ship. They were on the very lowest level. People in various uniforms were bustling about. Most seemed to be maintenance crew members, but here and there, Flint saw medical workers and people in uniforms for service industry businesses. The corridors were surprisingly large. Some people were walking, others were on a track that was continuously running down the straight sections of the corridors.

"That's me," Flint said, sticking out a hand.

"I'm Lieutenant Jenson, but you can call me Tad," the man in uniform said. "I'm head of personnel. Sort of the police HR if you will."

He grinned and waved for the squad to follow him. He led the way to a temporary workstation at the junction between the long row of berths and the midships sections.

"I can't tell you how sorry we were to hear about Sergeant Heath," Jenson said. "Terrible tragedy. But now you're here, and that is, well... a relief to say the least."

He settled heavily into a chair at the workstation and opened a drawer. Inside were files, the old-fashioned kind. He thumbed through a few and looked inside.

"Here it is," he said, pulling out a set of ID cards. "These are temporary, of course. We'll get you all set up in due course, but for now, you can get settled in your berths. The numbers are on your IDs. And hang onto those. You'll need them to get in and out of your rooms and to get food in the dining hall. Right now, we're just operating down here on Eighteen. Only officers and engineers are going up to the other levels. The passengers start arriving in two days. There's a lot to do still."

Flint took the IDs. They were standard smart cards, but without pictures on them. Each one had a name and a berth. His was eighteen Starboard dash four hundred and six. After looking at them, he handed out the IDs to the rest of his squad.

"Looks like we're sharing berths," he said.

"Awesome," Jeopardy said in a sarcastic tone.

"All ship personnel save for senior officers are in combined quarters, I'm afraid. But you'll have private bunks."

"How many berths are there?" Dave asked the Lieutenant.

"For ship personnel, twenty-five thousand," Tad Jenson said. "All double occupancy rooms. You get a locker, a bathroom, and a bed. A ship like this needs a lot of crew members."

"Spacious," Becky said.

"How many security people are on board?" Flint asked.

"Eight hundred," Jenson replied. "Plus, one dog."

"Really?" Becky said. "That kind of sounds like a lot."

"Does it?" Jenson said. "This ship is basically a city, with eighteen decks, so roughly two hundred and eighty-eight square miles. We'll have patrol officers paired up and assigned four-mile zones on every deck. The goal is a three-minute response time. And that's with perfect conditions, which we all know do not exist. I'd say we're understaffed."

"You expecting a lot of trouble?" Logan asked respectfully.

"I'm expecting that we'll have a lot of people from different backgrounds, speaking different languages, all trying to adapt to small quarters on a crowded ship. Some will find healthy ways to cope, others... others will need help."

"Good answer," Flint said. "Sounds like we're in good hands, gang. Everyone, find your berth, then we meet up in two hours in the CLE headquarters, which is..."

"Most of Eighteen is maintenance, storage and crew quarters, but there is a small detention center, along with our admin offices in the fore section."

"Special Investigations?" Flint asked.

"Your squad has a small office on Deck Nine, that's Yellow Upper Deck. Commissioner Forrest thinks it's best if you stay in a central location. But those decks aren't open yet, so you can borrow a space in the main Law Enforcement admin space in the fore section. It's a long walk."

"Make it three hours," Flint said. "Let's go, people."

They were in three rooms. Becky Nash and Jeopardy Bess were on one side of the ship, and Dave Bannon and Logan Keys were on the other. They were bunked with crew members of the same gender. Deck eighteen was like a massive industrial complex with rows of apartments squeezed between warehouses along the wide corridors. There was signage everywhere, which they were all grateful for since the ship felt like one giant maze.

Sergeant Sawyer Flint was in a room with the head of the detention facility team, a short Japanese man named Oto Iagowa, although he was there when Flint arrived. Oto had taken the lower bunk. Both beds were recessed into the wall with panels that closed over the outside edge for privacy. Inside the pods, there was a shelf for personal items, power outlets and climate controls. There was even a wide display screen that folded down from the ceiling above the mattress. Flint didn't intend to spend a lot of time in the tiny berth, but he supposed it was comfortable enough.

There was a narrow table built into the wall opposite from their bunks that could fold up so that it took up a minimal amount of space. A pair of wide lockers was the only other furniture in the berth. At the rear was a small space with a shower stall, therapy lights, and a stainless steel vanity with a medicine cabinet above. It was clearly utilitarian, which was fine with Flint. He was a worka-holic who only needed the basics at home. But he could see that a two-year stint with very few amenities could be hard to take for some people.

There was a wide drawer beneath his bunk and above Oto's. His roommate had a similar one beneath his own bunk. Both had a keypad locking mechanism. Flint went through the process of setting the combination, then stowed everything except for their special order pistols inside. He checked his locker and set its combination too. He hung up some clothes inside and stowed his extra shoes. Special Investigations were plain clothes officers, but there was a set of patrol blues and another of dress blues already hanging in the locker. He double checked everything and then set out for the admin area.

Lieutenant Tad Janson had been right. It was a long walk. The people movers were essential. The wide corridors had three color sections. The smallest was yellow, with the conveyor belt people movers. They traveled slightly faster than Flint would consider a brisk walk. And while some people just stood there, letting the belt move them down the long, street-like corridors, others walked on them, doubling their speed.

Beside the yellow section of the passageway was a wide green section. Most people not in a hurry, strolled along the green section. Flint saw no one on the blue section.

He passed banks of elevators several times before reaching the admin section. Signs there pointed him to the law enforcement divi-sion, which consisted of several offices for the higher-ranking commanders, a set of four detention cells and one larger detention room for low-level offenders that wouldn't be held long. Tad Janson was already there.

"Long time no see," he said, chuckling.

"Seems like a while. It's a heck of a walk," Flint said.

"Indeed. Tomorrow, your team will get their orientation, at which time you'll be approved for vehicular travel."

"Vehicles?"

"So, to speak," Janson said with a grin. "You'll get prepped and trained tomorrow. I wouldn't want to spoil the surprise. Let's get your weapons logged in and you can issue those. And I'll need to get biometrics for your team."

The rest of the day was taken up with what Flint and his squad were assured was standard info. Normally, it was all done before arrival. Every person on the ship had their fingers and palms printed, their retinas scanned, their voices recorded, facial and gait scans were recorded, and DNA was taken. Blood type was also recorded and each person had a full body scan to ensure that no medical emergencies were imminent.

Flint passed out their pistols. Normally, law enforcement officials chose their own service weapon from a variety of options. On the *Colossus,* they would use special weapons meant to disable, not harm.

They ate dinner together in a dining hall that was like most other spaces on the lower deck, designed for utility. The food was good, but obviously not real. It was made from rehydrated foods, which meant it often had a strange texture. After their meal, the squad returned to their quarters. Flint took a shower and discovered he was only allowed sixty seconds' worth of water. He used ten seconds before pausing the flow, soaping up in the tiny stall, and finally rushing through the last fifty seconds, rinsing off. When he was finished, he was clean, if perhaps a little stressed out over the new bathing routine. The shower also had a set of high-powered lights, almost like an old-fashioned tanning booth. The purpose wasn't to tan his skin, but to encourage his body's vitamin D production and help him avoid the dangers of Seasonal Affective Disorder. It also dried his body about ninety percent, which would allow him to use the same towel for at least a week before it needed to be washed. Water was a high-value substance in outer space. Every drop had to be taken care of. Wastewater had to be cleaned and reused. It was a serious matter on a vessel with hundreds of thousands of people. If the water supply was contaminated, a lot of people could get very, very sick. Flint didn't like thinking about how desperate people might get if they were to run low on water.

In his bunk, he settled his meager personal belongings, then closed the privacy panel. The bed was a bit small, but the walls were padded and he had complete control over the temperature in the enclosed space. Plus, it was dark and soundproof. He had no trouble sleeping, although when he finally woke up, he had no idea where he was.

CHAPTER 7

BECKY NASH'S roommate was a tall woman from South Africa who worked in the food services division. She had dark black skin and a bald head. They were friendly, but a little reserved.

Jeopardy's roommate was an American who worked as an engineer's mate. They had nothing in common and ignored one another for the most part.

"You guys are just unlucky," Dave said. "My roommate and I stayed up playing video games until one in the morning."

The four Special Investigation officers had gathered in the dining hall before their scheduled day of training.

"What about you, Logan?" Becky asked.

"I don't have one."

"What?" Jeopardy asked.

Logan shrugged. "It's just me."

"You are so lucky," Jeopardy said.

"Things will get better," Dave said optimistically.

"Yeah, look at the bright side. We'll be in great shape after walking for miles every single day."

They ate bowls of oatmeal flavored with dehydrated fruit. The coffee was good and the dining hall was a noisy place. They settled at the table and ate their food, all the while their eyes scanned the crowded room for signs of danger or criminal activity.

"What do you want to bet this is the most boring assignment of your career?" Dave proposed. "I mean, who wants to commit a crime here? Everyone will be too busy gawking over the fancy ship."

"At first, maybe," Becky said.

"Two years is a long time," Jeopardy added. "Plenty of time for people to get up to no good."

"Has anyone been to the fitness center yet?" Logan asked.

The others shook their head.

"Didn't even know there was one," Dave replied.

"It's on the far end of the ship," Becky said. "The stern."

"Eight miles is a long walk home after leg day," Dave said, waving his spoon in the air as he talked.

"You don't walk the whole way," Jeopardy said. "You go up to the top deck and ride the tube to the nearest bank of elevators."

"Seems odd," Dave said, then grinned and started singing, "I guess you gotta get up to get down."

"Very funny," Becky said.

They finished their meal and put their trays in the cleaning racks before going to the admin center. Flint was there, waiting for them. He had a tall container with a lid from which he was sipping coffee.

"This way," he said. "We get eight hours of orientation today."

There were looks between the members of the squad. No one liked sitting around watching instructional videos for hours on end, but it had to be done. Only when they reached the room that had been assigned to their squad, there was no sign of a video display.

"I guess we're early," Flint said.

The room contained two empty desks and a few more generic chairs for visitors. They waited nearly ten minutes and when Lieutenant Janson arrived, he was sweating a little.

"You're here. Great! That's what I was hoping for," he said.

"Something wrong?" Flint asked.

"Just getting all my ducks in a row," Tad said. He had two large, heavy-looking cases. He sat one on each of the empty desks. "Today, we're going to do a real tour of the ship!"

The squad looked concerned. Becky didn't like the idea of walking for miles on end through the long corridors. And she wasn't the only one. Even Sergeant Flint looked concerned.

"Sounds like a long day," he said.

"Oh, it's going to be fun," Lieutenant Janson said. "First, we get your smart cuffs set up," he said, opening one of the cases. "Everything on the ship is tied to your digital identity, which will be programmed onto these."

He held up his hand. The sleeve slid back, revealing a dark band around his wrist.

"This does everything a smartphone does, and also works as a key for your cabins, the dining hall and anything else you might need. Once we've got those programmed for each of you, we will learn to use these."

He opened the other case and pulled out a sleek-looking hover-board with a T-shaped handle.

"What is that?" Jeopardy asked.

"The fastest way around the ship," Janson said. "They're for official use only, so you can't ride them for fun, but you're going to like it."

"A scooter?" Logan said. "We're going to ride around on scooters?"

"Trust me," Lieutenant Janson said. "You will love it!"

It took half an hour to program everyone's data cuff. Their files on the ship's computer network were completed and the smart devices linked to each member of the squad and had their security clearances included in their file.

"With these, in case of an emergency, we can open almost any compartment on the ship, even the VIP suites on deck two," Janson said. "What they don't do is keep track of a person's location. There's too much machinery for total ship connectivity. Instead, the system is linked to hubs, such as doors and the elevator banks. But there are dead spots. And while it's not recommended, they can be removed."

"Too bad for us," Dave said. "Twenty-four hour tracking would have made the job a lot easier."

"You don't value personal privacy?" Jeopardy asked.

"Not for criminals," Dave replied.

"And who gets to make the decision of who is a criminal and who isn't?"

"Let's not get bogged down in the weeds," Flint said quickly. "We set our own political views aside and enforce the laws that are set by the government."

"Which brings me to an important point," Lieutenant Janson said. "For the next two years, we will be living and working, not in a democracy, but under the standard naval protocols, which means that Captain Walter Hastings is the ultimate authority. His word is effectively law while we are underway. I'm sure you all understand the necessity of this. We do have a civilian board which has been entrusted with creating laws and governing the passengers on the ship. To that end, I have forwarded the *Colossus Charter and Passenger Rights*. It's essentially the criminal code while aboard this ship. Most of it will be familiar to you, but there are some changes. Our task will be to enforce the law, but also to help the passengers on board live together in harmony."

"Five hundred thousand people from a hundred and seventy different countries," Jeopardy said. "What could go wrong?"

Janson smiled, ignoring her sarcasm, and said, "That's the spirit."

With the data cuffs programmed and on, they started their tour, which took them from the Law Enforcement admin offices to the nearest bank of elevators. There were eight of them in a row. The group already knew there were banks of elevators evenly spaced along the outer portion of the ship. And there were more scattered around the interior of the ship. When Lieutenant Janson pressed the elevator button, a chime sounded, and one of the elevator doors opened immediately.

"That was quick," Dave said.

"We're operating at a fraction of total ship capacity," Janson said. "Soon, these elevators will run constantly."

He allowed the others to board the elevator before him, then stepped inside. There were no buttons, just a blank touch screen beside the doors. He waved his data cuff, and the panel lit up.

Welcome, Lieutenant Janson, a computerized voice said. *Which deck are you traveling to?*

"Seventeen," Janson said.

All passengers are approved, the computerized voice said, before the elevator car immediately started upward.

"My rank accesses a special program in the elevators," Janson said. "Most people will use the touch display."

"We have to be approved?" Becky asked.

"That's right," Janson said as the elevator chimed and the doors opened onto the seventeenth deck. He stepped out, and the group followed. "Passengers will have access to certain areas. Someone from Deck Nine can't just go wandering around anywhere on the ship they want. Their access is dependent on their job and assigned deck. Your data cuffs will allow all the members of your team to access ninety-nine percent of the ship."

"What's the other one percent?" Dave asked.

"A few spaces in the Officer's Section, including the Bridge. Those areas are for the senior crew members only," Janson explained. "Now, let me show you the best part."

He waved his arm at a panel between the elevator doors. A chime beeped and the panel slid forward. Janson reached inside and pulled out a hoverboard.

"Go ahead, there's one for each of you between the elevator doors," Janson told them.

Flint walked over and held his wrist out toward one of the panels. It beeped and opened. He pulled out the hoverboard by the handle. There was a button on the connecting rod that released the folded deck down and activated the device. It hovered just a few inches over the floor.

"Let's all mount up," Janson said. "These puppies will reach a top speed of thirty miles an hour. But we'll start slow."

Flint stepped onto the deck of the hoverboard. He expected it to descend under his weight or bounce a little on a cushion of air. It did neither. The device seemed solid. The handle had a simple thumb lever that made it move forward, plus a hand brake. Janson started down the corridor and the rest of the Special Investigation squad followed. Occasionally, the Lieutenant pointed things out. Every deck was different. Some had massive storage rooms the size of commercial hangars. Others had maintenance compartments of all sizes. Some were filled with machinery, others with computer servers, and still others with tanks of various liquids and gases that were vital to the survival of the people on the ship.

"Everyone approved for passage on the *Colossus* speaks English," Janson said. "That was one of the requirements for application. Of course, not everyone will be proficient in it. Many will inevitably prefer to speak their native languages. When you are on duty, you will wear a simple comlink device that will be synced to your data cuff, which has a translation device. In theory, it will recognize a foreign language and automatically translate it for you."

When they got back to the bank of elevators where the hoverboards had come from, they returned the devices to the hidden charging stations and went to the sixteenth deck. The process was the same on every level. It was like touring vast neighborhoods, each one different. There was a variety of decor, most of which was specific to the nationalities of the people who were assigned to the various areas. There were nursing stations, schools, communal dining halls and recreation spaces.

"What about work?" Flint asked when they were halfway through the tour. "What will the passengers do for work?"

"As you can guess, there's a wide variety of people from all kinds of backgrounds," Janson said. "Some, such as artisans and researchers, will continue their work independently. Others are assigned to work groups. Carpenters, for instance, will divide their time on Secundo between private work and group work. The groups will begin meeting while on board. They'll start working out the details of their assignments while in transit. As you can imagine, there will be a lot to get done when they arrive. All the various work teams will need to be integrated to ensure that things are built up for the entire community at first. Once their basic needs are seen to, the people will have more and more freedom to do as they wish on the planet."

At the ninth deck, they took a break from the tour inside their new headquarters, which was really just a series of small rooms. Flint had an enclosed office that overlooked four desks with computer stations and adjustable chairs. There were two interrogation rooms and one holding cell, along with a restroom and a tiny break-room. It was positioned in the center section of the ship among a cluster of other civil administration offices, including a nurse's station with a robotic emergency medical physician (aka, 'REMP') that could perform full body scans and even emergency surgery, if needed. There was also a legal representative in a small office that could be called upon by both the law enforcement members of the crew and the civilian passengers as needed.

The Special Investigation Squad took full advantage of the beverage dispensers in their new break room. Flint used one machine to brew himself a cup of coffee, while Logan used another to dispense a fruit-flavored cold drink. Once everyone had their beverages and each squad member had claimed a desk, Janson continued his orientation.

"Questions?" he asked.

Becky's hand went up. The Lieutenant nodded at her. "I've noticed that the amenities and facilities have gotten nicer as we've gone upward. Why is that?"

"I'd venture to say that the *Colossus* is a step up for seventy-five percent of the passengers coming on board," Janson explained. "But you're right. The designers tried to match the ship's comfort level to those who would be using the space."

"They missed the boat for us," Jeopardy said.

"Crew members aren't expected to spend a lot of time in their berths," Janson said. "No one is discounting the fact that this will be a grueling two years for the crew, but the designers needed to house a lot of people on a single deck. We can't expect a scholar who works half a day from his home office to move willingly into a crew-man's berth. And so, cabin assignments are based on a person's function, as well as their anticipated time in their personal spaces. Families, for instance, need more room, with persons in the family group needing more privacy than a crew member. While many of the passengers were chosen via lottery, there are many who were picked because of their expertise. They have been asked to give up luxuries on Earth to start new lives on a colony planet with few, if any, of the niceties they were accustomed to. And so, they were given special consideration in regard to their personal spaces on the ship."

"Makes sense," Dave said.

"It also makes for resentment for the people on the lower decks," Becky countered.

"Which is why we're here," Logan said.

"Our hope is that the first few months will be relatively calm," Janson said. "For a lot of people, just the availability of three square meals a day will be a massive upgrade over what they're accustomed to. By limiting access to other decks, we hope to stave off any jealousy or covetousness."

"They'll still see it," Becky said. "They may not be allowed to go onto an upper deck, but they'll see it on their way to the surface."

"Topdeck," Janson corrected her. "We call it Topdeck, or Colossus City."

"She's got a point," Jeopardy said.

"Crime in any community is inevitable," the Lieutenant continued. "Fortunately, we have law enforcement to protect and serve."

Flint knew the standard motto, just as he knew that most police were reactionary and did more clean-up than serving or protecting.

"Alright, let's continue the tour, shall we?" Janson said.

They did. The second and third decks were reserved for the VIP passengers who had helped to fund the project by purchasing wildly expensive tickets for the two-year trip. Some were simply individuals and families who wanted to establish a home on Secundo. Others were business owners who would open stores and restaurants on the *Colossus*, which would eventually return to Earth and start the process all over again. There were restaurateurs, fashion designers, and even retail manufacturers. There was more wealth represented by the passengers set to come on board than in many of the nations which had been part of the lottery.

When they eventually reached the topmost deck, Janson gave the squad time to marvel. The elevators opened onto a sparkling new city. There were high-rise buildings and neon signs. Most buildings had large glass fronts. There were streets with automated passenger vehicles, wide sidewalks and colorful shops. But most impressive of all was the massive dome overhead. It was transparent with sweeping views of the Sol system and outer space beyond. Thousands of stars twinkled in the vast expanse. And right down the middle of the dome, arching from the port to the starboard side of the ship, was a massive beam. It was twenty feet wide and covered with lights.

"Welcome to Topdeck," Janson said. "Home away from home."

"It's massive," Dave said.

"Sixteen square miles," the Lieutenant explained. He sounded more like a salesman than a law enforcement administrator. "Half of which is urban and half is green space. The four corners are dedicated parks with lots of the most oxygen-producing plants from Earth, such as Areca Palms, Snake Plants and Pothos. There are also plants that will be useful to the passengers, such as Aloe Vera, fruit trees, and herbs. The oxygen on the Topdeck is pumped back down to the lower decks. It's not enough to provide us with all the oxygen needed for the two-year trip, but the air up here is rich and clean."

"You can tell," Logan replied.

"A city of half a million people and no smog," Dave said.

"That's an accomplishment," Jeopardy said.

They retrieved more hoverboards. They were not the only people on the top deck of the ship. They saw maintenance people delivering goods to various business locations and putting the finishing touches on a variety of storefronts. They took their time cruising up and down through the city streets and exploring the green spaces. In an ideal world, they would have weeks to really get to know the ship. While other law enforcement officials would need a cursory knowledge of the ship, they would only need to be intimately familiar with their own four-square-mile beat. Flint worried that it might take months to learn everything there was to know just about the top deck city, not to mention the over two hundred and seventy miles of lower decks. A person who committed a crime could hide easily in such a vast complex, especially if they had help. The tracking system would help, but there were places that would be invisible to the computers and surveillance cameras. And how long would it take the passengers to find ways to disable those security devices?

The taller buildings were mostly office spaces. The colony's government would be formed during the transit, and there were plenty of professionals, from civil engineers to cartographers and architects, who would need workspace. Cities would need to be planned, national boundaries established and environmental systems created. There were historians who would document the journey and establishment of the first colonies on Secundo. Anthropologists taking the trip just to study the dynamics of life on the *Colossus*. Never before in human history had so many people from so many different countries lived in such close quarters. It was, in some ways, a researcher's dream come true.

There were also churches, temples, synagogues and mosques on Topdeck. Every world religion was represented. There were art galleries, performance theaters and clubs specializing in all sorts of personal interests. Two of the green spaces included sports fields.

Baseball, soccer and American Football were just a few of the sports that would be active on the trip for passengers of all ages. There was even a series of sound stages that would allow filmmakers to create stories in space.

"So, people work," Becky said as they left their hoverboards and gathered in a pavilion in one of the green spaces. "Does that mean they have money?"

"Of course," Janson said. "The *Colossus* has its own bank. You will all be paid your normal salaries on top of the room and board you are provided on the ship."

"We can eat at the dining halls or we can pay for food up here?" Jeopardy asked.

"Correct," Janson said. "Some passengers will take advantage of the situation to be frugal, and others will enjoy amenities they have never had access to before. For instance, your data cuffs and tablets will connect to the ship's information system, which in turn has a massive digital library of books and entertainment programs. All that is free for every passenger to enjoy. But if you want to go up to Topdeck and enjoy a specialty coffee made by a professional Barista, you will need to pay for that."

"What about laundry?" Logan asked.

"Work clothes and uniforms are laundered by the crew," Janson said. "But if you choose to play in a soccer league, you'll be responsible for cleaning your own jersey."

"We're plain clothes officers," Flint said. "Is that covered?"

"Yes, anything you designate as workwear will be laundered for you at no expense."

"Let's talk detaining suspects," Flint continued. "What are our rules of engagement?"

"Non-lethal means only," Janson said. "There is nowhere we can go on this ship that won't be subject to other passengers watching and even recording our actions. We must maintain law and order at all times without spreading undue fear or resentment against the authorities of this spacecraft."

"Okay," Becky said. "But what if the suspect is using deadly force?"

"Your firearms will effectively disable any suspect," Janson said.

"I doubt that," Logan replied.

"Do we have training facilities?"

"Yes, Deck four has designated space for law enforcement training. We stopped at that cluster of compartments, if you recall."

"Live gun range?" Dave asked.

"Simulated," Janson said.

Flint, like the other members of his squad, suppressed a groan. Administrators and bureaucrats loved simulators. They offered training at a fraction of the cost. But anyone who worked with firearms knew they needed time actually shooting them to become proficient. Firing a simulated gun wasn't the same.

"You'll have access to stun batons, plastic restraints and hover sleds if needed," the lieutenant continued. "The goal, as always, is de-escalation and peaceful detention of suspected persons."

"When do I get to meet my K-9 partner?" Jeopardy asked.

"He'll be coming aboard tomorrow," Janson said. "And speaking of tomorrow, I have your squad down to help passengers find their quarters once they come on board. That will help you get to know the passengers, as well as better learn the ship. Now, there's one more thing to see before we call it a day. Let's take a ride on the tube."

CHAPTER 8

JEOPARDY DIDN'T LIKE theme parks. She had never gone skydiving or jumped off a cliff into a lake. Her life had been lived on the gritty underbelly of the sprawling East Coast megapolis. The shuttle ride up to the *Colossus* was her first experience in zero gravity and it made her a bit queasy. The Tube was no different.

"There are actually four separate trains," Lieutenant Janson said proudly. "They move from stop to stop in ninety seconds."

"There's no gravity in the Tube?" Becky asked.

"No," Janson said. "And the cars are propelled by electromagnets."

The doors opened and inside was a standard public transport train. Jeopardy had ridden in enough of them, but never one so clean. The oddest thing about the Tube was that the roof was padded and there were small handles between the seats so a person could pull themselves into one and not just float randomly around.

"Won't people get hurt crashing into one another?" Dave asked.

"We'll have personnel on the Tubes for the first few months. Once the novelty wears off, it shouldn't be a problem."

As the Lieutenant was explaining that riding around in zero

gravity wouldn't be a problem, Logan and Dave were bouncing around while Becky drifted up by the roof. The doors closed and the train slid through the tube. It covered the two miles quickly and then stopped at the next depot, but no one made a move to leave. They would ride the entire circuit and get off at the same spot they had entered.

"It's kinda fun," Dave said.

"You monkeys stop fooling around," Flint scolded them.

Jeopardy thought the Sergeant was insulting monkeys. She had learned to love animals at an early age. As an only child, she had taken in stray cats and known a few older ladies in her apartment building with canaries. When an opportunity to join the K-9 unit opened up, she jumped at the chance. While most police don't want to get stuck in a fringe division, Jeopardy saw an opportunity to work with a partner she felt she could really trust.

The hardest thing about police work for Jeopardy was overcoming the wounds and disappointments of her past. Her father was a narcissist who cared nothing for children, not even his own. Jeopardy knew she had three step-siblings, all from affairs her father had with students from the university. There were probably more. He urged all of them to terminate the pregnancies, and when the three that Jeopardy knew of didn't, he cut off all contact. Jeopardy knew about them after running her father's police report and discovering that he had been sued for child support by three different women. He had broken promises to Jeopardy until she was seven years old, at which time he stopped making promises to her at all. Despite his mistreatment of her, she still loved him. He was her father, and she longed for his love. His absence and failure to show her any kind of familial affection had left a deep wound in her soul that made it hard for Jeopardy to trust anyone.

Her mother had not been much different. She had given birth to Jeopardy and stayed home for a year to nurse her. That year had hurt her career and the subsequent resentment she had for Jeopardy had been palpable as the years went by. She continued to dance, but never quite regained her form and certainly never landed the lead. There weren't a lot of opportunities for classically trained dancers. Jeopardy's grandparents on her mother's side were well off, but disagreed with their daughter's decision to keep the baby, and so withheld their love the only way they knew how, by withholding the financial assistance that their daughter and granddaughter needed. It wasn't until Jeopardy was old enough to be sent away to boarding school that they gave in and paid for her schooling.

But private school was not the grand opportunity many considered it to be. Jeopardy was behind academically and struggled socially. Without parents to build her up and encourage her, Jeopardy withdrew. She found solace in isolation and learned to distrust the world.

After they rode in the tube, the group split up. Sergeant Flint had reports to file and Lieutenant Janson was going to take him to meet the ship's captain. Everyone else was free to do as they pleased. Dave returned to his berth, anxious to dive into the rules and regulations specific to the *Colossus*. Logan went to gather his workout clothes and hit the gym. Becky was returning to the Law Enforcement center on deck four to practice with her new weapon. That left Jeopardy all alone, which she didn't mind.

She was nearly back at her berth when the device on her left wrist buzzed with a new message. Glancing at it, she read **K-9 Officer Requested in boarding section Alpha.** There was only one reason why the K-9 officer would be requested and she hurried back through the ship to meet her new partner.

Boarding section Alpha was the same point of entry that she and the rest of the SI squad had entered through. It was essentially a wide hallway leading to an airlock, which was left open while the ship was docked to the receiving station. Gear and supplies of all sorts had been stacked along the walls. A ship's officer was near the airlock with a large tablet. He used a stylus to tick off items on his inventory as they were brought on board. There were several crew members in coveralls of different colors. She had just learned earlier that day that each division among the crew had different colors. Navy blue was the engineering division. Green coveralls were the life support maintenance division. Orange was for janitorial. Laundry was a light gray color, food service wore white, and law enforcement wore black. She was happy that her tiny squad were plainclothes officers.

"Help you?" the ship's officer, in a royal blue uniform that included a small, brimmed hat, asked as she approached.

"I got a message to come down. I'm the K-9 officer."

"Cuff," the officer said.

For a second, Jeopardy didn't know what he was talking about. Then it hit her, he wanted to see her data cuff. She held out her hand. He used the tablet to scan it. Something beeped and he looked at the information that came up. Then he pointed toward a pet carrier against the far wall. She felt a flush of heat at all the gear stacked around it.

"That thing is your responsibility," he said. "Including cleaning up after it."

"Understood," she replied. "You might remember that it's a trained law enforcement officer, not a thing. And it needs access to air just like us."

"Sure thing," the ship's officer said, his focus back on his list.

She knew his response was typical, even among other police officers. K-9s were highly trained and useful in a wide variety of law enforcement applications. Still, they were often seen as outsiders, as were the human officers who worked with the animals.

It took her a few minutes to move the gear stacked on top of the animal crate. She heard a deep-throated growl before she could even see the dog.

"Aus!" she said in a firm tone.

The growling stopped immediately. She felt a little sorry for the dog. It was in a new environment, which was hard on anyone, especially when they had no say in being moved. And the ride up from Earth was stressful. She imagined the dog had been loaded with the cargo and left to deal with zero gravity with no help, not even a familiar voice or scent.

Once she got the crate uncovered, she knelt down by the door. The crate was standard plastic with just a few holes for ventilation. The door was a metal grate. Jeopardy held her hand by the door, but didn't put her fingers through the crate. She waited. The dog was standoffish for a moment, then she heard it sniffing her. She didn't rush it. Once the animal had familiarized itself with her, she heard it whine in distress. She didn't have to wonder what was wrong. The smell of urine and solid waste was palpable. It had probably fouled itself during the flight up. And she knew immediately what she needed to do.

"Braver hund," she said. It was German, as all police dogs were still trained using commands in German. Braver hund meant *good dog.* "Braver hund, bleib."

She could hear the animal panting, but it stopped whining and growling. She got back to her feet and started back down the passageway toward a bank of elevators about two hundred feet from the airlock.

"Hey!" the officer shouted at her. "You can't leave it there."

"I'm not leaving it," she said. "I'm moving it."

"Just carry it," he barked.

She waved her digital cuff at the panel near the elevator door. It opened and she pulled out a hoverboard.

"That dog weighs eighty pounds," she said.

"So, walk it," the officer suggested.

"It's covered in feces and urine," she told. "But if you want me to walk it through the ship..."

"No, no, no!" he said. "Just get it out of here."

She wanted to say that's exactly what she was doing, but she held back. The man was frustrated, probably because he didn't like his job. She wouldn't make things any better by being prickly. When she got the hoverboard back to the kennel, she unfolded the device. It hovered a few inches off the deck. The one thing she had been wrong about was how much she had enjoyed riding the hoverboard. It was fun to go racing down the long corridors of the spaceship and it made covering the long distances a breeze.

Lifting the heavy box wasn't easy, but she managed it, setting the crate onto the hoverboard. It would have been smart to strap it down, but she didn't have a strap and she wasn't going to be moving fast. She walked beside it, leading the device through the hallways and back to her berth. Her roommate wasn't there and she whispered a prayer of thanksgiving for that small favor. She had to take her time with the dog. Her cabin wasn't where it would stay, but it was standard procedure for a handler to spend a few days with a new animal. They needed to build a solid rapport.

She put the crate on the ground, then moved the hoverboard over beside the door. For a few minutes, as she got things ready, she just let the dog watch her through the bars of the crate door. Jeopardy got a towel and an extra blanket from her locker. It was one she had used and knew that it smelled strongly of her scent. On the bunk, she had linens from the ship, but she had brought the blanket from home specifically to help her new partner bond. She also got a bag of small dog treats from her locker. While the other members of the SI squad had packed snacks and things that reminded them of home, Jeopardy had packed goodies for her K-9 partner.

She opened the dog crate and waited. If she had given the order, the dog would most likely have come out, but she didn't want to force it. She let the animal take its time. After a few moments, she shook the bag of treats, then ripped the top off. The dog whined but still didn't come out. She knew it was embarrassed and afraid. She tossed one little treat just outside the crate. At first, nothing happened, but then a long, dark muzzle appeared. It gave the treat one small sniff, then used its tongue to lap it up. It chewed fast and gulped the goodie down.

"Braver hund," she said, then tossed another treat. The second one was a little farther out from the crate. The dog stepped out, looked around for danger, saw none, and lapped up the treat.

"Braver hund," Jeopardy said again. Across the top of the crate was a name printed in black paint: **Stürmer.** She knew that meant *Striker* in English, but she decided instead to shorten the name. "Braver hund, Stu."

She tossed a few treats. By the time she finished, the dog was out of the crate and sitting in front of it. He was dirty, but she could see he was young, maybe only eighteen months old, with black fur, pointed ears, and bright brown eyes that watched her intently. The one good thing about her berth was the size. It was small enough that the dog felt comfortable.

"Stu, *fuss*," she said, getting to her feet. The dog moved around and stood beside her. She walked to the door of the small cabin. It stayed right beside her. She turned and walked back to the bathroom. It never left her side. "Braver hund, Stu," she said, petting the dog affectionately. "Braver hund."

Her next task was getting it into the shower stall. "Bleib!" she ordered it to stay, and to his credit, Stu did as he was told. She filled a small container with water. The shower would only give her a minute's worth of water every twenty-four-hour cycle. She knew she was going to get messy cleaning the dog and his crate. So, she saved her shower water and used a cup at a time from the little lavatory. The bath took a while, and Stu obviously didn't like it, but he didn't seem like being dirty either. At least not in his own excrement, so he endured it. She used the towel to dry him off, then moved Stu back into the room and onto her blanket from home. He curled up, but kept his eyes on her as she took the crate apart and scrubbed it clean. Finally, she took her own quick shower. When she came out of the bathroom, Stu was still watching her. She got dressed and sat down beside the dog. It lifted its head and put it on her thigh.

"Braver hund, Stu," she told him as she scratched around his ears. "We're going to be good friends. Yes, we are."

CHAPTER 9

FLINT HAD TO WAIT. He didn't mind too much. There was no doubt that the captain was a busy man. And his office on the ship was opulent. Lieutenant Janson had taken him up to the Control section of the ship, which was essentially a huge building that spread across the front of the *Colossus* right on the top deck. The interior side of the building was covered by a massive display like the kinds used in sports stadiums. The outer side had what looked like floor-to-ceiling windows. Flint knew the transparent material wasn't glass, but it was spotless. In fact, it felt in some ways like the entire office he was waiting in was open to space.

He sat on a curved sofa. In front of him was a round coffee table with a carafe and several thick mugs with the *Colossus* logo printed on them. The tops of the mugs were covered like tumblers in a fancy hotel. Opposite from where Flint sat was another curved sofa. The pair nearly formed a circle. Flint thought the space felt very futuristic.

Across the room was a desk with a slate colored surface that flowed down to form the sides of the desk, as if the floor had been pushed up from below. There were shelves behind the desk, but no books or binders. The shelves were mostly empty, with just a few little keepsakes that the Captain of the *Colossus* had collected over the years. One was a framed pinboard with military medals neatly arranged. Flint didn't know what they represented, but it was clear the Captain was proud of his military service. Another was a globe that hovered over a round base. There was no visible attachment of the globe to the base. Flint guessed that it hovered via magnetics, but wasn't sure. It was clearly the Earth and painted to match their home planet. It slowly rotated above its base and was slightly tilted, just as Earth was. The only thing missing was the moon.

Lieutenant Janson had stepped out to make a call. There was no need for phones on the *Colossus*. Every member of the crew had a comlink. A few taps on their data cuff would connect their communication devices with anyone on the ship as long as they weren't in a dead zone. Flint tried not to think about the fact that there were so many spaces on board the massive transport that had no security cameras and where the computer signals were blocked. They were ideal places for mischief, and as a lifelong police officer, he had spent most of his career searching out such places where criminals naturally gathered to plan their devious capers. There was little doubt in his mind that he would soon continue doing exactly that.

In a perfect world, the *Colossus* would be filled with law-abiding citizens who had a firm grasp of the importance of their journey and the need to maintain order for the two years when they were crammed onto a ship like sardines. But nothing was ever perfect. The system used to ensure fairness was, in Flint's mind, a mistake. Yes, there needed to be equity in how people were selected. All the developed nations of the world, and many that weren't, had invested billions into the project. But a random lottery was not as fair as it seemed and it certainly didn't account for the types of people who were selected.

In North America, a person who won a space on the *Colossus* via the national lottery system had to first be put through a battery of tests, both physical and mental. Their criminal background was checked. Their associations and memberships in private and civil groups were examined. The purpose was to identify anyone who might not be up to the challenge. There were lottery winners who lost their spots because of a genetic abnormality or mental condition. There were people who discovered they had a rare disease that had yet to show any symptoms. Those people were not allowed to join the passengers on the *Colossus,* but they were given the chance to head off their disease before it became so widespread in their bodies that it cost them their lives.

But Flint understood there were a lot of people who could pass every test and still held anti-establishment leanings. Or, who, despite everything else, were really just one bad decision away from turning to a life of crime. In his mind, the passengers should have been chosen on merit. And some certainly were. It was one of the best ways to circumvent the lottery. If you had a skill or expertise that would be useful on the colony expedition, it wasn't hard to leverage that skill or expertise into a spot on the ship. Flint had no illusions about the lottery itself. Criminals were well-versed in rigging such systems and they had no moral qualms about doing so. They could easily hack into the criminal database, as well as their medical records, in order to fool the approval committees. Not to mention, a simple bribe was probably the easiest way to get on board. There had been hundreds of arrests made around the world by good law enforcement officers working tirelessly to keep such miscreants out of the lottery, but it was inevitable that some got through. That left Flint wondering why they would want to join the expedition. What nefarious plans might criminals be fomenting as the shuttles made their way into orbit with thousands of passengers, enabling them to hide in plain sight?

When the door opened, a tall, thin man with silver hair cut short and neatly styled entered. He wore a royal blue uniform. And his face was pinched into a frown. But he did his best not to scowl as he peered at Flint.

"You must be Sergeant Flint," the captain said. "I'm Captain

Hastings. It's a pleasure." The captain extended his hand, and Flint shook it, appreciating the firm grip. "Welcome aboard the *Colossus*. I hope you've been given a good tour."

"It was excellent," Flint said.

"Good. Then you know we have problems."

"Sir?"

"Please, sit down. Coffee? I'd offer you something stronger, but there's too damn much work still to be done."

"I'm fine, thank you," Flint said.

Captain Hastings tossed the paper cover off one of the thick mugs and poured himself a cup of coffee, then settled into the sofa opposite Flint.

"I asked to meet you. I've read your file, Sergeant. You have an impressive resume."

"Thank you," Flint said.

"I was in His Majesty's Royal Navy for twenty-five years, and I only retired to take this job. It's a massive undertaking. We've been working for months to get ready, and tomorrow the real job starts."

Flint knew he was talking about the passengers arriving.

"My job," the captain continued, "is to get the passengers to Secundo safely. And when it comes to the operation of the ship, we shall surpass all expectations. I have a top-notch crew who know their business. As I'm sure you know your people, Sergeant. You know that not everyone on this ship will be law-abiding citizens."

The captain sipped his coffee and it was Flint's turn to frown. "I know you're making a point here, captain, but I'm not getting it."

"My point is that as fine as this ship is, it has issues. The truth is, we've got too many passengers coming aboard. A week-long cruise to exotic locations is one thing. People can handle close quarters and crowded conditions for a short time, but two years? No, we'll have problems. There will be disgruntled people on this ship. While we have an excellent law enforcement division, the real heavy lifting will be carried out by Special Investigations and Logistical Operations.

Your team, Sergeant, is a vital part of this crew. I want to know you are up for the challenge."

"If you read my file, then you know I've been a cop as long as you were a naval officer," Flint replied coolly. "There's nothing I haven't seen. No crime that I haven't worked. I've got an excellent squad of special investigators. We won't be able to stop every crime from taking place, but we will catch those responsible and maintain order on the ship."

The captain studied him with a steely gaze for a long moment while neither man spoke. Then the captain sighed.

"Thank God," he said. "I was afraid they had replaced the SIU team leader with a complete imbecile. Not that I thought that from your record, Sergeant, but the temptation of a supervisor to use this as a chance to get rid of a difficult employee isn't unheard of."

It was Flint's turn to smile. He wasn't the easiest person to get along with, but he didn't have enemies in the department. His statistics were very good. He was neither a dirty cop nor an incompetent one. He was confident he and his squad could do a good job.

"I understand," Flint said. "... and I'm aware of the inadequacies of the ship. But to be honest, even if every inch was under video surveillance and there were no dead areas anywhere on board, those looking to make trouble would still find a way."

"Then I'm counting on you and your people to find a way to minimize the damage. I wish we had far fewer passengers on this voyage, but I'm keenly aware that every soul on board is needed on Secundo. We must do all we can to ensure they are ready to hit the ground running."

"Yes, sir," Flint said.

"I'm also aware that there is some distance between us on this ship," Captain Hastings said. "I don't mind that with most of the crew. There's a chain of command that must be respected. But I want you to know, Sergeant, that for you my door is always open. I've instructed my people to understand that. It's not that I want you to run up here every time you have an issue, but I want to know if there is a problem."

"Anything you need to know, sir, I will make sure you know it."

"That's all I ask," Hastings said. "I can only help when I know it's needed."

They shook hands again. The captain apologized that he didn't have more time, but Flint understood. In fact, he had a lot to do himself and it was getting late in the day. A hot meal, a quick shower and a good night's rest were in order. Soon, he would have very little downtime. That was fine with Flint, but he was smart enough to make the most of what time he had. His mind was buzzing with all the new sights and sounds he had experienced on the tour of the ship. It would take a bit of work to calm his mental faculties enough to actually sleep. Starting the next day, there would be thousands of people on the ship without a lot to do to keep them occupied. His grandmother had always said idle hands are the devil's playthings and in his decades of police experience, he knew that old saying to be true. At some point, there would be crime on the *Colossus*. When it happened, he wanted his squad prepped and ready. That meant setting a good example for the team. He would take care of business and set the tone for what he expected of each of them. There was still a lot he wanted to do with his squad and it was clear that they would have to pitch in and help with the security work, right off the bat. That didn't leave a lot of room for team-building exercises or just getting to know one another. But he would find a way to bond with his team and build rapport. That was what good leaders did and Flint was determined to do his very best while on the *Colossus*. After that, his future was a blank slate. But, in the meantime, his squad would be the best in the business.

CHAPTER 10

TAY MATTOX WAS NERVOUS. He was not a people person and preferred solitude to being in crowds. He was not crazy. He wasn't afraid of crowds, but in his personal philosophy, it was better to keep people at arm's length.

He had grown up in rough conditions. Never the fastest or the strongest, he had been the target of many cruel people until he discovered a rare talent. Technology spoke to him. He discovered his gift when, as a teenager, he was sent to collect old computers from the municipal recycling facilities. Most people went there to dump their trash, but Tay had gone to collect. The old, old computers often had trace amounts of rare minerals in their circuit boards and processors. The tech might not function any longer, but the composite parts still had some value, from the copper wiring to the lithium in batteries, and cobalt in the semiconductors. Tay didn't know much about minerals, but what he discovered was a knack for taking random parts and building something new. And not only could he build the technology, but he found its operation to be intuitive. Some people could speak multiple languages. Tay spoke the language of computer programming. Within a few years, he was known by his hacker name, Crank ... and he was busy running scams for the same people who had tormented him before.

Crank being on the first wave of passengers was no accident. JD had wanted it that way, and what JD wanted, he got. The man was a master of strategic planning. Had he gone to West Point or the NATO Military Academy, he would have climbed up the ranks swiftly. Instead, he had joined the East Side Boys, where he became a shot caller by the time he was just seventeen years old. He was instrumental in merging the ESB with the much larger and rougher Ghetto Kings. And after just a few years, he was the top dog in the criminal enterprise. They were a gang, and there was plenty of wanton violence associated with the teenagers and young men in the organization. But they had widely expanded their illegal trade, moving beyond guns and drugs, to more sophisticated types of crime: insider trading, stock manipulation, government assistance fraud, and blockchain hacking.

They were successful and Crank was at the center of it all. Yet, for all their success and bounty, they were still locked into the system.

After years of defrauding the system with little they could show for it, JD got the idea to expand to a new world. Secundo was the promised land, the gang leader proclaimed. After using Crank to get himself and his lieutenants on the manifest, the crime of the century was planned. They were going to steal an entire planet and rule the new world like kings. It all started with Crank getting on board and locating what was needed to ensure they could communicate and plan their heist in complete secrecy. They would be under the nose of Johnny Law for a solid two years, hiding among the thousands of ignorant cattle being sent to prepare Secundo for the future that would soon belong exclusively to the Ghetto Kings.

Crank wasn't the only criminal on the shuttle. There were close to a thousand passengers waiting anxiously as the aircraft docked at the transit station. They were strapped into their seats, a wide range of people, but almost exclusively young men and women. There were no children in the first wave of passengers, just as there were none of the VIP or special skills passengers. Those would come later. Crank was among the young hopefuls, single people on a mission to reach Secundo, who had been selected via the nation-specific lottery. None of them were fat. None had visible, identifiable ailments or infirmities. Crank didn't know it, but he hadn't seen any wedding rings on the fingers of the women he had quietly been staring at. He was himself a skinny man, shorter than average, with close-cropped hair and dark black skin. There were gang tattoos on his arms, chest, and legs, but they were all covered and would remain so. In his carry-on was what appeared to be an out-of-date laptop computer. It had been scanned at the airport and again at the space port. He had no doubt it would be scanned again before he boarded the *Colossus*. He didn't mind the scrutiny. Unless a person was a computer expert and could open up the hard case to see the components inside, they wouldn't know how powerful it really was.

Crank had built the laptop PC himself. He used an old version specifically because it had more room inside. And he had replaced all the interior parts. It wasn't built for gaming or for business. It was, instead, a powerful control center, created specifically for breaking into secure servers and networks. If a person had opened the computer and booted it up, they would have gotten an old operating desktop system, that was in fact just a false front, almost like a screen saver. Crank could minimize it via a hidden command and then access the powerful system properly.

"I can't believe this," the man sitting next to Crank said. He had a swarthy complexion. When he boarded, he had a scarf wrapped loosely around his neck. Once they broke free of Earth's gravity, he had been forced to remove it to keep the garment from floating up in front of his face. "We're almost there."

"Yeah," Crank said.

"My name is Ido," he said.

"Tay."

"Nice to meet you, Tay," Ido said. "I'm just so excited to get on board."

"What deck are you assigned to?" Crank asked.

"Seventeen. You?"

Crank could have hacked the manifest and put himself in one of the VIP staterooms on the second level of the massive ship. But his orders had been to stay under the radar.

"Fifteen," he said.

"When we get on board, we should exchange info," Ido suggested.

Crank had no desire to give out his personal information to a stranger. And he felt no bond with the man just because they were leaving Earth on the same ship. But he nodded along, doing nothing to attract attention.

Three rows behind Crank was another man who wasn't what he seemed. Beside him was a woman, his partner, although they pretended not to know one another. They, too, had rigged the lottery system and even the shuttle manifest so that they would be among the first passengers on the ship. At a glance, they seemed completely normal. He had the look of a Greek or Italian citizen with jet black hair and a heavy five o'clock shadow on his square jaw. The woman was Asian, with her long black hair in a thick braid and a tiny little scar on the high cheekbone beneath her left eye. They were not only seatmates in the shuttle, but they were also roommates in a double occupancy berth on the seventeenth deck. And both had been paid an enormous amount of money via fake companies and stock options on Earth, to ensure that Everett Goddard didn't reach Secundo alive.

In fact, there were a variety of people on the shuttle who shouldn't have been. Some were people who felt the rules simply didn't apply to them. Others saw the journey and life on a new planet as the perfect hustle. All around, the rule breakers and bad actors were good people with good intentions. They were anxious for a new chapter in life. Getting off an overcrowded, highly controlled planet was, in itself, a step up. But the opportunity to chase new dreams on a world where people had freedom and space was almost too good to believe. There were some doubters among the passengers. It was inevitable that pessimists found their way onto the *Colossus*. There were people who were convinced that Secundo was not what it was promoted as being. Through a wild twist of fate, they had been chosen to go there and help populate the new world. Some of those people had given up their spots. Others had been quietly replaced with people who assumed their total identity. Others were going just to prove that they had been right all along.

Fortunately, for most of the crowd, the naysayers couldn't put a dent in the enthusiasm of their fellow passengers. When the shuttle safely docked with the transit station, they were released in groups. It was better to make the transition in small groups simply because too many people set loose in zero gravity was the recipe for disaster.

Crank made his way off the shuttle and through the transit station, then onto the *Colossus*. The sudden return of gravity was difficult for the young cyber-criminal to deal with. He was not strong. Long hours spent sitting in front of a computer had not increased his physical abilities. But he managed to cope. His group was lined up. They met with a dour-looking junior officer who checked them on a state-of-the-art tablet. Their physical identity had already been established on Earth and the data had been uploaded to the *Colossus'* computer. Facial scans were confirmed by voice recognition and each passenger received a device that wrapped around their wrist. The ship's crew members called them, "cufflinks". The smart device interacted with the ship's computer system and was the key to their cabins and various amenities.

They had all gone through a virtual orientation before leaving Earth. Their only task upon arrival was to find their cabins and get settled in. What luggage they were allowed to bring on the trip would be delivered to their cabins and the passengers were strongly encouraged to stay on their assigned deck for the next several days, while thousands of people would be boarding the colossal ship.

Crank took an elevator up to deck fifteen. From there, he had a long hike to reach his room but when he finally did, he was relieved to find it well-appointed. He had a private room with a low, recessed bunk, a wide work desk and a personal entertainment console. There was an office chair near the desk and a more comfortable reclining chair near the display for the entertainment station. The tiny berth was not big enough for many visitors nor did it have appliances for keeping food or beverages. It did have a closet and a tiny bathroom. What mattered most to Crank was that it was new. He had lived his entire life in old, government-assisted housing. The hallways were dimly lit and rank with foul smells. The elevators were unreliable. Graffiti covered the walls and the housing units were tiny. Half of the things he ordered using his ill-gotten gains were stolen before they even reached his apartment. But his berth on the Colossus was different. It smelled of fresh paint and new furniture. There was tightly woven carpeting on the floor from the front door to the bathroom. Outside, the corridors were wide, well-lit and graffiti-free. Nor did they smell like urine and body odor, or worse. The ship was bound to have its own problems. Crank was a realist, after all. He also knew there were over twenty thousand crew members whose sole job was to look after, fix, and maintain the ship's many systems.

In his room, he forced himself to wait for the rest of his luggage to arrive. When it did, he thanked the crew member and locked himself inside. Only then did he settle down at his new desk and open his computer. The system was fast. It booted up with record speed. That was the one drawback to his masquerade. Anyone who knew computers would know that an old system like he was pretending to use would take a long time to work through its opening routine. But no one had bothered to check it. No one suspected that he had hacked into the lottery and rigged the system to put himself and the men he worked for onto their acceptance lists. He was a complete unknown, and he intended to stay that way. But not before he penetrated the defenses on the ship's computer systems and established himself as the shadow in the machine. From there, he would be in control. The crew might call the shots, but at any time, he could step in, override their commands and gain a stranglehold on the system. When JD arrived, Crank would either be inside the ship's computer system or close to it. Whatever they wanted would be within their grasp.

CHAPTER 11

"WHO IS THIS?" Logan asked as Jeopardy came out of the locker room with Stu.

"My new partner," she said proudly. "He's a fast learner, too. His name is Stu."

Logan knew better than to pet a police dog. They were friendly and full of love, just like a pet, but they were also trained to keep a close watch on the people around their handler. Instead of trying to pet the dog, he held out a hand.

"Stu, freund," she said, reaching out and touching his thick forearm. "Logan ist ein freund."

The dog dutifully stepped toward Logan and sniffed the man's open hand. After getting a good scent, he stepped back. It was as friendly as he cared to get, no matter what Jeopardy said about him.

They were in the law enforcement training center. The large space was divided between meeting rooms for classes, simulators and exercise equipment. Many of the law enforcement personnel enjoyed cardio equipment, but some still preferred to jog, so an eighth of a mile track was mounted above the large workout space below.

Logan approved of the training area. It was large and well-equipped. There were all the usual resistance training machines, free weights and exercise devices. There were long rows of cardio equipment, from ellipticals to rowing machines. Then there were combat spaces with thick mats for training in various martial arts. There were heavy punching bags, speed bags, and devices for all sorts of martial training. Just like any gym, there were people who gravitated to one section or another. Logan liked it all, but spent the majority of his training time on the mats or working the heavy bags.

Jeopardy had never been a big fitness fanatic, but once she started training with police dogs, she recognized the value of running with her four-legged partners. It was a way for the pair of them to exercise and bond at the same time.

"Stu, *fuss*," she ordered as they began walking around the track. The dog stayed right beside her. There were only two other people on the long track, and both were jogging with headphones over their ears.

"How was your day?" Logan asked as he walked on the other side of Stu.

"Fine, I guess," Jeopardy said. "Stu and I worked luggage. He did all the heavy lifting. I stood around and tried not to fall asleep."

"That bad, huh?"

"I get it," she replied. "We have to be careful. If someone is smuggling something onto the ship, we should catch it now. But their bags have all been checked and scanned before they left Earth. What did you do?"

"I played tour guide," he said. "Helping people find their rooms."

"At least you were around people. We stood by a conveyor belt while Stu sniffed the bags that went trundling past."

"Isn't that a lot like what you did back on Earth?"

"I suppose, but with much lower odds of actually finding something. There's excitement getting called in and working a vehicle or checking a suspicious object when you find something that shouldn't be there."

"Can Stu smell explosives?"

"He can do it all. They should have named him Krypto super-dog," Jeopardy said. "Stu, joggen."

They began to jog. The German Shepherd seemed almost bored with the slow pace, but it didn't take long before he was panting.

"Do you do this every day?" Jeopardy asked Logan.

"Six days a week," he said. "Weights, martial training of some form or other, then cardio."

"You run last?"

He chuckled. "Yeah, that's my routine."

"Well, we didn't mean to mess things up."

"You aren't," he said. "I did a full workout this morning. It's hard getting used to a new place."

"So, you've already worked out today?"

"Yeah, but I don't mind hitting it twice. Maybe I'll sleep better tonight."

"Or maybe you're crazy," she said and they both laughed.

They picked up the pace, and the conversation was held in short bursts as they worked their way around the track eight times. When they finished, they walked another circuit, cooling down and continuing their talk.

"Do you think there will be much to do on this ship?"

"Lots of entertainment options," Logan told her.

"That's not what I mean."

"Do you want there to be police work on the voyage?"

"Yes and no," Jeopardy said. "Obviously, I don't want there to be crime. But spending all day searching for something that isn't there was mind-numbing. What if the whole trip is like that? What if we just do nothing all day, every day?"

"If there were only fifty people on this ship, there would be crime," Logan said. "It's human nature to break the rules."

"Sure, I guess so," Jeopardy said.

"And when they do, we'll find them and lock them up. I don't think too much is getting past your partner."

"No," Jeopardy said with a smile. "He's a good cop."

She reached down and scratched his ears. They made their way back through the ship, getting their share of odd looks from the crew, who were mostly surprised to see Stu walking between them. Eventually, they split up as they got closer to their own quarters. And after getting Stu settled in his crate, Jeopardy joined the rest of the squad in the dining hall.

"How was it?" Dave asked.

"Fine," Logan replied.

"Boring," Jeopardy added.

"Great. We've got a twelve-hour shift tonight," Becky said.

"This is what we signed up for," Flint said. "Sometimes it's working the streets, sometimes it's helping people find their new homes on a giant spaceship."

Later that evening, the first crime was reported on the *Colossus*. Dave and Becky's cufflink alerted them to a complaint coming from the fourteenth deck. They had been helping passengers on different parts of the ship, but caught up near the elevators on the fourteenth floor.

"You get a ping?" Becky asked.

"Not even a full day on board and someone is complaining," Dave said.

They reached the apartment a few minutes later and were met by a woman with frizzy hair and bulging eyes.

"They stole my bag," she said.

"I'm sorry, what?" Becky asked.

"My luggage! I had two suitcases. One with clothes, the other with heirlooms. The second one is missing."

"And you know this because..." Dave asked.

He wasn't a sarcastic person. He could joke around when he was with the squad, but he took his job very seriously.

"Are you even security?" the woman asked.

"Special investigators," Becky said, holding up her new badge, which was in a special wallet with a photo ID card that was more for civilians than anything else. All their pertinent information was on the cufflink, including any access they might need to the ship and crew. But the badges and IDs were familiar to the passengers and would be used for that purpose.

"Well, a crew member brought one suitcase, but not the other. And when I asked him about he got defensive."

"Did you get his name?" Dave asked.

"No."

"What did he look like?" Becky questioned.

"He was wearing orange coveralls and looked like a criminal."

Orange had become the standard color for the scrubs worn by inmates in detention centers, at least in North America. The woman they were talking to was clearly American, although Becky was starting to wonder about the woman's mental stability.

"How's that?" Becky asked.

"He had dark eyes," she said. "And his hair wasn't combed. I could tell there was something wrong with him right off the bat. When I asked about my other bag, he pretended like he didn't know what I was talking about. We're allowed two pieces of luggage. I checked them both together. They should both be here, but someone stole my bag."

"What did the bag look like?" Dave asked.

"It was silver, a hard case Samsonite. I paid a lot of money for that suitcase," the woman explained. "My name is on the tag."

"Helena Grisolm?" Becky asked.

"Yeah, that's right. And I'm not leaving without that bag."

Becky wanted to explain that a single lost suitcase wouldn't keep the *Colossus* from setting off for Secundo, but she saved her breath. "I'm sure it's just a mix-up, but we'll do our best to find your missing luggage."

"It's got all my heirlooms in it," the woman said, suddenly emotional.

"Items of value?" Dave asked.

"It's invaluable to me," the woman said, her voice cracking.

"Try to stay calm," Becky said. "We're going to look into this right away."

"And we'll be in touch soon," Dave added.

They turned away from the woman's cabin and waited for the door to close. Becky glanced over his shoulder before saying, "Looks like we've got our first case."

"Should I alert the team, or do you think we can handle it?"

"Let's take a crack at it," Becky said. "What could possibly go wrong?"

CHAPTER 12

JD'S real name was Jerome Donalds. He never knew his father, but his mother had a permanent scar on her face where he had burned her with a hot pan, and her left eye was slightly misshapen from where the utensil had shattered her ocular socket. He had left her shortly after the incident, which landed her in a hospital. Yet for some reason, she hadn't pressed charges against him and had even given JD his last name five months later.

His home life had been stable but his mother had done nothing to discourage him from a life of crime on the streets. It was expected, in her world, that boys would be rough and wild. JD hadn't seen his mother in years. Like his own father, he had abandoned his mother and never looked back.

Life on Earth was predictable. JD had a knack for identifying patterns and trends. One of the easiest to identify was the amount of crime that government officials were willing to live with. Half of all robberies went unsolved and cybercrimes were the least investigated of all such felonious activities. That was one of the reasons JD had shifted much of what he was personally involved in to online scams. While many of the thugs on the streets didn't really understand what the Ghetto Kings were up to, they had no problem with the money that came rolling in. Digital currency, with its blockchain trail, was harder to wash and often made spending it almost impossible. Unless said currency was used in what the establishment wanted it used for. Large, lavish purchases were almost immediately flagged by the system and investigated by cybercrime specialists, but lots of little purchases flew completely under the radar. On the streets, goods were bartered on a regular basis. JD still slung plenty of good dope to those who wanted it, but he also had soldiers on the street scoring tech hardware, trading perishable goods and supplying the neighborhoods the GKs controlled with whatever the people needed, from protection to medicines.

In exchange, his people really did live like kings. His lieutenants had entire apartment building floors, with harems of women that did their bidding. Cooking, cleaning, laundry, it was all traded for the goods people needed. The Ghetto Kings couldn't drive fancy hovercars or travel to exotic locations, but they transformed their world into a kingdom that was under their control. And because of the stability they created in the city blocks they controlled, the GKs had no trouble with law enforcement. When it came to crime, the squeaky wheel got the grease. And JD had his gang transformed into a well-oiled, money-making empire.

But eventually, the thug life lost its appeal. Real power was in the hands of politicians, many of whom were criminals just like JD, only their crimes brought them more than wealth and control; it afforded them respectability. But that system was out of JD's reach. There were plenty of people from the streets who took a run at government office. Some even managed to win their local elections, but the glass ceiling was low when it came to politics. There were big machines behind the political parties, except they decided who would run for office and who would serve in what capacity. JD didn't like the idea of being anyone's puppet. He had nearly settled for life as a thug king when the announcement was made about the Secundo colony.

A new world was a place rife with opportunities. There would be roadblocks and difficulties, but JD was convinced he could seize real power on the new world. He was in the first-class section of the shuttle. On Earth, airplanes had been flying the lucky winners of the lottery to space ports for several days. Shuttles with hundreds of passengers had been running nonstop for a full twenty-four hours. JD was among the first VIP passengers taken up. He was a slim black man. He had traded his blue jeans and leather coat for khaki pants, loafers and a cashmere cardigan over a short-sleeved golf shirt. It was a disguise of sorts, as was the woman posing as his wife and the two children posing as his family.

Crank had given JD a new identity. On the manifest, he was a specialist with a family, which meant he got a three-bedroom suite on the third deck, but he was scrubbed from the lists of job duties required of the scholars, technical advisors, and specialists with expertise in what were considered to be essential fields.

When he stepped on board the ship, he was met by an officer, who assigned him to a crewman who would show the Donaldson family to their new quarters. They took the elevator up to the third deck.

"I think you may be the first passenger on this level," the crew member said.

"We were excited to come on board," the woman posing as JD's wife said.

"It's a great ship," the crew member said. "Really first rate. Here's your berth, three-three-seven. Your luggage will be brought up once it gets processed."

"Thank you," JD said.

He walked into the cabin. It consisted of a large main room with a full kitchen in the back. There was a dining table large enough for four and, near the entertainment console, was a two-person sofa and a pair of matching chairs. They looked comfortable, but everything felt a bit small to JD. He was used to making do with whatever could be gotten by his crew, which sometimes meant second-hand furniture or jewelry. He knew that thousands of other passengers were living in much smaller quarters and some were even forced to live with roommates.

"Take the rug rats and wait for Crank," JD told the woman as he pointed to the small bedroom that was meant to be shared by the children. It was a small space, with a desk built into one wall, two recessed bunks, and a pair of matching lockers with veneers over the metal to make them seem more appealing as furniture.

He looked into the other bedroom. It was more to his liking, if a bit small. There was a double bed with nightstands on either side, a closet with built-in shelving, and a single chair under a lamp in the corner. The bedroom led to the bathroom, which had a single wash basin on the oversized counter and a second mirror with lights for a lady's vanity. The shower stall was standard, as was the sixty-second water limit. And the toilet was in its own small compartment.

"This will do," JD said. He could have paid for a nicer berth on the second deck, but that would have put him into contact with the other VIPs, and he knew no matter how good his cover story, or how well he played the part, there would be suspicion about him from the rich and nosy VIP passengers.

He went to the beverage dispenser and studied it for a moment. Hot water and coffee were available from one side. Cold water, fruit-flavored beverages and cold tea from the other side. JD preferred beer or even hard liquor, but that would have to wait. He settled for coffee and found cream and sugar in small packets on a rack built into the wall above the counter. There was no stove in the cabin's modified kitchen, just a refrigerator, freezer, microwave, and dishwasher. There would be drawbacks to living on a spaceship for two years. JD would have to compromise on the quality of his lifestyle, even with a larger suite to live in.

On one counter were the cufflinks given to each member of his pseudo-family upon arrival. And JD didn't have to wait long before Crank showed up. The small man was a wizard with technology, a fact that had probably saved his life on the streets. JD wasn't surprised that his tech guru knew he had come aboard. It would have been a problem if he hadn't.

A soft chime announced a guest at the door. JD pressed the release button beside it, and the door slid sideways to reveal the small hacker carrying a duffel bag.

"Glad to see you made it," Crank said.

"Was there a reason I wouldn't have?" JD asked, wondering for the first time if his tech slave might have sabotaged his leader. A simple email could have done it. Cast a little shade on JD, or the other shot callers, and it wouldn't take long for the authorities to realize their lottery system had been tampered with.

"The shuttle could have exploded," Crank said. "I'm not a fan of flying."

"You're not a fan of anything you have to do outside your little desk chair," JD said. "You soil yourself on takeoff?"

"No," Crank said.

"Maybe there's hope for you, yet," JD replied as he watched the smaller man work.

Crank set his duffel bag on the floor and pulled out his chunky laptop computer. He opened it, typed in the security code and then reached back down to pull out a series of cables.

"We can hack the cufflinks," Crank said. "Takes a while, but the security on the ship is weak. They got locators running, trying to keep tabs on everybody all the time."

"But you can fix that," JD said. It was more of an order than a simple statement.

"I'm on it," Crank said. "What do you want me to do with the kids?"

"Don't care," JD said. "Just so long as they ain't bothering us here."

"Got it," Crank said. "The others ain't on board yet."

"Fine," JD said. "We ain't in no hurry. You bring what I told you to have ready for me?"

Crank leaned back down and pulled out a bottle of booze. He set it on the coffee table next to JD's nearly empty mug.

"That's what I'm talking 'bout," he said, lifting the unopened bottle and reading the label. It was whiskey, and JD had never been picky about his liquor. He broke the wax seal and popped the cork off. There were clean glasses in the cabinet above the drink dispenser, but JD just turned the bottle up and drank it straight. After taking a mouthful and swallowing it slowly, he exhaled, letting the heat from the booze waft from his mouth. He hadn't eaten in a while. The liquid burned down his throat and scalded his stomach, but it was a familiar and welcome burn. The heat spread through his body and he felt the tension releasing from his shoulders.

"You want me to do anything else?" Crank asked, as he unplugged JD's cufflink from his computer and plugged in the next one.

"Finish up, and get rid of them kids," JD said. "Viv!"

"Yeah?" said the woman from the children's room.

"Time to earn your keep. I need a massage."

JD stood up. "Soon as the others get here, you disable that tracking feature," he ordered. "Then we can gather up right here. Start making our plans."

Jerome Donaldson went to his bedroom, followed by the woman posing as his wife. Crank watched her go, trying not to be jealous of his boss, but it wasn't easy. He had made arrangements for the children. JD had insisted on no less than seven women being at his beck and call. The children would be shuffled between them, go to school, and live a somewhat normal life with no connection to JD or the Ghetto Kings. They were still in the small bedroom and Crank eyed it once he was alone. He didn't like kids, didn't like most people. He preferred solitude. He would get their cufflinks hacked and take them back down to the lower decks. Then he, too, could disappear for a while, before his boss gave him more work to do.

CHAPTER 13

"I'VE GOT it checked in on the shuttle, but not checked onto the ship," Becky said, staring at her computer screen.

She and Dave Bannon were in the SIU office. They had already talked to the crew member in charge of cargo. He admitted that it was possible that some bags didn't get scanned.

"We got a lot to do, and it happens," the crew member said. "Once we make the majority of the deliveries, we'll double-check what's left."

Becky had no desire to go digging through the mountains of suit-cases in search of one missing bag. She had sympathy for the woman who had lost her luggage, but it didn't feel like a real emergency.

"Shouldn't there be a note on the system when you scanned her other bag?" Dave asked. "She registered two suitcases."

"Doesn't mean the other one is on board yet. The shuttle crew unloads," the crew member they had questioned explained. "If they missed it, we can't do anything about that. We'll just have to wait until that shuttle comes back around."

With nothing more to be done, they had gone up to their office and filed a preliminary report. Everything they did had to be reported. There were files for all sorts of crimes and issues, even lost luggage.

"Looks like a Greg Gilbert," Dave said from his computer. "Delivered the bag to her room at 0210 ship time."

"I guess we need to find him and have a chat," Becky said.

"This is sad," Dave said, sending the information on Greg Gilbert's berth, which was where his cufflink was located at that moment, to his own smart device on his left wrist. "We've been relegated to investigating stolen luggage."

"Look at it this way, if you ever lose your job, you can apply with TSA. You've got experience now."

"Funny," Dave said. "You want to go talk to this guy?"

"It's what we do," Becky said.

She knew that a large percentage of good police work was talking to people. There were times when she wanted to lock herself away and solve crime from her desk. But that wasn't how crimes got solved. It wasn't like a murder mystery novel. There were often little or no *clues* leading to a revelation of guilt. In most instances, it was an accumulation of seemingly innocuous data, collected over time and through dozens of conversations, that revealed the truth. People could be excellent liars, but with enough data, holes often emerged in a suspect's story. With enough legwork, those holes could lead to proof. But none of it happened if a detective stayed comfortable behind their desk.

They left the SI office and took an elevator up to the top deck. Greg Gilbert, like all other crew members except for senior officers, had a berth on the lowest deck. But Greg's was on the far side of the ship. And while they could have used hoverboards to travel the eight miles, it was actually faster to go up and take the tube around.

Ten minutes later, they reached the berth they were looking for and pressed the call button mounted beside the door.

"Think he's home?" Becky asked.

"He should be sleeping," Dave replied.

"Unless he's a criminal mastermind. In that case, we could be walking into a trap."

"Are you always this flippant about your job?" Dave asked.

"Oh, loosen up, Bannon. We're looking for lost luggage."

He frowned, but didn't respond because the door opened before he could think of what to say. Dave loved to joke around and have fun, but there were times when his mind locked into a rigid framework and wouldn't allow him to focus on anything but the work. It made him a tenacious investigator, but a poor partner.

"What?" a bleary-eyed man in a long sleeping gown asked. He had thinning hair and his stomach was round against the front of the strange garment. It wasn't a woman's gown, but an old-fashioned garment that reflected an obscure religious belief that only natural fabrics that weren't combined with other materials should be worn against the body.

"Are you Greg Gilbert?" Dave asked.

"No," he said. "He's still asleep."

"Wake him," Becky said, holding up her badge. "We've got some questions."

"Oh, okay," the man in the sleeping gown said. "Sure. Just a second."

He stepped back into the berth, which was exactly like Becky's, only messier. It had clearly been lived in longer. There were towels hanging on a rack near the bathroom, and what looked like a tabletop game still in progress on the fold-out.

"Could have been worse," Becky said. "He could have been nude."

Dave just frowned at her. He had his hand on the door frame. A sensor inside kept the door from sliding shut. Becky leaned against the wall on the other side of the frame. She knew what was coming. There was no great mystery to solve. It was almost certainly just a logistical mistake. While she joked about the seriousness of the supposed crime, she did relate to how the supposed victim felt. Leaving Earth and everyone you had ever known was a serious undertaking. The woman had been allowed one bag of keepsakes. And, as she had said, that suitcase was invaluable to her.

"What's going on?" Greg asked as he stepped to the door, shading his eyes from the bright light in the street-wide corridor outside his tiny domicile.

"You Greg Gilbert?" Becky asked.

"Yeah."

"We have some questions for you about luggage that was reported stolen," Dave said.

"Did you take a suitcase up to a Helena Grisolm?" Becky asked.

"Huh?"

"Helena Grisolm," Dave said. "Up on deck fourteen."

"I delivered a lot of suitcases," he said. "That's all I did my last shift."

"You might remember this one," Becky said. "She was expecting two bags, but only got one. I'm sure she let you know about it."

Greg began to nod. "Okay, yeah, there was one passenger who complained. I didn't think much of it."

"Why?" Dave said.

"She asked where her other bag was. I told her that I only had one assigned to her cabin. She didn't like that. But I assured her if she had another bag, it would get sorted out and sent up. That's what we're instructed to say. It's usually true. Probably just a mix-up in sorting."

"Did you look into her suitcases?" Becky asked.

"No," he said. "That's against regs. Besides, I got no time to look in the bags."

"Maybe it was heavy, or you saw something that caught your eye, and you thought you would just check it out?"

"They're all heavy," Greg grumbled. "That's why they put wheels on 'em. Come on, you guys don't really think I would steal someone's luggage, do you?"

"Would you mind if we take a look around in your berth?" Dave asked. "Just to confirm the bag isn't here."

"Sure, whatever," Greg said. "Some things never change."

"What's that supposed to mean?" Becky asked.

"I mean, you're wasting your time looking at me. I think you both know that. I'm just a maintenance mate. Why would I steal some-one's luggage? It's not like I could do anything with it. Only a fool would steal something when they've got no possible way to escape the authorities. Yet here you are, waking me up in the dead of night, rifling through my berth like I'm a criminal. There's a reason why people don't like the police, you know."

"We're just doing our jobs," Becky said. "And that means we check every possibility, no matter how far-fetched."

"Besides," Dave chimed in, "you could be the kind of person who views the situation differently."

"What?"

"He's saying you could be a complete idiot who hasn't thought about the fact that you've got nowhere to run on a starship for the next two years, only he's being nice about it."

The search only took a few minutes. Both men opened their lockers and the drawers beneath their bunks. They were both guilty of being slobs, but nothing else. There was no evidence that they were stealing luggage.

"Sorry to have bothered you," Becky said when they finished.

"We appreciate your cooperation," Dave added.

"Not like I had a choice. Can I go back to bed now?" Greg asked.

"Sure," Becky said.

The pair of special investigators started back down the hallway. It was still very early by ship's time, which was a standard 24-hour cycle. But there were always people on duty, just as Becky and Dave were. The corridors between the berths and storage compartments on the humongous ship were well-lit all the time. Only on the top deck, with its great arch representing the sun, did it ever go dark.

"He could have been a sociopath," Dave said.

"What?"

"Or suffering from delusions," Dave continued. "Idiocy was just a possibility."

Becky laughed. Dave glanced over, with just a hint of a smile on his face.

CHAPTER 14

LOGAN DIDN'T SLEEP MUCH. Four hours was his average. Six hours was rare. Nor did he feel groggy when he woke up. His body just seemed to brim with energy. Sitting still was difficult for him, and going more than a single day without pushing his muscles hard was unthinkable, which was why he was up at 0500 ship time and jogging to the law enforcement training center on deck four. The jog from the elevator nearest his berth to the TC was nearly half a mile, plenty of distance to get his blood pumping and his joints loosened up before a workout.

He went right to the resistance machines. He preferred free weights, which could have been utilized on the *Colossus* with her artificial gravity, but whoever made the decisions about the fitness areas on the ship opted for devices that contained heavy plates that could be selected with the use of a metal pin. And even that was kept on a bungee tether. The machines themselves were bolted to the deck. In the off chance that the ship's artificial gravity failed, the TC wouldn't be filled with dangerous metal weights drifting around.

Logan was no bodybuilder, although he was a little bigger than average. His frame was packed solid with powerful muscles. After working out hard for an hour on the weight machines, he gloved up and moved to the martial training area, where he pounded on a heavy punching bag in intervals of three-minute rounds with one-minute breaks in between, for a full forty minutes. After that, he moved up to the jogging track, where he sprinted down the long straight sections and jogged slowly around the ends. It was how he started every morning.

A shower and shave followed, then breakfast at 0630. He was at the Special Investigations office by 0715. Jeopardy was there with Stu and their boss, Sawyer Flint. Assignments were handed out, and Logan went down to help with the new passengers. He wasn't tired, even after a hard morning workout, but neither did he feel antsy. He wasn't buzzing with energy, although he could feel his energy levels building back up. It was better to be busy than to be bored, and while he didn't care for escorting people through the ship, it was better than sitting all day at a desk. Sitting for hours on end was a special kind of torture to Logan Keys.

It was officially the second day of passenger arrivals. They were scheduled for seven, but it only took two for the first blood to be spilled in anger on the *Colossus*. It was inevitable that there would be disagreements. Everyone knew it would occur. With passengers from all over the world, there were bound to be differences in customs, or even how the various groups perceived things. People from cultures that did not get along on Earth were separated on different decks, but the same old animosities and insecurities from the old world were brought on the new ship.

Logan saw the inciting incident. He was on his way back from showing a family to their berth on deck ten when a passenger in a compression shirt, with shoulder-length hair, bumped into a woman in a flowing dress. Logan was not immune to the charms of women, and the female involved in the incident was classically beautiful. Her husband, on the other hand, was a short man with thinning hair and a thick waist. He was following his wife and struggling with their carry-on luggage, which was clearly heavy.

The long-haired man could have been a professional athlete. He certainly had the build: wide shoulders, thick pectoral muscles, a narrow waist, and very little body fat. Logan knew the type. The long-haired man had chiseled features and was obviously very popular with women. Logan couldn't say for certain, but he felt confident that the stumble into the ugly man's pretty wife was no accident. The long-haired man caught her arm and then flashed her a brilliant smile.

"Oh, sorry about that," he said.

"It's alright," the woman replied, returning his smile.

"Thanks," the long-haired man said, still holding the woman's arm. "This place takes some getting used to. I'm glad there are people on board with some patience for an oaf like me."

"Nonsense," the woman said. "We are neighbors."

"You're on this deck?"

"Yes, room—"

"Hey!" the husband shouted. "Get your filthy hands off my wife."

"What?" the long-haired man asked, never taking his eyes off the woman.

"Let go of her before I break every bone in your body, you ignorant baboon."

Logan appreciated the insult. He hadn't heard of someone called a baboon in a very long time.

The long-haired man finally turned to the woman's husband. He was a full head taller and, from the looks of things, much stronger.

"Please," the woman said. "No offense was intended. We will go."

"Beat it, loser," the husband said.

"Better watch your mouth," the long-haired man said. "Or someone will shut it for you."

"Touch my wife again, and you will regret it," the husband said.

The long-haired man turned back to the man's wife, and Logan knew instantly it was a mistake. He hurried forward, but he was still twenty paces away.

The long-haired man said, "How much money does a cretin like that have to wed a beautiful woman like you?"

The shorter man dropped both of the bags he was carrying and drove his fist hard into the taller man's groin. The punch drove the man backward and caused him to double over. The shorter man followed up with a strong uppercut. Logan was running by then, but he still noticed how the husband set his feet, bent his knees, and put his entire body into an upward thrust that powered his punch. It landed flush on the long-haired man's nose and sent the bigger man rearing backward as blood fountained through the air.

"Stop!" Logan shouted. "Police!"

The smaller man had been about to pounce on the taller man, who had crashed to the floor on his back. The husband glanced up, saw Logan, probably noticed that he wasn't in any sort of official uniform and pivoted to take on what he considered a new threat.

"Hands up," Logan shouted.

"Screw you!" the husband snarled.

Logan had been in a thousand fights. They started when he was young. He had grown up in a rough neighborhood. His father had been a professional boxer and successful enough that people knew his name. Unfortunately, that success had not carried over into his personal life. His wife, Logan's mother, left him when his boxing career — and the money that came with it — ended. Logan had been taught to face every bully and every threat head-on. And while he struggled with the loss of his mother, and school didn't suit his high-energy personality, fighting was second nature. He was a firm believer that nobody really won in a street fight. Since becoming a cop, he used his experience and skills to end conflicts as quickly as possible. Which was why he anticipated the short man's attack and pulled back just beyond the smaller man's reach.

A powerful, looping punch flashed by Logan's face just inches away. Logan let it pass, then used the man's momentum from the missed blow to turn him. A strong shove in the back smashed the man into the wall, and Logan leaned in, pressing his weight into the center of the man's back.

"Stand down!" Logan shouted. "I'm police."

"Let him go!" the man's wife screamed.

The man was screaming too, like an enraged animal. Logan felt the woman grab his short hair and pull, trying to move him off her husband, who was pinned to the wall and had no leverage in the struggle. The woman pulled hard enough to make Logan's head crane back. He had no choice but to reach up, grab her narrow wrist and squeeze.

Bone snapped. Logan didn't possess a magical strength, but he was stronger than he looked ... and the woman's thin wrist didn't offer much resistance. She screamed, letting go of him. Logan was wearing cargo pants and a thick, black tee-shirt over a ribbed tank-top. His police ID and badge were in one pocket. He normally carried his firearm on his belt, but with the escort assignment working with new passengers on the ship, he had been asked to conceal it. The gun was strapped to his ankle and covered by the cuff of his pants, which bunched above his high-top sneakers. Nothing about him revealed his profession, but he didn't have time to pull out his credentials and verify his authority. Instead, he grabbed hold of the husband's shoulders and flung him to the floor. The woman was wailing in pain and shouting, "He broke my wrist! He broke my wrist!"

Other passengers had come out of their rooms and down the wide corridor to see what was happening. A pair of men started to intervene, but Logan raised a hand palm upward.

"Stop!" he shouted. "I'm police."

He was down on top of the husband, who was still struggling to get free. Logan settled astride the man, pinning one arm to his side with a knee. When he was certain the struggling husband couldn't get free, Logan pulled his badge from his back pocket. "I'm police," he said again to the people around. "Everyone, stand back."

He stuffed his badge back into his pants and hit the transmit icon on his cufflink.

"Emergency services, this is Special Investigator Keyes on deck ten, requesting back up and medical assistance. I have two injured passengers and one agitator in custody."

The response was immediate. "Copy that, Officer Keyes, we have your location. Medical help and patrol officers are on their way."

Logan pulled a set of plastic restraints from the big pocket on the thigh of his pants. The man he was holding down screamed as Logan pulled his free hand backward.

"Stop resisting," Logan ordered. "Hands behind your back."

For the first time in the altercation, he picked up on the alcohol that was heavy on the husband's breath. He had obviously been drinking on the flight up to the *Colossus*. Logan made a mental note of that fact and tightened the restraints on the aggressive man's wrist. He had to shift his weight to free the man's other arm. The husband struggled again, but Logan put a hand on the top of his back, right on the spine below the neck and leaned forward. He waited a moment until the man beneath him realized that getting free was hopeless.

"I didn't do anything wrong," the man argued. "Let me go."

"I'm detaining you for assault and battery," Logan said. "As well as resisting arrest."

"I'm not resisting," the man declared, even as he fought to break free of Logan's grip.

It would have been funny if not for his wife's weeping and the long-haired man bleeding all over the deck. Logan forced the plastic restraint over the man's free hand and tightened it. Only then did he get off the man's back.

"Logan," Sergeant Flint's voice crackled through the comlink in his ear. "What's your status?"

"I've got one man in custody on deck ten," Logan said. "Another is semi-conscious with a broken nose, and an adult female with a broken wrist, Sergeant."

"Wonderful," Flint said. "I'm pulling up the video from that area now. Are you okay?"

"Right as rain, sir."

"Good to hear it," Flint said. "Let's do an immediate recording for the record. You alright with that?"

"Yes, sir," Logan said. "Just one second."

A pair of uniformed patrol officers was hurrying toward him. Logan pulled out his badge again. "Officer Keys, Special Investigation and Logistical Operations," he said, as he pointed down at the husband in restraints. "Can you get a breathalyzer on this suspect?"

"Yes, Officer Keys," one of the patrolmen said.

The other dropped to one knee beside the long-haired man and helped ease him onto his side. Logan stepped back and rolled his shoulders, loosening the muscles that were clenched under tension from the arrest.

"I'm ready, Sergeant Flint."

"Go ahead then, Logan. Tell me exactly what happened."

His report lined up with the video footage perfectly. The cameras in the wide walkways had no sound and were wide-angle cameras that took in large portions of the corridors, which made the people small. The video wasn't as precise as a person usually wanted, but with Logan's report, what had happened was clear. They would get witness testimonies to add to the report, but it seemed like a clear case of battery. It didn't matter that the long-haired man, who had been identified as Cristolf Vulane, had been out of line in flirting with the married woman. Her name was Vivian Okios and her husband was Raul. There was still enough time that the couple could be put off the ship, and if the criminal court on the *Colossus* was smart, they would make an example of the pair. They had no children, so there would be no innocents. At least to Flint's way of thinking, since Vivian had attacked his officer, she too was complicit in the assault.

Logan stayed with Raul as the medical personnel arrived. A field splint was put on Vivian's wrist. Meanwhile, Cristolf appeared to have both a broken nose and a concussion from the savage upper cut. Logan guessed his testicles would be bruised as well. It was enough that a gurney was used to transport him to the nearest medical facility. More law enforcement officials arrived. They took statements, Then Logan went with a pair of patrolmen to book Raul into the nearest detention facility, which happened to be the tiny holding cell inside the SIU offices.

"You look no worse for wear," Flint said, after Logan completed the intake form on the suspect.

"His wife messed up my hair," Logan said.

"Looks better," Flint joked. "You sure you're okay?"

"Fine," Logan said. "A little tense maybe."

"Mr. Vulane is lucky you were there or he would have been worse off."

"Some might say he had it coming," Logan said. "He overstepped his bounds."

"Not legally," Flint pointed out.

"Would you have reacted differently in his shoes?"

"Probably not," Flint said. "But then, both of my wives stepped out on me. It's just par for the course. You can't take it personally."

"Kinda hard not to if she's doing it right in front of you," Logan said.

"We're still connected to Earth's network," Flint explained. "I got on the Greek police database. Raul is not squeaky clean. He doesn't have an arrest record, but he was involved in several bar fights. And there were domestic calls to his residence. No arrests were made, but..."

"I thought the system was supposed to filter out people like that."

"I suppose, since no arrests were made and no charges filed, there was nothing the lottery committee could do. Maybe they didn't even know he was violent."

"How's a guy like that not got a record?"

"He knows the right people, I suppose," Flint said. "Hopefully, he gets the boot."

"I suppose I should head back down," Logan said.

"As long as you're okay."

"I'm fine," Logan said. "Let me know when I'm needed to testify."

"I doubt that'll be necessary. It's a clear case. The video and your report line up perfectly."

"Right place at the right time," Logan said.

"A good cop keeps his head on a swivel. You've got good instincts, Logan. You may have been Johnny on the spot, but you handled the situation perfectly. It was a textbook arrest."

"Thanks, boss," Logan said.

He left the SIU office feeling like he was in a bubble. It happened, especially after violent altercations. As a kid, his peers steered clear after a fight. They didn't want to accidentally get onto his bad side. Even after a martial competition, people were often put off by his natural ability to utilize violence.

On the ship, hardly anyone knew what had happened and yet he felt like they were all staring at him. It was hard to shake. Logan feared that someday he wouldn't be able to get past the way he felt in those situations. He hadn't been hurt, but it felt inevitable that somehow, someway, violence would catch up with him. Even if it eventually came from himself.

CHAPTER 15

"OUR FIRST CRIME, and it seems your people were right on top of things," Captain Hastings said.

"Yes, sir," Flint replied. "Logan Keys was nearby when the assault occurred.

"We're still technically in dock, which means that our unruly passenger will be turned over to Earth's authorities. His cabin has already been reassigned to someone on the wait list."

They were in the officer's lounge, a private space in the Command building on Topdeck. Flint didn't technically belong there. He wasn't an officer on the ship's crew, but rather a team leader in what was being called Logistical Staff. Although he had met with plenty of higher-ranking officers in the police force during his career. They always seemed to prefer to get word about a case from someone involved. In this case, it was Flint.

Joining them was Commissioner Monty Forrest and the ever-jovial director of law enforcement personnel, Lieutenant Tad Janson. The officer's lounge was essentially a break room for the command staff, but it was richly appointed. There were tall-backed, leather sitting chairs in small groups, ornate rugs on the deck and the walls between large video display screens were decorated in some sort of wallpaper that looked like wooden paneling. All the lamps and sconces were polished brass, there was even a full bar that was stocked with bottles of whiskey, gin, vodka, and tequila. There was also a large espresso machine where a barista was busy making specialty coffee for the officers. Flint had been offered one but declined. He was a drip coffee man and he took it black.

"That was fast," Commissioner Forrest said.

"The wait list is extensive," Captain Hastings said. "And I won't have stragglers slowing us down. We're in the final week before we begin our cruise. My people are working around the clock to ensure everything is ready."

Flint understood that. Even he had taken a turn showing new passengers to their cabins and answering questions as shuttle after shuttle brought more people to the *Colossus*.

"It sends a message," Forrest declared. "This ship will not tolerate lawlessness."

"We can't expect passengers to share our sense of discipline or duty," Hastings said. "But we must insist that they follow the rule of law. And I must say, Sergeant Flint, your team handled the situation with the sort of ruthless efficiency that I prefer when it comes to such matters."

"Let's just hope we can keep it up," Flint said.

"What's that supposed to mean?" Janson said. "Of course, we can keep it up."

"Let's not kid ourselves," Flint said. "There will be people on this ship who will try to subvert the law."

"And when they do, we will stop them," Forrest said, frowning in disapproval.

Flint didn't press the point any further. The ranking officials wanted to revel in the glory of their grand ship and the noble mission. They were the first people to leave Earth and make a new home on a new world. It was historic and there was no room in their minds for the ugliness that was going to plague the voyage. It was his place to make sure it was cleaned up, which was exactly why he had been invited to the Captain's gathering in the first place. They settled into the big, comfortable chairs.

"What's the status on our passengers?" Captain Hastings asked.

His first officer was a woman with icy blue eyes and blonde hair cut very short. She was tall and thin. Her uniform was a close fit, but she had almost no curves. And while Flint, who was a student of people, knew she could be beautiful, the severe look on her face made her seem intimidating.

"We're at twenty-two percent," she replied without looking for the information on any sort of tablet or device. "VIP's are starting to make their way to the transfer station. We're ahead of schedule by one hour and forty-seven minutes."

"Excellent," Hastings said. "The last of our stores have been brought on board. All we need now are the passengers and we shall make history."

Several of the large wall displays showed an elevated view of the cityscape known to the crew and passengers as Topdeck. In some ways, it reminded Flint of a downtown section of any large city, only without housing. The buildings on Topdeck were for working or entertainment. The people lived below in the maze-like lower decks, sandwiched between warehouses and engine compartments. The lowest decks had the most people and the greatest chance for tragedy.

The group finished congratulating themselves and drinking their coffee at the same time. The little meeting broke up. Flint was on his way out when the first officer, Commander Lova Koll, tapped his shoulder. He turned and was greeted by a tight smile.

"We haven't met. I am Lova."

"Sawyer Flint, it's a pleasure, Commander."

They stepped out of the lounge and started down the corridor together.

"I'm not sure how familiar you are with ship command, but as the Executive Officer, the passengers fall under my purview," she said. "I agreed with what you said, back there. We have a potentially volatile situation on this vessel."

"The designers did their best, but the ship is just too large and too complex. There are dead spots on every deck; some of them are pretty big. Law enforcement personnel will patrol those areas as often as possible, but any large city is really just a balancing act. We can't prevent most crimes."

"It is the same on military ships," Lova said. "Not every regulation can be enforced."

"Good to know we're on the same page," Flint said. "My team won't knowingly permit any criminal activity, but my guess is we're going to be pretty busy."

He reached the elevator and pressed the down button.

"I just want you to know I'm here," she said. "If you need anything."

"Thanks," Flint said.

They shook hands and Lova held his in both of hers. It was a very friendly gesture, but he knew she was Scandinavian and didn't know their customs.

"We're on the same team," she said. "I look forward to working with you, Sergeant Flint."

"Yes, ma'am," he replied.

She released his hand and he stepped onto the elevator. After hitting the button for the ninth deck, he looked up. First Officer Koll was already walking away. She was tall, her back straight and she moved like a proper officer, but there was something about her Flint found intriguing. He watched her until the elevator doors shut.

Two floors down, JD's door opened. There was music playing from a stereo, and laughter could be heard from the bedroom. The head of the Ghetto Kings looked hungover. The three men waiting outside his posh suite chuckled at the sight of him.

"Long night, homie?" Slash asked.

"Looks like the boss man started the party without us," Nova added.

"Get in!" JD said. "Anyone see you?"

"Nah, we ain't seen nobody on this floor," Fever said. "It's real quiet up in here."

"These bigwigs ain't on board yet," Nova added. "Least that's what Crank said."

"Will be soon," JD said. "Can't have no gangstas like you three coming up here all the time."

"Wouldn't want to upset the neighbors," Slash replied. "We feel you, G."

"What's news?" JD asked.

"Just checking in," Nova said. "Crank got us set up. We're golden."

"Good," JD said as he sat down and rubbed his face with one hand.

There was stubble on his jaw and over his normally clean-shaven head. He picked up a glass of water and took a drink while his lieutenants looked around his new home.

"They call this boat the *Colossus*," Slash said. "But everything is small."

"Yeah, our rooms are half the size of this," Nova said. "Just a bed and a couple of lockers."

"But you've got private berths, right?" JD asked.

"Yep," Fever assured him. "Can't be sharing digs with no stranger."

"Then get back to 'em," JD said. "Play nice and get the lay of the land. We don't make a move until this ship is underway. You hear about the fight last night?"

"Heard a pig got involved," Slash said. "Put some dude down pretty quick."

"Yeah, that's what I heard too," JD said. "We'll worry about the law down the line. Right now, what I care about is that fool who started static got sent packing. We don't want to start nothing until that's not possible. We ain't going back."

"I don't know, boss," Nova said. "The old neighborhood is looking pretty good compared to this place."

"What's wrong with the ship?" Fever said. "It's clean and loaded with lots of honeys."

"And lots of law, too," Slash complained.

"Don't none of that matter," JD said. "We gotta keep our eye on the prize. Won't take long, and things will shake out. Once we know what's really moving people, we can start collecting, you dig. Till then, we don't do nothing. Keep your product to yourselves, no pimpin' either. We just bide our time and let the riches flow to us. Follow my lead and we'll be kings on a new world."

"Sounds good," Fever said.

"You really think the rich pricks on this boat will fall in line?" Nova asked.

"They's two things that run every group of people, money and power. We got the first, but outside the street, we're capped. Can't rise to real power back in the world. Ain't nobody gonna stand for that. Been that way for a thousand years. But everything's new here. We got us a chance to build something strong. I ain't gonna give that up for a quick fix, ya feel me?"

The three lieutenants nodded.

"Good," JD said. "Now get gone. From now on, we maintain that low profile. Don't come knocking on my door. I'll reach out when it's safe to start planning things."

"Kinda hard just sitting around not doing nothing," Nova said.

"But not impossible," JD told him. "Won't last long. Enjoy some downtime. Might not be much of it after this. We take control, there will be a thousand others looking to snatch it from us."

"Ain't gonna ever let that happen," Slash said.

The trio of high-ranking gang members left, and JD picked up his glass of water. His head was pounding hard. He pushed the glass against his left temple and closed his eyes. From the bedroom, his guests giggled. Opening his eyes, he looked around. The suite was small and nondescript, like a hotel room. The throb from the stereo matched the one in his head. An empty whisky bottle was lying on its side on the counter. He would send the girls to the other bedroom, and then he could get some sleep until his hangover passed. It was a lame way to start things on their new adventure, but he felt the constriction he had lived with his whole life starting to loosen. It might not make sense under their present circumstances on the ship. Yet JD was a forward-thinking man who saw opportunities where others saw problems. And it was only a matter of time before his chance came calling. When it did, he planned to grab onto it with both hands and never let go.

CHAPTER 16

THE BAG WAS FOUND by a crew member and checked into the system, which immediately sent an alert to Becky Nash's cufflink. She was escorting an elderly man to his berth. He was a famous historian with a string of best-selling narrative non-fiction books that had made him wealthy. He had paid a premium to get around the age restriction. But his gray hair and cane made him an outlier on the ship.

"I can't thank you enough for the help," he said.

"It's no problem," Becky said. She was carrying his satchel. It contained a brand new computer still in the box, a set of solid-state hard drives with all his accumulated work and hundreds of sources for his historical research. It was literally a library in a bag.

"But you have other tasks," he remarked.

"Just the mysterious case of the lost luggage," she told him with a smile. "Maybe you can write a book about it."

"That's not the kind of books I write," he replied. "I like to read them, though. Perhaps, you'll write it and be a big hit."

"I doubt it," she said. "Writing isn't where I shine."

"The same could be said for helping an old man to his room, but you are surpassing my greatest expectations."

"What are you working on, if I may ask?" she said, ignoring the pain in her shoulder from the satchel's narrow strap.

"You may," he said, grinning broadly to reveal crooked teeth stained yellow from thousands of cups of coffee. "I am writing a history of the legend of Robin Hood."

"Really?"

"Yes, there is a rich tradition, and some very interesting individuals who either played a role in the creation of the myth, or may have been the source personally."

"You think there will be a big market for books on Secundo?"

They were almost to the historian's room.

"Oh, doubtful," he said. "I'll send the manuscript back to Earth."

"Here you are," she said. "Deck three, room eight-sixteen."

"You are an angel, I must insist on giving you a small token of my gratitude," he said, waving his cufflink in front of the door lock. The door slid open and Becky tried not to look inside.

She failed and was filled with regret. Unlike her tiny berth, which she shared with another crew member, the old historian had a spacious cabin with a living room, a small kitchen, a bedroom and a separate office.

"Oh, this will do nicely," he said, reaching for his satchel. Becky held it out, pasting on a fake smile. "Can I offer you some money for your time?"

"No," Becky said. "This is just part of my job. Knowing you is its own reward."

"Well said," the old man replied, setting the satchel on the ground with a sigh, "even if it isn't true. And if you won't accept a tip, then I must insist on buying you dinner at some point on our grand journey. I may eat a bit early for a young woman like you, but the offer stands. You know how to find me."

"I do," Becky said. "Good luck with your book."

"Thank you," he said.

Becky might have lingered. Most of the passengers she had met were so enthralled by the ship and the journey they were embarking on, they ended up hardly saying a word to her. The historian was different, perhaps a bit too friendly. She found it odd how often older men would flirt with her. Few people seemed as interesting as the historian, but she bade him farewell and set off to reclaim the lost luggage.

Along the way, she met back up with Dave Bannon and the pair of them collected the missing bag and checked its contents.

"Full," Dave said.

"Looks like it's alright," Becky agreed. "I suppose Ms. Grisolm will be relieved."

They took it right up to her cabin and were surprised when Helena Grisolm treated them as if they had lost, rather than found, her missing bag.

"It's about time," she insisted. "I've been worried sick."

"We're sorry it took so long," Dave said. "It was on the shuttle. The work crews must have missed it."

"They should lose their jobs," she snarled. "And if I find out that anything is missing, I will go straight to the authorities."

Becky wanted to remind the unpleasant woman that she was the authority to which Helena Grisolm was referring, but she had dealt with enough unruly people to know it did no good to correct them. The sad fact of police work was the reality of dealing with a lot of very unsavory people.

"If there's anything else we can do for you, please, let us know," Becky said, pasting on her fake smile again.

"You've done little enough already, thank you very much!"

The woman smacked the door control switch hard and her door slid shut.

"I guess that's that," Dave said as they both walked away. "I guess it was too much to screen for crazy on this trip."

"Crazy comes in a lot of guises," Becky said. "Some people would say that we're crazy for doing what we do."

"True that," Dave said. "It takes a certain kind of insanity to work in law enforcement."

A few hours later, the first of the VIPs occupying deck two arrived. She was introduced to Evan Kitterling by one of the ship's officers who had come down to welcome the shuttle of VIPs.

"Officer Nash will show you to your rooms, sir," the officer said.

"Thank you," Kitterling said.

Becky thought the remark was dismissive. Evan Kitterling was obviously accustomed to people hurrying to do anything he needed. And why not? He was a semi-famous inventor who had helped develop the engine technology that was powering the *Colossus*. He was also filthy rich and a constant source of material for the sensationalist podcasters. He was usually with a beautiful model or actress, but he had come on board the *Colossus* alone.

"You're on the far side of the ship," she told him. "We'll take the elevators up to Topdeck, then ride the tube around to the far side."

"Excellent," he said.

She expected more, but he was content to keep his thoughts to himself. She led the way to a bank of elevators. All around them, people were pointing and whispering. It was a strange new experience for Becky Nash, who had always been lost in her surroundings.

"How long have you been on the ship?" Evan asked when they stepped onto the elevator.

"About a week now," she said.

"How is it?"

"Takes some getting used to," she admitted as the elevator started up.

"I'll bet," he responded. "Strange to think of how much we're all leaving behind."

"And yet, people were clamoring to do it."

"The grass is always greener on the other side of the fence, or across outer space, I suppose."

"I certainly hope so."

"How come you aren't in a uniform, Officer Nash?"

"Special Investigations is a plainclothes unit," she said.

"Oh, I didn't realize we had detectives on board."

"We're an unfortunate necessity, I suppose," she told him. "Have you had much contact with law enforcement?"

"Oh, yes. I've been a target of criminals and scam artists all my life," he confessed. "On Earth, I employed a private security firm to provide protection for all my assets. That's one of the things that drew me to this journey. We're all starting from a level playing field, aren't we?"

Becky knew that wasn't true. The *Colossus* wasn't an experiment in Socialism. That flawed ideological system had failed in every corner of the world where it was tried. While the passengers on the *Colossus* might be starting on Secundo at the same place, there was a wide variety in the resources they would bring to bear. Evan Kitterling had more resources than some small countries.

In person, he seemed almost too normal. He wore wool slacks, a black tee-shirt and a dressy coat, the kind she thought of as a Pea Coat. All he carried was a small pouch with his tablet computer inside. There were no throngs of people around him, no security besides Becky herself and no beautiful date to keep him company. He was all alone.

The elevator dinged and the doors opened. Becky held the doors open and let Evan Kitterling pass through ahead of her. He stepped off the elevator and looked around. The top deck was more like a small city with a cluster of high-rise buildings, a shopping and entertainment district, as well as four distinct green spaces. Displayed across the Command Building's integrated display was a bright welcome sign that said *Welcome to Topdeck.*

"Impressive," Evan said quietly.

"I imagine it will be," Becky said. "It seems a bit like a ghost town at the moment."

"A taste of home as we rocket through space," he said with a chuckle. "Very good."

They went directly from the bank of elevators to the nearest hub for the fast train that cruised around and around the upper deck. They were the only occupants as they rode to the far side of the city-ship. There, they took another elevator down one floor. The second deck was called "VIPsburg" by the crew. It was obviously a much finer space than the other decks and the corridors were wider. There were no warehouses and no engineering clusters. The floor was lined with fancy carpet tiles. The berths were different too, starting with the doors, which were double the size of the rest of the ship. They slid apart in the center, with each half sliding in opposite directions.

Becky took Evan to his cabin. He waved his cufflink at the security reader, but also had to place his hand on a bio-scanner. His identity confirmed, the doors opened. Becky almost gasped in surprise. The cabin was huge. There was even a grand piano on a raised dais and a glass wall that was actually a wine rack filled with aged vintages. There were long sofas in the living space, a long, narrow dining table with twelve seats around it. The kitchen was in its own compartment and Becky counted four other doors leading off the main room.

"Home sweet home," Evan Kitterling said.

"If there's nothing else, Mr. Kitterling," Becky said, suddenly in a hurry to leave. She had been jealous of the historian's cabin, but she could have fit three of the old man's berths in Evan's main room. There were huge paintings, ornate tiles on the ceiling, gleaming fixtures and polished floors.

"Actually, before you go," he said, turning toward her. "I'm sure it's not your job, but I like to be thorough. Can you let the kitchen staff know that I prefer my main meal at eight pm? And remind them that I'm gluten and dairy-free."

"Gluten and dairy," Becky said. "We're on ship time here. It's a twenty-four-hour cycle, so eight pm is twenty-hundred hours."

"Ah, good to know," he said, flashing her a smile.

She was shocked at the difference between the famed historian and the billionaire inventor. Evan Kitterling had perfect teeth. They were so white they almost didn't look real, or as though he had just stepped off a movie set. His jaw line was smooth, his hair perfectly styled. There was no denying that he was handsome, but Becky felt it was all bought and paid for, just a facade that hid the real man.

"Have a nice voyage," Becky said as she left.

He had been right about one thing. It wasn't her job to inform anyone about his dietary preferences. But she made a quick oral report and filed it. Hopefully, the message would get to whoever needed to receive it. She had no idea who was in charge of food for the residents of VIPsburg. The rest of her shift was taken up with VIP escorts. None had as opulent a berth as Kitterling, but some were close. Almost everyone else on the VIP level was partnered up, and a few even had a child, although never more than one. All the VIP couples with a child also had a nanny. Becky couldn't imagine the wealth it must have taken to purchase VIP tickets for one's hired help. Was it more than she made in a year? Or more than she would earn in her entire career. She thought it was likely the latter.

That evening, when she made it back to her berth, she frowned. It was small, which hadn't bothered her much at first, but after seeing the wide cabins on the second and third decks, she felt robbed. Of course, the real benefit to working her way across space in the *Colossus* was getting to Secundo. She would even have a lot of money banked as she continued to draw a salary, although she had no bills. The only money she would spend on the trip would be on entertainment or perhaps some new clothing. Once they got to the new world, she would have a nice nest egg, but her mind went back to Evan Kitterling saying it was a level field. She knew if she saved every last credit she earned on the two-year voyage, she wouldn't be starting with even one percent of what he would begin with.

She took her one-minute shower, trying not to think that the VIPs had longer access to more water. Then she climbed into her bunk. Her roommate was neat and worked long hours, which was fine with Becky. They rarely saw one another. Becky lay in her small, enclosed sleeping nook and tried not to let the bitterness take root. The *Colossus* was no different than life on Earth. Back in the East Coast megalopolis, there were huge apartment buildings with multi-storied penthouses, and massive apartments that took up entire floors of their building. She, meanwhile, had lived in a small, one-bedroom apartment in a building with a host of problems. Her elevator hadn't worked, but she was only on the third story, so two flights of stairs every day was not an issue. What it lacked in aesthetic, it made up for in safety, with cops in apartments on every floor. Her landlord had given her a discount, which was a fairly common practice in most apartment complexes. But her berth on the *Colossus* was barely the size of her living room on Earth. That made it feel like she was a second-class citizen. She fell asleep wondering how she was supposed to keep the peace on a ship that was so unfair to the passengers on board. If she had any doubts about the probability of crime and violence on the ship, she knew that when the poor masses huddled down on the sixteenth and seventeenth decks learned of the VIP berths, there would probably be riots.

That night, she dreamed of the wide open spaces on Secondo. But in her dream, she could only see the new world through a tiny window on a ship that was flying her farther and farther from the new life she hoped for.

CHAPTER 17

SERGEANT FLINT WAS WAITING along the corridor across from the elevators. A new shuttle had just arrived. He was one of about a hundred crew members waiting to help the new arrivals and the only member of his squad in the queue that morning. Dave Bannon and Becky Nash had just gone off the night shift. Jeopardy Bess and her K-9 partner, Stu, were working the baggage area. Somewhere on the vast ship, Logan Keys was already helping someone. It wasn't what he imagined when he had been told he would lead his own team on the *Colossus*. But he had worked in law enforcement long enough to know that at times, it was all hands on deck.

Flint stood out from the other crew members in his street clothes. It was the one thing he had invested in back during his time on Earth and the only prized possession he had brought along on the trip. In his little bag of keepsakes was a signed football card, a letter written by his mother the year before she passed away, a small folding knife that had been passed down from his great, great grandfather through the men in his family, and the divorce papers he had received just before leaving Earth. But what he really cherished were his suits. He owned five, one black, three navy blue, and one dark gray. They weren't tailor-made, but they had been adjusted slightly and cost him half a paycheck each. Detectives in suits were no longer the norm. Most wore cargo pants, compression shirts and body armor. It was a distinct look, but there was something about a good suit and clean tie that made people feel like Flint had authority. Most of the people he dealt with were either victims or witnesses. Flint had never taken a poll or done any real research, although he felt that it set people at ease, which made his job just a little easier.

He was in the gray suit with his badge snug in the inside pocket of his jacket, which he left unbuttoned for easy access to the firearm that was clipped on his belt at his right hip. He wore a clean white shirt and a necktie. His shoes were polished wingtips with athletic soles. Hidden by his jacket was a pair of old-fashioned handcuffs, a telescoping baton and two clips of spare ammunition. It was doubtful he would ever need them on the *Colossus,* but he was big on showing up prepared. Everyone else in the queue was wearing the standard coveralls that almost all the crew members were required to wear. There was a variety of colors, each one related to the various job divisions. The only color Flint didn't see was white. The culinary staff was already busy. Food service on the *Colossus* was an around-the-clock task, with certain groups being urged to dine at specified times. It wasn't a hard and fast rule, but rather a way of helping spread out the number of meals that needed to be prepared at any one time. Flint knew it would also keep the passengers from getting unruly waiting in long lines for a meal.

There were other crew members working around the queue. Not every person in the ship's various divisions was called upon to help the new arrivals. Flint saw a pair of janitorial crew members polishing the deck with a wide machine that was self-propelled. A member of the engineering division was taking readings on a special device, which he plugged into a control panel. There was the junior officer in charge of greeting the VIPs who were about to cross over the transfer station. The officer was in a dress uniform, dark navy blue with some ribbons on his chest and a flat-topped hat. He was the only person with shoes shinier than Flint's.

Years of paying attention to details had honed Flint's mind so that he was always on the lookout. His brain categorized the various details in an almost effortless fashion, cataloging them in case he needed to recall them later. He stood still, leaning against the wall of the corridor like everyone else in the queue, but his eyes never stopped scanning the people around him. He was, in fact, like most accomplished law enforcement officials, a student of human nature. Deduction on the scale of Sherlock Holmes was impossible in most instances. There were just too many reasons why a person might have ink under one's fingernails, or an impression on their elbow, but it was in taking note of such details that one could begin to flesh out a person's nature. When Flint noticed those types of oddities about an individual, especially one suspected of a crime, he used them to stake down what the person was telling him. Truth was always the goal when trying to solve a crime, yet people were inherently liars, especially when they felt like they were being called on the carpet by someone in authority over them. Flint used the small details he could see about a person to get them to be honest. They might have a well-rehearsed story about their actions or whereabouts when it came to the crime in question, but if he could get them talking about mundane things, like why there were grease stains on their pants or a tear in their favorite tee-shirt, those little facts could, in many instances, box a person in. When their fabricated story began to bump up against the truth, they either doubled down on the lying or broke down completely.

What many people didn't realize was that lies were easy to poke holes in. The best criminals succeeded in lying to authorities because they fabricated as little as possible.

When the first person to enter the *Colossus* through the open port settled into the ship's artificial gravity, Flint found his curiosity piqued. It was a man in a designer tracksuit, with silver hair and bright eyes. In one hand, he carried a glossy leather attaché case and he looked just a little bit green around the gills.

"Oh," he said as his feet settled on the deck. "That's better."

"Welcome aboard the *Colossus*," the junior officer said. "Please place your hand on the scanner and state your name."

Flint didn't need the man to say his name. He recognized the wealthy mogul. He had been one of the founders of Aurora Tech, but after masterminding some of their most popular devices, he was ousted from the company in a very public way. There were rumors of inappropriate behavior with co-workers, but no charges were ever filed against him. Within a year, he had gone from giving keynote addresses at tech symposiums to becoming persona non grata. Which had certainly played a role in his decision to leave Earth.

"Melvin Starmer," he said in a clear voice.

Flint heard murmurs behind him. There would be plenty of famous passengers on the *Colossus*. Melvin Starmer was given a cuff-link and assigned an escort. When he passed Sawyer Flint, the police Sergeant offered a polite smile, the one given to people brought into the station who hadn't been informed that they were suspects yet.

A few more VIPs passed before Flint was up next for escort duty. The passenger in line happened to be a woman. She wore a business suit, comfortable but classy shoes, and had a rather heavy-looking backpack as her carry-on luggage. Her shoulder-length hair was in a ponytail, and she had a small scar under her left ear. The scar intrigued Flint. The jagged white line ended at her jawline.

"Welcome to the *Colossus*," the junior officer said as Flint approached the check-in area. "Please place your hand on the scanner and state your name."

The woman put her hand on the glass surface of the palm reader and said, "Harmonia Lukid."

She had an interesting accent that he couldn't quite place. Her skin was tanned and there were light streaks in her dark brown hair. Flint waited while the junior officer explained how the cufflink worked and fastened it around her wrist. She waited politely, but had a look of tired resolution on her face.

"This is Sergeant Sawyer Flint," the junior officer said. "He'll show you to your berth. All the information you need will be on your cufflink."

"Thank you," she said, stepping toward Flint.

"Can I help you with your bag, Ms. Lukid?"

"Yes, thank you. It feels like I weigh three hundred pounds for some reason."

"Readjusting to gravity takes some time."

"I was only in zero-gravity for a little more than an hour," she said. "I don't think I've ever felt so tired."

"Welcome to space lag," Flint said as he took the backpack from her. It was heavy, but he shouldered it without problems and led her to the bank of elevators.

"Why are you in a suit?" she asked.

"I'm a detective," he said. "The suit's standard issue."

"Wow, I've only just arrived and already in trouble," she said. "Why are you escorting me, Sergeant..."

"Flint," he said.

"Call me Harmony, everyone does," she said.

"It's very nice to meet you, Harmony. I'm just helping out new passengers."

"There's no crime to investigate?"

"Not unless you count missing luggage," Flint said. "So far, it's been pretty quiet."

They got on the elevator and Flint pressed the button for deck two. Since being on the ship, he had come to think of it more like a high-rise than a spaceship. The eighteenth deck, where the crew lived, was like the ground floor, with all the other levels built on top of it. But spaceships, much like sailing ships on Earth, were designated from the top deck down.

"Well, that's encouraging," she said. "I would be frightened to think I was stuck on a ship for two years that was rampant with crime. How long have you been aboard?"

"A week, but I'm a late-comer. I think some of the crew have been on board for over a month already."

The elevator beeped and the doors opened. Flint held a hand over the door and let Harmony exit first. He followed and they stopped for a moment just outside the elevator bank.

"This is different," she said. "From the other part of the ship, I mean."

"You came aboard on deck eighteen. That's the crew level. This is deck two, VIP section."

"I shouldn't be surprised, I guess, but... it seems a bit lavish."

"Oh, this is nothing. Wait until you see your berth."

Her cabin was right next to the elevators, which some of the VIPs would have complained about. Harmony didn't seem to mind. Her's was an L-shaped cabin that wrapped around the elevator shaft, and had large windows on the back side with sweeping views of outer space.

"Oh, wow," she said. "This is better than the pictures on the website made it out."

They entered from the wide corridor into the cabin's kitchen area. Unlike most of the other cabins, her berth had a large work area with an island, and all the appliances were commercial grade.

"Are you a chef?" he asked.

"How did you know?" Harmony asked.

"I've seen a few of these cabins," he replied. "None has a kitchen like this."

"I'm a chef, but also a food scientist. My job on Secundo will be testing new foods and helping create recipes using native ingredients."

"Wow," Flint remarked. "That's pretty cool. I never thought about needing something like that on a new planet, but it's really brilliant."

"I'm flattered," Harmony said. "Most people never think about how the foods we eat came to be recognized and developed. Martin Lawrence wrote an excellent book about it, if you're interested."

"I'll have to check it out," Flint said.

Harmony took her backpack and unzipped it. Flint was surprised to see her pull out a set of fancy skillets. But it certainly explained the weight of the backpack.

"They wouldn't let me bring my set of knives onto the shuttle," she said, pulling out powders and dried herbs.

"Looks like you've got everything else," Flint said.

"Just the essentials," Harmony replied.

"Well, unless there's anything else I can do for you, Ms. Lukid, I'll leave you to it."

"Thank you, Sergeant Flint," she said, looking up. "I'm quite squared away here. They'll bring up the rest of my luggage?"

"Yes," Flint said. "It's being brought on board. Someone will deliver it to your cabin shortly."

"Wonderful," she said.

Flint left the cabin and headed back down to join the queue again. He would be escorting people to their rooms all day. They were the final arrivals. Once everyone was on board, the *Colossus* would leave the transfer station and set out through open space. There was nowhere on the ship, other than Topdeck, with views like the one he had just seen in Harmony's berth. He did his best not to think about it. In space, there wasn't much to see, just stars and more stars. They were distant specks of light and yet he wished his cabin or office on deck nine had a view from the ship. He was the kind of guy who liked to see where he was going, even when he wasn't going where no one had gone before.

CHAPTER 18

IT TOOK twenty-six more hours before the *Colossus* was ready to leave the transfer station. They were asked to wait another two hours as a shuttle full of media reporters flew in to film the auspicious occasion. During that time, passengers were asked to remain on their floors, yet all through the ship, celebrations sprang up. Dozens of localized parties started and stopped on every floor. In places, people got drunk and rowdy. Others got stoned with a variety of recreational drugs. Smoking and vaping wasn't allowed on the *Colossus,* even though there were bags of marijuana and tobacco seeds in the stores for Secundo. But the ship didn't have the ventilation appropriate for smoking, so the passengers relied on edibles, pills and sniffable powders.

There were all the usual difficulties that went along with parties. Alcohol was limited, but available, and fights did inevitably break out. Fortunately, the law enforcement personnel were out in force at all times, making their presence known. There was a camaraderie among passengers so that even those who fought were also helping one another avoid trouble with the police.

On the transfer station, cameras were set up, and news reports were given with the *Colossus* in the background as it slowly moved away and rotated toward the outer system. It was a historic event; the first group of colonists leaving the Sol system had to be recorded and celebrated. On Earth, there were watch parties and celebrations in every nation. People would always remember where they were and what they were doing when the *Colossus* left port and headed for a new world.

Flint and his squad of Special Investigators gathered together in their new office on deck nine. They drank sparkling cider rather than champagne, just in case they were needed. Stu was with them too and given a special pillow in the corner, which he quickly made his own. The best they could do was to pull up the video feed from the ship's external cameras. They settled on a feed that showed the transfer station. They could also see Earth in the background. They watched the ship drift back from the station, then turn away. There was no sensation of movement on the ship. The engines engaged but accelerated slowly. There was no sound of the big engines inside the ship, just the video feed showed them moving away from the only home they had ever known.

"No turning back now," Flint said.

"If I can make it through the last week, the next two years should be a piece of cake," Becky said.

"I don't mind boring," Logan said.

"Says the only guy that saw action," Jeopardy teased.

"We've been living vicariously through your heroic deeds," Flint said. "I must have watched the video of that fight ten times. But I hope it's the last."

"Here, here," Dave said. "Fisticuffs are overrated."

"I don't want a fight," Becky said. "But something else to do would be great. Escorting passengers around isn't my cup of tea."

"Trust me, it's better than eight-hour shifts in the cargo receiving center," Jeopardy said. "Poor Stu had to smell every bag."

"Find anything interesting?" Dave asked.

"One passenger had bags of cured meats," Jeopardy said. "We

found two antique pistols brought on board by two different passengers."

"Both VIPs," Flint said.

"They claimed the firearms were historic pieces, but we confiscated them anyway. They will be returned in two years on Secundo."

"Funny how some people think the rules don't apply to them," Becky said.

"It's in our nature to think of how to get around the rules," Flint said. "We're always looking for loopholes."

"That's what lawyers do, right?" Dave suggested. "They write contracts and legislative bills that aren't supposed to be broken, then other lawyers do their best to poke holes in them and find workarounds."

"Don't get me started on lawyers," Becky said.

"I have to agree with her there," Flint said. "But don't worry, tomorrow we start working."

"Doing what?" Logan asked.

"Topdeck opens tomorrow," he replied. "We'll make the rounds posing as passengers and identify hot spots."

"Excellent," Becky said.

"On the ship's dime?"

"Sure," Flint said. "We can't go crazy, but we can't be expected to pay our own way. Just notate all expenditures made while on duty and the ship will reimburse you."

"Including alcohol?" Dave confirmed.

"Beer only, nothing hard," Flint said. "We're not paying you to get drunk on the job. And if you buy anything that might compromise your mental facilities, you have to turn it in."

"That's not fun," Becky said.

"There was a time when all those fun little narcotics were illegal," Flint said. "A lot of cops spent their entire career fighting an endless battle to keep that stuff off the streets."

"And now there are government-funded centers where a junkie can get anything they want," Becky said. "I'm not sure that's better."

"Less people die," Flint said. "Besides, if you want to stem the tide of an illegal substance or activity, just regulate it and tax it. That's a fact."

The first twenty-four hours after launch, the ship's crew monitored every system around the clock. There were a few inevitable glitches, mostly in the wiring and monitoring systems. For instance, the air filtration system on deck seven was working fine, although the monitoring system glitched and had to be restarted. But no major systems had problems. Everything was modular, meaning that when something malfunctioned on the ship, it could quickly be exchanged. The malfunctioning units could then be taken apart, repaired or scrapped, depending on what was needed with each part.

Topdeck was then opened in stages. At first, only the people who worked in the space city were allowed up. There were several high-rise buildings filled with offices. The executives lucky enough to have corner offices on the top floors had outstanding views of both the city below and outer space through the transparent dome.

Next, the employees who would work in the restaurants, cafes, tailor shops and entertainment establishments were allowed up and did run throughs with their managers and owners. They had to have their schedules down pat, including how long it took to get from their berths down on deck eighteen, up to Topdeck and across to the location in the city. Crew members worked the trollies that ran in a grid around the city.

Eventually, the passengers were allowed up. They came in waves. Thousands of people worked their way up the ship's elevators and around on the magnetic train. They window shopped, walking the streets and sidewalks, marveling at the colossal arch with bright lights that mimicked the sun back on Earth. They visited the parks, played soccer on the wide pitches and basketball on courts. Children frolicked on playgrounds and everyone marveled at the bees that buzzed among the rows of blooming flowers. It was a paradise and a marvel of design and engineering. But there were problems, too. People forced to wait in long lines grew impatient and, in some cases, belligerent. A few had to be restrained by law enforcement, but few held their grudges long enough to need to be arrested. The beat cops that worked Topdeck were masters of de-escalation and had wide latitude in helping people adjust to their new environment.

Flint and his squad dressed in their casual clothing and joined the throngs of people on Topdeck. Only Stu was left behind. He was the only animal on the ship. People in need of service animals were excluded by the selection committees and pets were not allowed. There was only one animal on the ship and, at times, Jeopardy would bring him up to the green spaces to run and play. Yet, as they were working in an undercover fashion, Stu had to be left behind.

They weren't really undercover in the sense of trying to infiltrate organized crime or bust people doing illegal activities. Their job was to observe and report, not just the places where it was likely that crime would take place, but the people who seemed prone to lawlessness. It was profiling in a sense. People that Flint's squad identified were put into a database. All their relevant information was open to law enforcement. Cultural differences had to be learned and noted. When a person was stopped and questioned, or held for disturbing the peace, the officers involved needed to know everything relevant about that individual, including observations made by the Special Investigation squad. One scan of their cufflink opened up a world of information for law enforcement personnel.

Days passed. The squad rotated through different parts of Topdeck, including the business district. They explored the big buildings and checked the emergency exits for any signs of unauthorized activity. It was busy work but it was police work, and everyone felt more comfortable doing what they loved and had been trained to do.

But they weren't the only ones working on Topdeck. The Ghetto Lords crew made the rounds. They were experts at spotting victims, but they held back. Their goal was not to con the other passengers or shake down the business owners. JD had a larger, more ambitious idea. They gathered at a bar called the Iron Butterfly and drank beer in a dark corner in the rear of the store.

"Gotta admit, the beer is good on this ship," Slash said.

"Better than the food in the dining hall," Nova said. "That is some bland—"

"On purpose," JD said. "It's bland on purpose, dawg. How else are they supposed to motivate you to spend money up here?"

The three lieutenants nodded. Crank was the fifth member of the group, but not actually a lieutenant. He didn't hold a position of power in the gang, which was a little odd, as he was a major player in JD's criminal enterprises. But he wasn't a people person and couldn't have intimidated anyone, even if he was capable of carrying around a bazooka. Still, his mind was sharp and he was JD's right-hand man when it came to getting things done.

"Don't feel like I'm spending money," Fever said. "I just wave my wrist thingy and they give me what I want."

"That's cuz my man Crank is hacking the bank system on this burg," JD said, offering Crank a rare fist bump. "That's the real play. He who controls the money has power."

"I know that's right," Slash said. "Them bankers in the tall buildings already planning to grift the whole flippin' planet 'fore we even get there."

"Just like back home," Fever said. "Rich man's con game. They get a taste every time people spend money."

"That's a slick play," JD said. "Which is why we're getting in on that deal."

"How?" Nova asked.

"They's three execs in charge of the money on the ship, and that system is going to transfer to Secundo when we get there," JD explained. "Two VPs, one President. Our play involves getting close to them. They's the only ones who can catch us hiding in the digital code, but you ain't got to worry 'bout that side of things. Crank got that covered. What y'all gonna do is compromise the bigwigs."

"We catch 'em dirty, then hold it up from the back side," Slash said. "Smart."

"And easy," JD said. "Them playas are always up to something. They think the rules don't apply."

"Cuz they got money," Nova said. "They buy their way out of trouble."

JD pointed at him. "Only now they's in what Crank calls a closed system."

"It means there is no outside influence and a person can't get nothing that ain't already on this ship," Crank said.

"A closed system," Fever said.

"Smart, smart, smart," Slash added.

"That closed system means the big guys need a way to sow them wild oats," JD said. "Which is where we come in."

"We gonna supply what they need?" Nova asked.

"And get the proof," JD said. "That way, they can't risk shutting us out of their money system."

"Now, that's a plan," Slash said. "How we doin' it?"

"That takes time," JD said. "Gotta find out what they into and then make 'em trust us to deliver it."

"And then we get rich," Fever said.

"Rich is just a way to get what we really want," JD said.

"Which is what?" Slash asked.

"Legit power," JD said. "I want all them rich bigwigs bowing and scraping when I walk in a room, you feel me?" The three lieutenants nodded. "And when we get to Secundo, we gonna take control of the best places. They gonna be the GK kingdom, with us at the top."

"Hard to believe we could be kings," Nova said. "I ain't doubting, but..."

"Back in the hood, we didn't have no way to get close enough to that ring of power everyone was fightin' for. Here... we can do anything."

It was dark in the back of the bar. Nothing about the *Colossus* was seedy, but bars were the same all over the world. The light was low, the music was loud, and people nursed their drinks as they passed the time. JD couldn't see the faces of his lieutenants well enough to know if he had sold them on his vision of the future or not. But it didn't really matter because they had all proven their loyalty to him. All they needed to succeed in his new plan was patience. They had two years to get the banking people on their side. Once that was done, everything else would open wide for the Ghetto Kings. Secundo would be all theirs, at least as long as they were able to hang onto it.

"Hey," Slash said, nodding toward the bar. "Look who just came in."

They all looked. It was a man with pale skin and jet black hair. He wore jeans and a sherpa-lined denim jacket with a leather collar. There was nothing of interest about the man. He didn't stand out from the thousands of other people roaming through the streets of Topdeck, shopping, dining and having fun. But they all recognized him. Crank had hacked into the security system. They had seen the video of the fight between the passengers several times.

"What's the pig doing here?" Nova asked.

"Ain't on duty," JD said. "Just getting himself a drink like everyone else."

But the man wasn't like everyone else. He was a dangerous man, in many ways no different from the GKs themselves. It was as if a pride of lions had just spotted an interloper on their territory. Only there were no territories on the ship yet, at least if one didn't count the restrictions of decks, engineering spaces and warehouses.

"Makes me nervous," Slash said.

"Just chill," JD told him. "He ain't got no reason to suspect us of nothing. We're just a few pals out for a drink and good time."

"I hate all cops," Fever said.

"You had reason to on the old world," JD said, keeping his voice low. "They was the enemy on Earth. But up here, won't be long till they our dogs, doing our dirty work."

"Come on, man... be serious," Fever responded.

"I am," JD told him. "Trust me. The balance of power has changed. Here, we are legit. And soon, we'll be at the top. All the people on this ship will be doing what we tell 'em and thanking us for it, too. Even the cops. They'll protect us, just like they always been protecting the rich bigwigs back on Earth."

At the bar, Logan ordered a soda water with cherries. He took the small glass and swirled the cherries around until the bubbly water turned pink. He would have preferred a beer, but he was on duty. He didn't like to ingest anything that might dull his senses. The *Colossus* was full of people from all over Earth. He knew that most of them were good, decent people who wouldn't break the law because they felt bound to the rules of civilized society. Yet he also knew there were wolves among the sheep. Criminals were hiding in plain sight. His job was to identify the places on the ship where they might congregate. The Iron Butterfly was just such a place. It had the feel of an old watering hole. Everything was new, but it was staged to look older. The lights were dim, the booths along the side wall and in the back were large enough for conspirators to gather. He clocked the Ghetto Kings, although he had no way of knowing who they really were. They looked like a group of upstanding citizens. They wore nice clothes, no gang colors, or jewelry that would mark them as part of a criminal organization. Yet they were proof that the Iron Butterfly was the type of place to mark down as one of interest.

A woman came from one of the dark booths and flashed him a smile. He nodded, but said nothing. The woman ordered herself another drink and then leaned closer to him.

"Funny, meeting you here," Jeopardy said.

Logan turned toward her, using the opportunity to get a better look into the dark rear of the establishment.

"You come here often?" he asked.

"My first time," Jeopardy said. "Interesting place."

"Agreed," Logan said. He tried to stay professional, but he had felt an instant attraction the first moment he had met Jeopardy. She was different from many of the women he had known in his life and from all the other female cops he had worked with.

"You staying around?" she asked.

"Just long enough to finish my drink," he told her.

"Shame, we could have some fun."

"I'm sure we'll get the chance," he told her.

The bartender pushed her drink across the bar. She took it and walked back to the booth where she was sitting with Becky Nash. They weren't just in street clothes; they were made up for a night out on the town. The lights on the big arch were on their last position and would soon go out. Up and down the city streets of Topdeck, neon signs were coming on. On the decks below, the lights never dimmed. It was perpetual day where people lived, ate, went to school, and worked on the ship. But on Topdeck, there was a feeling of night. One could even look up and see the stars through the massive transparent dome.

Logan couldn't deny his attraction to Jeopardy, but the job came first. Normally, a relationship with someone in the same squad was frowned upon. If two cops formed a relationship, it was their duty to report it and one (or both) would be transferred. Logan guessed things might be different on the *Colossus,* but he didn't want to take the chance that he might get bumped down to patrol. And besides, he felt honor-bound to carry out his duty for the people on the ship. That meant filing a report about the Iron Butterfly ... and maybe even taking a closer look at the group of men gathered in the rear of the bar.

He swallowed the last of his drink, then put the glass on the table. When he went out, he looked up and down the street. There were still a lot of people perusing the wide avenues. But it reminded him more of a theme park than an actual city. He joined the throng and continued his clandestine inspection of Topdeck.

CHAPTER 19

IN BERTH seven-twenty-one on deck fifteen, a man waited for his roommate to return. His name was Filo, although he had gone by many names during his adult life. He had joined the army at eighteen and joined a special forces unit at twenty. At twenty-one, he had killed his first man, a terrorist in a grubby little apartment that was littered with bomb making supplies. He had been trained to make it look like a suicide and he carried out the mission with ruthless efficiency.

There were other people in his unit who balked at the taking of life. Some wrestled with a guilty conscience after carrying out similar missions. Filo didn't struggle. He didn't feel remorse for the lives he took nor did he lose sleep over the moral repercussions of his duty. To him, it was no different than stocking a shelf in a grocery store or sweeping the floor. He didn't take pleasure in the kills, as some people did, and certainly didn't fantasize about murdering people. To Filo, his ability to carry out assassinations was an interesting skill. He found pleasure in working through the process of identifying targets, planning missions and seeing them through to successful completion.

And, after his six-year enlistment in the army, he found that his skills were highly sought after in the private sector.

Unlike television or spy novels, Filo didn't earn millions by taking on hit jobs. In fact, while he earned a decent living, it was the chance to get to Secundo that made him take on his current mission. Normally, high-profile jobs killing well-known individuals were next to impossible. He couldn't just set up in a tall building with a sniper rifle and shoot a wealthy industrialist in broad daylight. That sort of task was much too risky, not just to his own life, but to the accomplishment of the mission. Long shots were difficult in the best of conditions. Once it was taken, the reality of the situation was undeniable. Most of Filo's clients preferred anonymity. A punk who had angered the wrong person was easy to kill. A rival among organized crime could easily be terminated without much fuss about who had done it. Killing a wealthy, well-known individual took a lot of planning and months of work. It was more like a con job. Filo had to get close to the target, gain their trust, then make the hit look like an accident or a self-inflicted act, rather than a hit. It could be done, although it wasn't Filo's preference. He worked smaller jobs for less money that required less of a time commitment and carried far less risk of being caught.

But he had taken the job of eliminating Everett Goddard, who was wealthy and well known, because it got him a slot on the *Colossus*. What Filo wanted more than money was solitude. Whatever faith he once held in the human race had been completely eroded away. While he was able to earn a living doing a job that he was both good at and enjoyed, he knew that there was no future for a hit man. He would either get himself killed carrying out a job or would get arrested. If he somehow avoided both of those scenarios, he could never retire. His former clients would not allow him to leave the life he had forged. They would send a rival to do to him what he had done to so many others.

But on Secundo, he had the chance to start again. His plan, once they reached the new world, was to gear up and disappear into the wild. He wanted to live the rest of his life in complete solitude; that way, he would never feel the need to depend on someone else. At base, he feared the disappointment of being let down. He had lost all faith in his fellow man.

In the small two-person room, Filo had spread a large sheet of paper. It was the type that would burn up within seconds of exposure to a flame. On the paper was a diagram of the second deck. It didn't have a lot of details beyond the doors to the berths and names of the people who live in them. Everett Goddard had a room just down the hallway from the main starboard bank of elevators. Getting to the second deck wasn't that big of a problem, but getting into the wealthy man's cabin was a different matter.

Filo didn't always take the time to learn much about his targets, but it was impossible not to know who Everett Goddard was. He was the architect behind the digital currency being used on the *Colossus*. It would also be the foundation for financial policy across Secundo. He was rich, well-connected and one of the foundational members of humanity's first colony on a planet outside the Sol system. He was also serving as the President of the *Colossus* bank, meaning he worked in one of the tall office buildings on Topdeck. Filo had already spotted his mark twice on his way to and from work. He took the same route each day, which only made sense given that they were on a spaceship with limited variations in the way a person could get from one point to another. There was no sense in going the long way, especially when most of it had to be traversed on foot.

The privacy curtain on the lower bunk slid open, and Evie sat up. They were the only mixed gender pair of roommates on the ship or, at least, the only two assigned to the same room. They were similar in many ways. Evie was also a stone-cold killer, with a resume just as impressive as Filo's. She also went by a variety of names or she had when she lived on Earth.

"Morning," Filo said without looking her way. "You missed breakfast."

"Great," she said.

To keep the dining hall running efficiently, all the passengers were assigned times for their meals that coincided with their work schedule. And like most roommates, they worked different shifts. Filo was a leather worker in one of the shoe stores on Topdeck. He used a small cutting press to make leather work boots and a variety of footwear from 2300 hours to 0700 hours, ship time. Evie worked as a waitress in one of the many restaurants on Topdeck from 1500 to 2300 hours. They saw each other only for a small stretch of time before Filo went to sleep and after Evie woke up.

It worked because they weren't lovers or even close friends. Evie wore thick, flannel pajamas to sleep in. She was a small person, only five feet four inches tall, and weighed less than a hundred pounds. She was attractive, but not overly so. Evie didn't turn heads and even added a few unnecessary accessories to ensure that she didn't. In a crowd, she blended in. She was Asian, although Filo didn't know from where exactly. She spoke flawless English without the hint of an accent and had training in chemistry, which she often used in carrying out her missions.

"I brought back some fruit," Filo told her.

"That was thoughtful. You're going to make me like you, if you keep that up."

She went into their shared bathroom and shut the door. He never looked up from the diagram. Filo liked women, although he was not adept at maintaining romantic relationships. He was not hip, didn't wear the latest fashions or keep up with trends. Nightclubs were not his scene and he rarely did anything that might attract attention, such as wearing close-fitting outfits that showed off his powerful build.

The goal, in their profession, was to blend in. To be as forgettable as possible. They didn't bond. They didn't make friends. Nor did they stay in any one place very long. In that regard, they would have been a perfect match on paper and they were at the beginning of a two-year journey in a shared space. From the outside, they appeared to be a couple, but in reality, they were simply roommates with similar professions.

Evie's target was not Everett Goddard, but his former lover, an independently wealthy chef and food scientist named Harmonia Lukid. Goddard's ex-wife fully believed that she was behind the hits. Everett had cheated on her, then divorced her. The prenuptial agreement she had signed before they married entitled her to only fifty million dollars. It was enough to live on, but not in the manner to which she had become accustomed. To make matters worse, Goddard and Lukid had purchased berths on the *Colossus*. When his ex-wife learned that Everett would sail away to a new life on a pristine new planet, while she was left behind on Earth with just a perceived pittance, she called her cousin, who knew some people with ties to organized crime. As it turned out, she wasn't the only one who wanted to see Everett Goddard dead.

There were people back on Earth with a vested interest in seeing the new colony fail. To that end, they had contributed to the contract on Everett Goddard, including getting Filo and Evie aboard the colony ship. They were not the kind of people one wanted to disappoint. Filo had no doubt that contingencies had been put in place. The only way to ensure those contingency plans were put into action was to take out Everett as quickly as possible. It was his entire focus. Every waking hour, his mind worked the problem. He needed to kill Everett Goddard, but do the deed in such a manner that it didn't fall back on him. There was nowhere to run to on the *Colossus*. It was a mammoth vessel to be sure, although that didn't mean a person could hide indefinitely on it. He needed a way to commit murder and get away with it ... scot-free.

CHAPTER 20

THE FIRST REAL crime took place on the *Colossus* only fourteen days into their journey. Blood was found in the corridor between a warehouse and a row of berths on deck fourteen. Dave and Becky were on call. They had separately made several rounds through Topdeck and felt they knew the city well enough to respond anywhere on the top level of the ship. Things might have been easier if the layout of the lower decks were all the same. But they were not. In some places, the warehouses were two, even three decks high. In other places, there were lots of little berths, and in others, there were larger cabins. It made the ship a giant labyrinth that would take weeks, maybe even months, to get a full grasp of. Fortunately, the same cufflink that alerted the two detectives to the call also showed them the fastest way to the crime scene.

When they reached deck fifteen, they took hoverboards to the scene of the alleged crime. There were four patrol officers loitering there, keeping the passengers away.

"What have we got?" Becky said, showing her badge to the first officer she encountered.

"Blood was found," a man with a broad chest and booming voice said. "We checked around, found more. No calls into medical were reported. Thought it needed to be looked into."

"Good call," Dave responded. He bent over to look at the blood. There was what appeared to be a gush of blood staining the wall and the deck.

"It's not just a minor accident," the big patrolman said. "I've got a trail leading back into engineering. We can chase it down if you like."

"I'll go with you," Becky said. "Dave?"

"Already on it," he said, hitting a few icons for a squad-wide call.

Becky's cufflink flashed and vibrated with the message, which she ignored. She walked after the big patrolman, taking note of the fact that he had no firearm, just a telescoping baton, pepper spray, and a close-contact taser. That was the way the international team of delegates arranged for law enforcement on the *Colossus* to be armed. Becky and the SIU were exceptions with their spring-loaded, non-lethal pistols.

The blood trail ran down another corridor. She checked her wrist cuff as they followed it. There was no signal near the engineering compartment they were moving around. Blood showed up every twenty paces or so, in dwindling amounts. It wasn't fresh either. The blood had coagulated to a sticky gel. Becky had seen enough such clues to feel certain someone had been seriously hurt. The only question was how? Had they hurt themselves? Had someone else done it? If so, was it on purpose or an accident? Was it a fit of rage, or a cold, calculated attack? They wouldn't know until they found the source of the blood.

On her comlink, which was a tiny in-ear device, she heard Flint's voice. It was thick with sleep, as he had been working the graveyard shift to allow the other members of the team the more favorable day and evening slots. Not that it was hard to adjust to life on the ship. Time was really a kind of construct on the *Colossus*. It was passing, but with no day and night, the cycle was artificial. On Topdeck, it worked because of the sun arch. But on the lower decks, there was no difference between day and night, other than the chrono built into their cufflinks.

"What's the call?" he asked.

"Blood trail," Dave replied. "Deck fifteen."

"On my way," Logan reported.

"Do you need Stu and me?" Jeopardy asked.

"Affirmative," Becky said. "I'm following the trail, and this isn't just a nosebleed."

"Did someone check with medical?" Flint asked.

"Patrol did," Dave said. "I'm double-checking that now."

"Alright, people, you know the drill," Flint ordered. "Get to fifteen and work the scene. Let's start knocking on doors. Someone had to see or hear something."

Becky felt a slight thrill, which she really wasn't proud of. It felt good to work a crime scene again. On Earth, there were serious crimes committed on a daily basis. At times, she had felt overwhelmed by the sheer number of cases that she had been forced to work. But since arriving on the *Colossus,* the job seemed remedial. She knew it was all good to learn the city and to make note of areas that might foster criminal activity. But it wasn't the same as running an investigation. She couldn't deny that she was happy to be doing what she thought of as real police work. Nor could she deny a deep fear that they would find someone hurt or dead, whose family and friends would be devastated by the crime. Too many lives were cut short by senseless violence and evil.

"Looks like it goes in there," the big patrolman said.

"What's your name?" Becky asked him.

"Cyrus," he responded. "Luke Cyrus."

"I'm Nash," she told him. "I agree with your assessment. We should go in."

The door in question was a maintenance hatch. The blood didn't lead to it exactly, but the trail stopped just before it reached the hatch, and there was no sign of it farther down the corridor.

Becky drew her pistol, but gave the patrolman the option. "You want to go first or shall I?"

"They took our sidearms," he said. "Best I can do is some pepper spray."

"Then watch my back, Cyrus."

Becky reached up and tapped her cufflink. One icon activated her comlink. She touched it, then tapped another that enabled her cufflink to open the hatches that were reserved for the ship's crew members with a need to access the area beyond.

"Sergeant Flint, we've followed the blood trail to maintenance hatch forty-four," she reported. "Patrolman Cyrus and I are going in."

"Copy that, Nash. Be careful. I'll be at your twenty in five minutes."

Becky looked up at Luke Cyrus. "Are you ready?"

"Let's do it," the big man said.

She waved her cufflink at the hatch, and it slid open. She held her pistol out in a two-handed grip. Like everyone else, she had fired a simulated version of the weapon. It was a lot like shooting an old-fashioned BB pistol. Only, instead of a spring or compressed air, the pistol utilized a mini-rail to propel the rubber bullets. That meant if she pulled the trigger, an electrical current from a battery in the rear of the weapon would send a plunger sliding along a metal hydrogen rail, pushing the bullet down the barrel with no friction. It wasn't rifled or made for long-distance shooting, yet could be very effective in close quarters without endangering the ship. The pistol was very lightweight. In some ways, it felt like a toy, but Becky knew the metal rail and barrel made the weapon very expensive and a bit delicate. She didn't favor it over her usual sidearm, but understood the danger of firing real bullets with gunpowder on a spaceship.

Inside the hatch, there was a narrow walkway between two massive machines that were built into the vessel. The stylish deck plates from the corridor were replaced by dull metal grates in the floor that allowed a person to see down into the space between decks.

There was no movement inside, just a dull rumble from the machines.

"Looks clear," she said softly to Cyrus.

He tapped her shoulder and she moved forward. The interior of the engineering compartment was large, but that said, there wasn't a lot of room. Most of it was filled with huge machines, leaving just narrow spaces where a person could walk, or shimmy, past or between them. Working on the machines must have been challenging, Becky thought.

"More blood," she said, as they came to another gush on the floor. It had dripped down into the space between. They pushed on, working their way through the engineering compartment, but finding nothing that seemed out of place. Whoever had been bleeding was nowhere to be found. And there was only one other hatch on the far side of the compartment. They went through it, but found no signs of blood.

"That's weird," Cyrus said.

"It's telling," Becky replied. "We've got two options. Either the bleeder found a way to stanch the blood, or..."

"They're still in there?"

"Bingo," she said.

"Maybe they bled out," Cyrus said.

"There's no evidence of that," Becky told him. "If they had been losing that much blood, the gushes would have been smaller."

"So, they might still be alive?"

"Maybe," she said as she tapped her comlink. "Jeopardy, we'll need Stu."

"We're on our way. Sixty seconds to your location."

"Come with me, Patrolman Cyrus. You'll want to see it."

They went back out the first hatch and waited. A minute later, Jeopardy arrived on a hoverboard with Stu sitting calmly behind her.

"Wow! That's some trick," he said. "I didn't know there were dogs on board."

"Just this one," Jeopardy said. "And Stu's a cop, just like you. What's up, Becky?"

"Blood trail ends inside, but no body," Nash said.

"Interesting," Jeopardy said.

"Patrolman Cyrus, stay here and guard the scene. No one goes in or out without my say so."

"Roger that," the big man said.

He turned his back to the hatch, and Becky led the way inside. She showed Jeopardy the blood spatter on the deck grates.

"Stu, *such!*" Jeopardy ordered.

The dog immediately bent his head and sniffed the bloody grate. Then he looked up and moved down the walkway, making a grumbling growl as he went. The two female officers followed him, but gave the dog enough leeway that when he turned back and forth several times, they weren't crowding him.

"Is something wrong?" Becky asked.

"No," Jeopardy said. "He's just working it out."

Stu began sniffing the side of one of the machines. He went back and forth several more times, staying locked on the machine to the right-hand side of the walkway. Then he sat down and barked twice.

"*Revier*, Stu," Jeopardy called out.

The dog got up, sniffed along the machine again in both directions, then sat back down and barked.

"*Guter hund*, Stu. *Guter hund.*"

"What is it?" Becky asked.

"The trail leads into the machine," Jeopardy asked.

They waited a few more minutes until Flint arrived. He called in an engineering supervisor. The machine in question was a cooling pump. It was the size of a house and pumped compressed nitrogen through the ship's main engines as needed. The engineer had a variety of tools hanging from his belt. He pulled off one that had three flat prongs. The prongs fit into an opening on the side panel of the machine. He twisted the tool to unlock the panel, then slid it back. Inside were huge pipes. A wave of cold air flowed out of the machine, creating a temporary fog around the officers.

Stu barked several times and had trouble sitting still.

"Careful, those pipes are extremely cold. They'll burn you if you touch them," the engineer warned.

Becky bent down. She could see something odd on the closest pipe, even through the fog of cold condensation billowing out of the machine. It looked like a cave formation, a stalactite.

"I've got blood," she said. "It's frozen."

"Will this fog clear?" Flint complained. "We can't see a thing."

"Yes, it will clear out in a moment," the engineer said.

In reality, it took nearly sixty seconds, but as the fog moved away, the scene became clear. A young woman had been murdered. Her body was stuffed into a space between the pipes of freezing liquid nitrogen.

"Ah, hell," Flint said. "Some things never change."

"Good hiding spot for a body," Jeopardy said. "It's got to be frozen solid."

"Which will make time of death impossible to calculate," Becky said. "At least we know it was an engineer."

"Excuse me?" the supervisor said. "That's a drastic conclusion to jump to."

"Is it?" Becky said, turning to the man. "Does anyone else have access to this compartment? What about that tool you used to open the panel? Can I find one just lying around somewhere?"

"Alright, alright, take it easy," Flint said. "Can we shut this down?"

"No," the engineering supervisor said. "The cooling unit is a vital component of the engines, which are still in operation."

"Well, then, call the medical staff. We'll borrow equipment from the engineers and pull her out. I don't guess her cufflink will still be operational?"

"After exposure to that much cold, I doubt it," the supervisor said.

"Alright, well, let's find the other end of the blood trail," Flint said. "I've got no signal in here. Becky, pull up a list of the engineers and engineer's mates on this floor. Can anyone else get in here? Maintenance? Janitorial?"

"Just the senior officers," the supervisor said.

"Is the lock monitored by the security system?"

"Should be. The flow of nitrogen creates interference with the ship's network, but the cameras and locks are hardwired."

The investigation went into overdrive. Jeopardy and Becky followed the blood trail back around the engineering compartment and down several adjoining corridors. It was a marvel to Becky that someone could hurt another human being and then move them down the corridor without being noticed.

Flint stayed by the body, waiting for the medical staff to arrive. When they did, they had to be suited up in safety coveralls, with two sets of gloves. The body was frozen. It was a teenage girl with light brown skin, although it had turned a strange gray from being frozen. Blood, and in some places tissue, had to be chiseled off the pipes. It left human remains that couldn't be taken off the pipes without risk of a major accident. Everything was photographed, including the body, which had been severely beaten. Her stomach was distended from internal bleeding. Flint surmised that she had been forced to stop and vomit up the blood, which left the trail to be found by the patrol officers.

Logan and Dave joined Becky and Jeopardy, who were following Stu down the corridor. The dog was sniffing the floor, his head down, tail straight out behind him.

"There's only a handful of engineers on this deck," Dave said, reading off his cufflink. "None of them are crew members."

"Makes sense," Becky said. "Crew are all housed with us down on deck eighteen."

"So, who had access to the engineering compartment?" Logan asked.

"There are a few passengers with experience who were assigned to help as part of their job on board the ship," Dave said. "They're pretty spread out around this deck."

It was unsettling to be on a spaceship, even one as huge as the *Colossus,* with a murderer. There might be another explanation for what happened to the girl, but Becky and the other cops were suspicious by nature. Years of dealing with people doing bad things had that effect. It was hard to see the good or believe optimistically that things would turn out in a positive light. People who are involved in accidents don't get shoved into a giant cooling machine's inner parts.

"Stu's got something," Jeopardy said as the dog stopped and sniffed hard at the foot of the door to one of the berths. "Cabin four-sixteen," she said.

"Four-sixteen," Dave repeated. "Four-sixteen, that's Henry Miller, his wife Kathryn, and their son, Johnny. He's fifteen years old."

"Let's see who's home," Becky said.

Jeopardy stepped back and called the police dog to her. "Stu, *heir... beilb!*" The dog trotted to her side, then sat obediently.

Becky put one hand on her sidearm that was in her hip holster, and with the other, she knocked on the door, pounding with her open palm.

Logan pressed the control panel. Each cabin on the ship had one just to the right side of the doorway. It contained a proximity scanner that connected with one's cufflink, as well as a biometric palm print reader that could be used if one's other device malfunctioned. It also had command overrides for senior ship officers and senior law enforcement officers. It also contained an intercom. Logan tapped the icon that would transmit his voice into the cabin.

"Mr. and Mrs. Miller, this is *Colossus* law enforcement personnel. We need to speak to you. Please open the door," he said.

They waited, and nothing happened. Becky turned back to Jeopardy.

"You sure this is the right place?"

"Absolutely," Jeopardy replied, putting a hand on Stu's head.

"Tell them we're coming in," Becky ordered.

Logan made the announcement through the door's intercom again. "Mr. and Mrs. Miller, this is *Colossus* law enforcement. We are entering your cabin now."

He pressed the override command and waved his cufflink at the scanner. It beeped, and the door slid open. It was a small space for a family of three. A narrow main room with a low-backed sofa against one wall, a small three-person round table near a cluster of kitchen appliances, and the obligatory entertainment console mounted to the wall between two bedrooms. Becky stepped in first, her pistol out of its holster, but still pointed at the deck. She kept her trigger finger straight up along the barrel and away from the trigger. Dave followed her. Logan stayed near the door, half in and half out of the tiny berth.

Becky looked into the first bedroom. It had to be the son's. It was a tiny space, with two bunks built into the wall, and a pair of metal lockers. There were clothes on the floor, and a few posters stuck to the wall. The lower bunk was converted into a chair of sorts. There was evidence of snacking in the small space, as well as wireless gaming controllers. The video entertainment screen was left folded down, with a screensaver scrolling through images from the child's phone. There was no place for anyone to hide in the tiny space and it smelled of sweat. Becky didn't know if it was from the dirty clothes or if someone had been exercising in the tiny space.

She moved on, Dave backing her up. He had his pistol out, too, but there was nothing imposing about Dave Bannon. He wore tan pants, a clean white shirt that buttoned up the front, and a light-weight, puffy vest that was long enough to cover his belt and the police gear he kept clipped to it.

"Is anyone home?" Becky called. "This is the police."

They weren't called police on the *Colossus*, or even cops; they were law enforcement officers, or LEOs. Becky referred to herself as police out of habit. But it didn't seem to matter. There was no reply.

She made her way to the main bedroom. It was slightly larger, with a double bed in the center, a narrow nightstand on each side, and to either side of the door, double lockers with faux-wood paneling. The room was neat, the bed made up with a light blue comforter and large pillows. There were a few personal items on the surface of the nightstands, and lights in sconces over the head of the bed.

Becky stepped into the room and looked at both lockers. They had a variety of clothes, shoes, and accessories inside. But no sign of where the passengers who lived in cabin four-sixteen were.

"Clear," she said.

"Maybe the dog was wrong," Dave suggested. "There's nothing to indicate a crime took place here."

"Perhaps it didn't," she said. "What if it started here? The girl in the cooling system was young. It was hard to make out much detail, but she didn't seem like an adult."

"The boy's girlfriend, maybe?"

Becky nodded. They were about to leave, but she stepped into the tiny bathroom. It was no larger than the one in her own berth. The shower was empty. She reached to open the door of the tiny closet where the toilet was located, only to discover it was locked.

"Dave," she said.

He looked over at her, and she pointed at the toilet door. He nodded. Becky then wrapped lightly on the thin door with her knuckles. It was made of molded plastic and was only an eighth of an inch thick. It was designed to give the user privacy, just not much of it.

"Hello," Becky said. "Please unlock the door. We're law enforcement, here to help."

There was no verbal reply; she heard someone moving in the small space.

"We're going to insist on talking to you," Becky said. "Either open the door or I will."

"Go away," a woman's voice said in a shaky tone.

"Can't do that, ma'am. Are you Mrs. Miller?"

"Please... just go... away."

She was crying. That wasn't surprising. Something terrible had happened and she was clearly traumatized by it. Becky had met many people in the same state. They weren't always the perpetrators of some heinous crime or even complicit in it, but that was the insidious nature of evil. The shock waves of it spread out and hurt the people around us. There was no such thing as a victimless crime nor any truth to the idea that immorality only hurt the person committing the act.

"We can't leave, Mrs. Miller. Open the door or we will break it in. You can cooperate with us or we will detain you for impeding our investigation."

There was a moment of silence. Becky wasn't sure how they would force the door open. It was hard plastic and built into grooves at the floor and the top of the door jamb. Instead of swinging open on hinges, it slid into a pocket. They would probably need a crowbar to break the lock and slide it aside. But just when Becky was about to send for one, there was a snap from the lock. The door opened just a few inches. Becky looked inside. A middle-aged woman was sitting on the toilet, fully clothed. Her dark hair was streaked with premature gray, and her eyes were swollen from crying.

"Mrs. Miller?"

The woman nodded.

"I'm Detective Nash, this is my partner, Detective Bannon. Can you come out of there? We need to talk to you about what happened here today."

The woman stood up and Becky slid the door aside. She holstered her pistol and took Mrs. Miller by the hand. Bannon followed suit, lending support to the other side of the woman. The three of them could barely navigate through the tiny space to the sofa. It was small, gray and stiff. Becky sat on it with her and Dave stood between them and the entertainment screen on the wall. Logan was still in the doorway and Becky could see Jeopardy in the corridor beyond. She had moved to get a better view of Mrs. Miller.

Becky tapped on her cufflink, activating the recording feature, then turned to the distraught woman.

"Can you tell me what happened here today?"

Mrs. Miller shook her head.

"We're here to help you, Mrs. Miller. Can I call you Kathryn?"

"Kathy," the woman said, holding a wad of toilet tissue under her nose. Tears were starting to well up in her eyes again.

"Kathy, I'm Becky. It's nice to meet you. Where is your husband, Kathy?"

"I don't know," she said very quickly, while shaking her head from side to side and looking down. It was classic body language. Most people did one or the other when they lied, usually without thinking about it. It was clear to Becky that Kathryn Miller was lying.

"Okay, what about your son, Johnny. Where is he?"

"School," she said, repeating the shake and downward look. "He's at practice, I think. He's on the wrestling team."

The *Colossus* had six educational facilities and only one was for adults. The other five were for children, of which there were nearly three thousand on board the ship. Two were for grades nine through twelve and offered the usual fine arts and athletic programs.

"Okay," Becky said, as Dave checked his cufflink. The device had a touch screen on the top of the forearm and a display screen on the bottom. Theirs were a bit larger than most cufflinks. The passengers had small, wristwatch-sized devices. But certain members of the crew had larger ones. The Special Investigators had the largest size. It was six inches wide and could be used almost like a computer to pull up information from the ship's network about the passengers.

"There was a crime committed today and I'm afraid that your husband or son might be involved," Becky said. "Have either of them been home lately?"

Kathryn Miller clamped her mouth shut and shook her head.

"You haven't seen them? We need to find your husband and your son."

"I don't know," she said.

"Did someone threaten you?"

"No."

"Did they threaten your family?"

"No," she said, weeping again.

"Did someone get hurt here?"

Kathryn looked down, shaking her head. "No," she said, the word coming out in a weepy whisper.

"Okay, Kathy, you don't know me," Becky said. "But my job is to keep bad things from happening. The sooner I find your husband and your son, the better off they will be. You want them to be safe, right? I know you do. Why don't you tell me where they are?"

"I can't?"

"Sure, you can," Becky urged. "It's best if you tell me what happened. Let me help."

"I'm not saying anything else," Kathryn said. "I want you to leave."

"We can't do that," Becky said. "And you can answer our questions here or we can detain you and question you in an interrogation room."

Kathryn started rocking back and forth. She shook her head and held her wad of tissue over her mouth. Becky looked up. She was frustrated, but not surprised.

"The kid's not at school. They haven't seen him all day," Dave said.

"What about the husband?"

"Logan's checking. These engineering guys roam around a lot. It's harder to pin down if he showed up for work and what he might be doing or where."

"Let's get her up to the squad room," Becky said. "She's not going to be any help."

Jeopardy took charge of Kathryn Miller, escorting her up to deck nine, where the SIU had their headquarters that included two small interrogation rooms and a holding cell. Jeopardy put Kathryn Miller in one of the interrogation rooms with a box of facial tissues. The distraught woman continued weeping all the way up from her berth.

Flint arrived at the apartment and found his squad discussing what to do next.

"We need someone at the school," Flint said, taking charge. "Logan?"

"Got it," Keys replied.

"Dave, go find out who's in charge of the day-to-day activities of the engineers and adjunct passenger engineers. Who has worked with Miller? What's he like? Where does he spend the majority of his time? Where might he go after a shift other than home to his wife and kid?"

"Yes, sir," Dave replied.

"That leaves us with surveillance," Flint told Becky. "We should get a report on the victim soon, too. And we'll have to notify her parents that their little girl has been murdered."

CHAPTER 21

LOGAN TOOK the nearest elevator and went up four floors. There were two high schools on the ship, one on deck eleven (the Red Wolves) and one on deck six (the Bulldogs). The vice principal met Logan. Classes were over for the day, but there was a wide array of after-school programs that took place. Many were a prescribed set of practical courses that were meant to help prepare the students for life on Secundo. Cooking, cleaning, building and repairing things were skills that everyone would need to utilize on a world without an infrastructure. Many of the high schoolers would be instrumental in making Secundo a safe place for other colonists to live. The classes weren't graded or even mandatory, but they gave the students a chance to practice doing things they couldn't do at home. There was a classroom filled with cooking stations, another that was lined with huge rolls of fabric and various consoles for cutting, pinning and sewing garments. There was even a wood shop class with saws, drill presses and actual lumber which could be used to build just about anything and a garage with long work benches where students disassembled and reassembled small engines, learned the ins and outs of basic wiring and plumbing.

There were also the regular extra-curricular activities of sports, music, theater and art. The vice president knew who Johnny Miller was, but not much about him. He escorted Logan to the gym, where wrestling practice was in full swing.

"Coach Barnes, can we have a word, please?" the vice principal asked.

"Yeah, who's we?" Barnes said without looking away from the two students struggling for supremacy on the mat.

"I'm Detective Logan Keys. I've got some questions about Johnny Miller."

"Good lord, what's Miller done? We're two weeks into the school year and Miller has a cop up here interrupting practice. Typical."

"Does he miss practice often?" Logan asked.

"No," Barnes replied. "But he's not a serious athlete either. He could be our best wrestler if he put in the work. Come on, Dalton! Don't let him take your back!"

"Who's Miller friends with?" Logan continued asking questions.

"Everyone. He's a popular kid. Hangs out with Gentry and Olson a lot. That's them, running laps. A pair of comedians, those two. They never take anything seriously."

"What can you tell me about Miller? Did he have a temper?"

"Sure, I guess. What teenager doesn't?"

"Has he ever hurt anyone?"

"Oh, no," the vice principal said. "We have a very strict code of conduct here. No bullying or violence is tolerated among the students."

"What about girls?" Logan continued. "Is he friendly with any of the girls?"

"Miller is friendly with all the girls," Coach Barnes replied. "Thinks he's God's gift or something."

"Has he been in trouble at school at all?"

"No, he has a clean academic record," the VP said.

"Nothing unusual," Barnes added. "Just the usual funny business all teenagers get up to."

Logan felt a rising sense of frustration. A young girl was murdered, but of course, that was classified information, and no one knew it yet. Logan couldn't tell the Vice Principal or the wrestling coach even if it would have made them more helpful.

"I guess I should talk to his friends," Logan said.

"Gentry, Olson!" Coach Barnes shouted. "Get over here. Hustle up."

The two teenagers hurried over. They were both Caucasians with sweat making their bushy hair stick to their foreheads.

"Who's Gentry?" Logan asked.

"That's me," the taller of the two said.

"You're friends with Johnny Miller?"

"Sure, we hang out."

"Is he sick or what?" Olson asked. "He skipped school today."

"We're looking into that," Logan said.

"We? Who's we?" Gentry said.

"We're trying to find Johnny," Logan said. "Do you have any idea where he might be?"

"He's not here," Gentry said. "Who are you, mister?"

"Celvin Gentry, show some respect to our guest," the VP said.

"My name is Logan Keys. I'm law enforcement. Where might Johnny hang out when he's not in school?"

"It's a big ship, man," Gentry said. "He could be anywhere."

"Movies, the park, dining hall, who knows," Olson added. "Sometimes he liked to just go walking around, you know."

The two boys glanced at each other, trying not to crack up laughing.

Logan sighed. He wished he could knock the two boys' heads together, but that would just make things worse, even if it would make him feel better.

"Look, I've got a job to do. We need help. No one knows where Johnny Miller is. Now, can you please tell me where he might be?"

Gentry folded his arms, but Olson grinned and said, "Have you checked Jenna Frankle's house?"

"Who is Jenna Frankle, his girlfriend?"

"I don't know that Johnny would admit it. But they've been hooking up," Olson said. "He goes to her cabin when her parents aren't home."

"Have either of you heard from Johnny today?"

They both shook their heads.

"Is that usual?"

"No, the students can message one another via their cufflinks," the VP said. "It's a bit of a problem with discipline, actually."

"And no messages from Johnny?" Logan asked.

The boys both shook their heads. Logan turned to the VP. "Who is Jenna Frankle?"

"A student here. She's one year ahead of Johnny," the school administrator said.

"I'm going to need to know more about her."

While Logan was led through the school, he called up the information to Jeopardy, who had just finished settling Kathryn Miller into an interrogation room.

"Frankle," Jeopardy said. She was in the joint offices of the SIU, where Becky and Flint were already starting to look at surveillance video. Her voice carried through the comlink to Logan down on deck eleven. "Father is Daniel, an agri worker. He's taking classes full-time. Her mother isn't listed. Looks like it's just the two of them. They have a berth on deck sixteen."

"Any chance..." Logan said.

He didn't need to say anything out loud that could be repeated. The Vice Principal was leading him through the school, but also listening to every word that Logan said.

"Maybe," Jeopardy replied. "We haven't gotten an ID or preliminary from medical yet."

"Okay, thanks," Logan said.

"Officer Keys, I did check just now. Jenna Frankle was absent without notice from classes today."

Logan nodded. He found that information to be both interesting and troubling. One of the things that arose from his career of dealing with evil people was the sheer number of innocent women and children who were targeted by criminals. It was part of what kept the fuse burning on his smoldering rage.

"Is that unusual?" Logan asked.

"According to her records, it's the first occurrence."

"But kids skip school all the time."

"Some do," the VP replied, "but things are a little different here on the *Colossus*. People not showing up where they're supposed to be puts things out of balance."

They entered a room with rows of small tables, each one with its own sewing machine. There were racks of fabrics and larger tables where students were pinning patterns on for cutting the various parts of a garment that they would eventually sew together. There were at least thirty people in the room, and not all girls, although they outnumbered the boys three to one. The teacher was a woman with kind eyes and long strawberry blonde hair pinned up into a coil on top of her head. She wore a quilted apron, as well as a red, long-tailed tailor's coat with big pockets. She had a tape measure around her neck and scissors in one hand.

"Ms. Ebberdean," the VP called out. "May we have a word?"

There were at least a dozen girls gathered around the cutting table. Several leaned close, whispering about the interruption. By the time the teacher arrived where Logan waited, there were giggles coming from the girls. Logan knew they wouldn't be giggling if they knew what he was there for. He wondered how many of the girls knew the victim.

"Is something wrong?" the teacher asked. She had a soft voice and a beguiling smile. Logan wondered briefly why none of his teachers had ever looked so attractive.

"This is Officer Keys," the VP explained. "He has some questions about Jenna Frankle."

"Jenna wasn't in school today," the teacher said.

"Do you know her well?" Logan asked.

"She's in my home skills class and first aid. But I don't suppose I know her as anything but an attentive student."

"Do you know who she spends time with?"

"Actually, I don't," the teacher said. "She's friendly enough, but I don't think she's found her friend group yet. It's still early, and this is a new school, after all. Why has something happened?"

"I can't talk about that," Logan said. "I'm sorry. I was just hoping to find out more about Jenna. And perhaps if you knew if she was spending time with Johnny Miller?"

That made the teacher blink her large eyes and take a half step back. There was a look of incredulity on her face.

"Johnny Miller?"

"That's right," Logan said.

Ms. Ebberdean looked at the VP. "With Jenna Frankle?"

"I think I'm missing something," Logan said.

The VP looked clueless, and Ms. Eberdean sighed. She was obviously frustrated by the VP's ignorance, but didn't press the point. Instead, she directed her opinion to Logan.

"I've been teaching kids for nearly ten years, Officer Keys."

"Call me Logan," he told her.

"I'm Abby. Anyway, Johnny Miller is a popular student, lots of friends, well-liked. In many ways, he is the opposite of Jenna Frankle, who is shy, reserved, and not exactly unpopular, but she doesn't run with the popular crowd. Frankly, I would be surprised if she was spending time with Johnny Miller. And if she is, well... that is troublesome."

"Why, exactly?"

"A shy young woman receiving attention from a popular boy is often... unhealthy. Insecure girls can be easily manipulated when their emotions are involved."

"Thank you, Abby, that's very helpful. By the way," Logan decided to ask one last question. "Do you know why Jenna is on this trip without her mother?"

"She passed away," the teacher said. Logan didn't have to look at

the VP; he could feel the reaction of surprise as the clueless administrator took a full step backward. "It's been just Jenna and her father
for several years, and he's busy. She was staying here after school, but
the last week or so she hadn't been around as much."

"Thank you. I think I've got all I need."

"If Jenna needs anything, anything at all, please look me up,"
Abby said.

"I will," Logan told her.

A look passed between them. Under different circumstances,
Logan would have looked forward to seeing Abby Eberdean again.
But he knew that if his hunch was correct, she would forever
associate him with a terrible loss. He had learned to put his feelings
about death away, but most people couldn't. And unless Jenna
Frankle was safe at home, the odds were stacking up that she would
never go home again.

CHAPTER 22

"YOU'RE SURE?" Sergeant Sawyer Flint said.

He was speaking to a member of the ship's medical staff. Most passengers would just be scanned by an automated medical unit if they had a complaint. There were nursing stations on every floor, but only a handful of actual nurses, and even fewer doctors. The medical units were good. They could detect all sorts of viral and bacterial issues from a simple breath sample. They could also scan for a person's temperature, detect abnormalities in a person's throat, ears, eyes and even look up their nose. Rashes and skin issues were usually diagnosed with a ninety-nine percent accuracy rating. There were a handful of specialists on board, including trauma surgeons. A few had thawed the dead girl's body. She had been officially identified and the cause of death was agreed to be internal hemorrhaging as a result of repeated trauma to the abdomen.

"That's pretty early to make a definitive assessment," Flint continued. "Alright, thank you."

He got to his feet and walked out to the bullpen where his officers were gathered. Logan and Dave were back from their interviews, and Becky Nash had collected all the surveillance footage.

"We have a victim. You were right, Logan. It is Jenna Frankle, sixteen years old."

A picture came on the large video display, with a list of information about the girl. She had mousy brown hair and freckles. But the more prominent feature was her mouth. She had broad, thick lips that the rest of her face hadn't quite grown into yet.

"The doctors say she was pregnant. Three weeks," Flint said.

"So, before we came aboard," Logan asked.

"Actually, gestation is counted from a woman's last menstrual cycle," Dave said. "The average fertility period is two weeks after that. A three-week pregnancy usually indicates sexual intercourse occurred just a week prior."

"How do you know that?" Jeopardy asked.

"That's not important," Flint said. "But the doctors told me the same thing."

"How do they know she was only three weeks?" Becky asked.

"Because she went to a nursing station early this morning. Probably before school," Flint said. "The medical unit records all that information from the patient. She was complaining of nausea, fatigue, thought she had cold, found out she had a bun in the oven. The med staff said her progesterone levels were very high for an early pregnancy. She was either very fertile, or possibly pregnant with twins, as that sometimes increases those hormone levels."

"So, our victim thought she was sick and found out that she was pregnant. Then she skipped school," Logan said.

"To tell the father," Jeopardy cut in. "Only he wasn't happy about that news."

"No," Becky said, "he killed her for it."

"How?" Dave asked.

"Doctors say she died of internal bleeding," Flint continued. "A result of traumatic injury to the abdominal area."

"How did that happen?" Dave wondered. "And why not go back to the nursing station for help?"

"Because the same person who caused it kept her from getting help," Becky said. She hit a control on her cufflink and brought up the ship's surveillance footage from 0730 hours that morning. It played on another large display screen beside the first. Their office had a series of them that allowed the investigators to keep pertinent information up at all times. The video showed a girl approaching the Millers' doorway. Flint recognized the type. She was a little tall for her age and not incredibly thin like most teenagers. She wasn't fat either, but her body was more developed than most at that age. He felt guilty for looking at her in that way, but he knew it was necessary to see her as her attacker had. From the report that Logan had given, it wasn't a leap to think that Johnny Miller had taken advantage of Jenna Frankle's shy nature and coerced her into a physically intimate relationship.

Becky sped the footage forward after Jenna went into the cabin. The hallways around the Miller's berth were busy from just before 0800 until a little past 0900. When the corridor was empty, the door opened and Mr. Miller was helping Jenna out of the cabin. He looked frightened and had to practically drag Jenna from his home. She was trying to walk, but could barely stay upright.

"Bastard," Logan whispered.

The surveillance feed changed three times before they saw Jenna fall to the ground. She vomited. Mr. Miller pulled her back upright and kept moving.

"We lose them as they approach the engineering section," Becky said. "They have fewer cameras there. Henry Miller must have gotten her into the cooling compartment before they were picked up on video again."

"He found out she was pregnant and what?" Bannon asked.

"He beat her," Logan said. "He hit her over and over in the stomach."

"Not him," Flint said. "Henry Miller is not our killer."

"Who then?" Jeopardy asked.

Becky brought up the surveillance footage outside the Miller berth again. Two minutes after his father left, a disheveled Johnny Miller stepped out and ran in the opposite direction.

"He ditched his cufflink shortly after this," Becky said. "It's off the network. I have been able to pick up the trail."

"I didn't think that was possible," Logan said.

"It's not supposed to be," Flint said. "If you recall, in the *Colossus* manual, the cufflinks even have a backup power battery that should enable it to ping the ship's location network even if the rest of the device is powered down."

"He removed it in a dead area," Dave said. "And hid it so that it wouldn't be found by someone passing that way."

"Why kill her?" Jeopardy asked. "He has to know he can't get away with it."

"I doubt he was thinking clearly," Flint said. "But, he was certainly surprised by the news and reacted to the baby. That's who he was trying to kill. The mother was just collateral damage."

"He may not even think she died," Becky said. "What are the odds that mom and dad heard him beating her. Maybe they even tried to stop him, but the damage was done. Henry Miller looks like a desperate man when he comes out of his cabin."

"He may have told his son that he would take her to another part of the ship and get her help," Dave said. "Instead, he took her where he thought no one would find her and stuffed her body into the cold."

"Bastard," Logan whispered again.

"He wasn't counting on Stu, though," Jeopardy said.

"Let's go talk to the wife again," Flint said. "Becky, take lead. Jeopardy, back her up."

"Me?" Jeopardy asked.

"Yes," Flint said. "She might respond better to two women."

Being a team leader was more than giving orders. Sawyer wanted his team to be the best they could be. And that meant giving them opportunities to grow. Jeopardy Bess had been added to the team because she had experience and training as a K-9 cop. But he had looked into her file. She had high marks on all her testing and glowing reviews from every superior she had worked for. Her choice to work the K-9 unit had stunted her career, and more to the point, stifled her growth. Flint planned to make sure she had plenty of opportunities to become the best investigator she could be. Including questioning suspects.

Becky led the way into the interrogation room. Not much had changed since she questioned Kathryn Miller in her cabin. The woman was still weeping. And why not? In one senseless act of rage, her world had been shattered.

"We put the pieces together, Mrs. Miller," Becky said, sitting down across from Kathryn. "Let me see if we got it all right. The girl, Jenna Frankle, shows up at your door unannounced and tells Johnny she was pregnant."

Tears began to flow in earnest at the memory. Jeopardy even felt sorry for the woman. She had raised a boy who had done the unthinkable, and her husband had tried to cover it up. They would both be arrested and face stiff penalties, probably for the rest of their lives. She would be all alone, the woman whose baby was a murderer. It was a story that would haunt her the rest of her days.

"I didn't," Kathryn said. "I didn't even know she was there."

"She probably messaged Johnny to let her in," Becky said. "He hid her in his room."

"He's not supposed to have girls in his room," Kathryn said.

"He's not supposed to manipulate girls who lost their mother to a horrible disease and who was having trouble making friends," Becky said. "He wasn't supposed to have sex with her without protection."

The mother moaned as if she were in physical pain.

"When did you hear them?" Becky pressed. "When he was hitting her?"

Kathryn shut her eyes and shook her head, trying to deny the memories.

"What about when he was trying to kill the baby he had made?" Becky continued, her voice rising with emotion. "Or when she screamed in pain that he was killing her?"

"No, no, no, no..."

"We don't need you to confess, Kathy. The story is clear. We have medical records. Jenna Frankle went to a nurse's station and got a medical scan. She thought she was sick with the flu; turns out she was sick with your son's baby."

"No," Kathryn said. "He's just fifteen. He's not old enough."

"He is and he did," Becky argued. "Do you want to know how she died?"

"No."

"Your son beat her to death. She had traumatic injuries to her abdomen. I wonder why he focused his rage on her abdomen, Kathy?"

"Stop, please," Mrs. Miller begged.

"She's bleeding so much inside she had to vomit it out," Becky said. "And then your husband stuffed her into the cooling mechanism that he works on. He tried to hide the body, Kathy. Your husband is now a co-conspirator in the murder of Jenna Frankle."

Kathryn Miller lowered her head and screamed.

CHAPTER 23

THE *COLOSSUS* WAS like any large city, with all sorts of services. The main difference was that because it was newly occupied, many of those services had become backlogged with work. The criminal court, of which there was only one, had done very little actual work to that point. There was one judge, Renee St. Pierre. She had been a young, talented star in the judicial world. She spent two years as a government prosecutor before making a small fortune as a defense litigator in just three years and was tapped to join the judiciary. In just seven years, she had risen through the court system, with a short stint at the International Criminal Court, before being recruited to join the *Colossus*.

There was a municipal building on *Topdeck* with all the ship's passenger services, including the court system. Renee had an office with views of a few other buildings and a courtroom that didn't see much use. There were arrests made on the *Colossus*, but they were for minor crimes and most were settled with a fine. She had held court officially once by the time she was contacted by Sergeant Flint Sawyer, who was requesting arrest warrants for a father and son, Henry and Johnny Miller.

Arrests could be made without warrants, but only to detain passengers for twenty-four hours. During that time, if the evidence justified an arrest of the detained individual, law enforcement personnel were required to make an official request to the Criminal Court Judge. An arrest warrant would then be issued that would automatically assign an advocate from the ship's crew. Advocates served as both prosecutors and defense attorneys on the colony ship. Their roles were assigned on a rotating basis, although not much work had been done. Crime was not rampant on the ship and, although Renee St. Pierre was thankful for that, she was also bored.

Once an arrest warrant was issued and a passenger was taken into custody, they had a right to hear their charges, make an official plea and have a date set for trial if that was needed. On paper, it was very neat and equitable. Renee knew that she would not only oversee justice on the *Colossus,* but she would also have the chance to guide judicial policies on Secundo that would last for centuries. It had been worth the sacrifice of leaving her career on Earth ... or so she thought. Two weeks of boredom and busy work were making her feel like she might lose her mind. The video call from Sergeant Flint was a welcome change.

"You have a case, Sergeant?"

"We do, unfortunately," Flint said. "A young woman was killed. A teenager, sixteen years old."

"Murdered?"

"Yes, it appears that way. We believe that Johnny Miller, age fifteen, was engaged in a sexual relationship with the victim. She found out this morning that she was pregnant."

"The age-old dilemma," Judge St. Pierre said.

"She went to tell her partner. We believe he responded in a fit of rage and severely beat her. The medical team is doing an official autopsy now, but the initial indications are that she bled to death from severe trauma to her abdomen."

"He tried to punch the baby out of her."

"Yes, Your honor, that seems to track. We have surveillance

footage of her arriving at the Miller residence. She stayed there for over an hour. At that point, she was taken from their cabin by the father, Henry Miller. He's an adjunct to the Engineering crew on deck fifteen. We found the girl's body stuffed into one of the engine cooling systems."

Judge Renee sighed. It was depressing to hear such stories. Human life was fragile and those who took it often had little or no regard for their victims. It was difficult not putting herself in the victim's place, but she had learned that she couldn't do that. Her job was to remain impartial and her sanity required that she stay on the outside of the stories she heard.

"We believe the father was trying to help his son," Sergeant Flint continued. "But whether he meant to let the girl die, or if she just expired before he could reach an aid station, is unknown. His wife is being questioned, but isn't offering much insight. She's in shock."

"Her child and husband are both complicit in murder," the judge said. "That's enough to knock anyone off their rocker, as you Yanks like to say."

"Indeed," Flint replied. "Both father and son are off the ship's network. They must have removed their cufflinks in dead areas. We've started searching for them, but I wanted to get the paperwork started for the arrest warrants."

"I'm not sure you have enough evidence for that yet," Judge Renee said.

"We have surveillance footage of the girl arriving at the Miller's residence in good health."

"You're certain of that?"

"She just left a nursing station," Flint said, with a clear note of exasperation in his voice. The man was ruggedly handsome, with strong features and thick salt and pepper hair. His gaze was steady, his words polite, but it was clear from the tone what he really thought of the judicial prerequisites of doing his job as a law enforcement officer. "We have a full scan. She was suffering from morning sickness, but otherwise she was in perfect health."

"Very well, continue," Judge St. Pierre said.

"We have video of her leaving the residence with Mr. Miller. She's obviously hurt. We have blood samples collected along their route to the cooling compartment. She was vomiting blood. There's no doubt that she was in great distress. And her body was found in a secured section of the ship. We have cufflink data access to that engineering compartment and the use of specialized tools that only a person working there would know to use to remove the panel from the machine where the body was hidden."

"How did you find the body?" the judge asked.

"Our K-9 team followed the scent trail," Flint said. "Otherwise, it's doubtful she would have been found until maintenance was done on that section of the cooling system."

"Alright, I'll issue a warrant for Henry Miller. But you haven't said anything about his son."

"He was in a relationship with the victim. We have direct messaging evidence and will have DNA when the medical teams finish their autopsy."

"And?" the judge asked.

"And she went to tell him about the pregnancy," Flint said. "Now, he's gone off grid. People with nothing to hide don't run."

"Running isn't evidence, Sergeant. You'll need a lot more than that to hold the boy."

"Okay, look, the mother all but said they found their son beating her," Flint said.

"If you can get her to say it on the record, with a clear understanding that what she is saying will be used in the prosecution of the crime, whether it incriminates her or her child, then you will have enough for a warrant. But it sounds like you are proceeding from a theory, not facts."

The LEO Sergeant grimaced. Judge Renee would never admit that she enjoyed disappointing people, but she did take great pride in being a voice for the rule of law. Perhaps she had always been that way. Even as a child, she felt boundaries and rules were important.

She never had any compunction when telling whoever was in authority that someone had broken those rules. It gave her a thrill to know that she held that power over the strong, handsome sergeant.

"We'll get more evidence," Flint said. "Thank you."

"It's my pleasure," Judge Renee said, meaning it.

The video call ended, and Renee got up from her desk. She went to the doorway that led to her assistant's cubicle.

"Begin drafting an arrest warrant for one Henry Miller, adjunct engineer, deck fifteen," she ordered the woman sitting at the desk playing a card game on her computer.

"Yes, your honor," the assistant said.

In most situations, judges didn't hold their co-workers to the etiquette of the courtroom, but her staff were all new, and she wanted it made certain in all their minds who was in charge. They could call her Your Honor for a few more months at least. There was, in Renee's mind, no harm in it.

She went back into her office. It was well-appointed. She had a coffee machine, as well as a floor-to-ceiling bookcase. She didn't use physical books any longer. The law was a system of precedents that was built up, one decision on another, to create a rigid structure that supported civilized society. But looking up past cases no longer required law libraries and hadn't for a long time. Computer databases and even AI law programs could find precedents and write entire briefs in seconds. But Renee liked the idea of hard copies. She had never opened any of the books in her library, but she admired the hardback, leather-bound tomes just the same.

There was a sitting area with two sofas and two high-back sitting chairs. There were overhead lights, but she rarely used them, preferring the lamps on the tables and on her wide, faux-wood desk. She also had a private bathroom, which included a locker with her judicial robes and a full-length mirror. There was no doubt in her mind that her office was larger and more lavishly appointed than most of the berths that her assistants lived in. But that didn't bother her at all. She felt that her accomplishments had earned such amenities.

Back at her desk, she opened the portal for the rotating list of legal advocates. The name at the top was Sven Hanson. She sent him a text message informing him that she was issuing an arrest warrant for Henry Miller, and that he would be the passenger's advocate. Another message went to Liev Gotteb IV, who would be the prosecutor for the case. Both lawyers were instructed to meet with Sergeant Sawyer Flint of the Special Investigation Unit to begin work on the case of Jenna Frankle's murder.

At the same time, on deck seven, Dave Bannon was waiting outside a classroom in the ship's higher education complex. The *Colossus* had a wide variety of scholars and professors from universities all over planet Earth. The ship didn't have the credentials to be a real university, nor had it seemed practical to the administrators to work through the steps necessary for accreditation. But with so many great minds on board, it only made sense to allow passengers to learn. The higher education complex offered a variety of courses, both academic and practical. Many of the passengers on board the ship were selected for their experience in agricultural sciences. While they couldn't work in their field while on board, they could apply themselves to learning new techniques, sharing ideas and planning. The initial colony on Secundo would require a great amount of farming and the raising of livestock to supply food and organic materials that could be used for a wide variety of needs. It was best for the individuals involved to know one another and to follow a plan of action that would ensure the colony wasn't in need after their long journey to their new home.

Dave wasn't a student and had no interest in agriculture. But he had on his cufflink the picture of a man, Daniel Frankle. He waited until the class let out, then approached Frankle.

Daniel was a big man, thick through the shoulders. He had grown up on a farm and had a Bachelor of Science degree in agriculture from Texas Tech University, where he had played football, met his wife, gotten married and then returned to the family farm. They had quickly started a family, having a daughter they named Jenna.

During the pregnancy, Daniel's wife, Lucile, was diagnosed with an aggressive form of breast cancer. After giving birth, she began a long series of treatments. The medical bills piled up until Daniel was forced to sell the family farm.

A year later, Lucile died, and Daniel was left to raise their four-year-old daughter on his own. He did his best, working hard and eventually getting selected to travel on the *Colossus* and become one of the first colonists on Secundo. He had no idea that Dave Bannon was about to rip his heart from his chest and destroy the little hope Daniel had left in his tragic life.

CHAPTER 24

BECKY HAD DONE the easy part. A simple set of commands set the surveillance system on the ship to search for their fugitives using facial recognition. It would alert her if they appeared. The ship's doorways and elevators operated using the passengers' cuff links. In theory, a person who removed their cufflink wouldn't be able to move beyond whatever deck they were on. But there were always tricks and workarounds. The elevators, for instance, were supposed to ping every passenger who boarded the car. Individual cufflinks were programmed with access for certain levels. For instance, anyone could go to Topdeck, but only the VIPs and their guests could go to deck two. A student from deck fifteen could go up to deck eleven, where their high school was located, but they weren't allowed into the elementary schools. And all the ship's vital areas were restricted for everyone except for ship's crew, and adjunct passengers with job assignments in certain areas. But if an elevator was crowded, a person standing in close proximity to others could fool the security system. Likewise, if a door was opened by an authorized person, the unauthorized individual might follow them in.

Becky knew that when people had crossed the line into criminal activity, they became desperate. And desperate people would and often did, anything. All their former morals and societal taboos were scrapped in a desperate attempt to outrun the consequences of their criminal actions. That meant that Johnny Miller, or his father, Henry, could force someone to open a restricted compartment or follow a group onto an elevator and flee onto another deck of the ship. She hoped the facial recognition would help them, but it could be fooled as well. The security system on the *Colossus* was supposedly state-of-the-art, yet in reality, it was just another set of parameters running through a program that collected data and spit out a reasonable conclusion. Facial recognition had failed before, as had gait recognition, fingerprints and DNA. No system was infallible, but then, she wasn't dealing with professional criminals. Most crimes were spur-of-the-moment reactions to something, such as being told that Johnny's girlfriend was pregnant. A fit of rage, a lover's quarrel, a person pushed around one time too many, that snapped and reacted with unreasonable violence.

Henry Miller didn't have a plan. He was simply trying to hide long enough to figure out his next move. Becky had no doubt that he would have tried to return to his cabin and go about his life if his secret hadn't been exposed. But Jenna's blood had been found. He had probably seen the patrol officers and changed his plan. He had removed his cufflink and gone dark, although that didn't mean he was invisible.

While Flint took care of the administrative tasks, and Dave went to find the victim's father, the rest of the squad were spreading out through deck fifteen in search of Henry and Johnny Miller. Becky didn't believe the father and son were together. They had gone in separate directions and blinked off the ship's information grid at far removed places. In fact, she would be surprised if they found Johnny Miller on deck fifteen. Word had come down from Sergeant Flint that they should focus on the father, which was good. Becky knew young people had ways of finding their way where they shouldn't be. Meanwhile, Henry Miller was more predictable.

On deck fifteen, there were two large maintenance compartments and four storage areas the size of airplane hangars. But all of those had steady traffic and security cameras. The one place that didn't was the sanitation cluster. Every floor had the same water treatment system. There were six in total, one for every three decks on the *Colossus*. The system was exceedingly efficient. Waste products were removed in stages, with the water flowing between larger filtration tanks. It was a stinky, dirty section of the ship, and completely contained to try and make the areas around it more habitable. The water treatment section on deck fifteen serviced decks thirteen, fourteen, and fifteen. It was manned by crew members and passengers on work details. Some manned the controls, others helped move the dried waste into containers that could be used on other parts of the ship. The composting facility would turn much of the waste, including food scraps from the dining halls, into usable fertilizer. There were chemists on board who collected a range of chemicals and utilized microorganisms to help break down the raw matter into usable elements.

To help facilitate the movement of the unsavory products between decks, there were freight elevators running up through maintenance sections on each deck. These were surrounded by pipes and large ventilation shafts. No one bothered to put up security cameras, although the elevators still required cufflink connections to operate. Becky didn't think that Henry could utilize the freight elevators, but there were plenty of places to hide in the water treatment complex. She had been in bad places with terrible odors before. Enclosed spaces with decomposing corpses were by far the worst. The smell of a dead body could and often did encamp in one's sinuses. It required harsh chemicals to remove from clothing. But Becky had also been to prisons with low sanitation, or flop houses where drug-addled residents frequently soiled themselves. There was a certain kind of stench in alleyways piled with trash in the summertime, and buildings where clogged pipes caused the sewage system to back-up and overflow. Criminals were rarely found in clean, sanitary places.

She searched through the water treatment complex for over an hour before she came to Waste Storage Room K. There were many such storage compartments. Some held plastic barrels full of dried waste matter. Others were empty and clean. Waste Storage Room K was filled with empty barrels. The overhead lighting was faint, but Becky had a small flashlight. She nearly missed Henry Miller as she did a quick scan. But her light played across a row of barrels that were stacked a little too close together. Had she not searched a dozen other rooms that were exactly the same, she wouldn't have noticed it. Most of the barrels were evenly spaced, but in Waste Storage Room K, half the barrels were pressed up against one another. That said, all it caused her to do was shift over slightly and take a second look. There were a thousand reasons why the barrels in that compartment were pushed together, but then she saw the edge of a rubber-soled work boot.

Without hesitating, she stepped out of the room as though she hadn't spotted anything. After walking away from the hatch a few paces, she stopped and used her cufflink to alert the rest of the squad that she had spotted a possible suspect. She could have done the same thing with her comlink, but she didn't want whoever was in the room to overhear her. Then, drawing her pistol, she returned to the room. Nothing had changed inside and, for a moment, she felt foolish. Maybe she was wrong.

"Henry Miller, I know you're in here. Please stand up and show me your hands."

There was no response but silence and she felt even more foolish than before.

"If you force me to come in after you, I'll use force," she said. "Come out, with your hands where I can see them."

At first, there was only silence and the feeling of failure. Then someone behind the barrels sighed and his hands came up.

"I'm coming out."

She waited, heart pounding in her chest, pistol pointed in his direction, but with her finger off the trigger. Henry Miller may have been guilty of murder, although he was not a killer. He was just a desperate man. She knew she could be wrong. For all she knew, Henry Miller was a serial killer who had tricked his way on board the *Colossus* and continued his evil spree of slayings. He might even have a weapon she didn't know about. The thought of it made her skin crawl. Becky was no coward, but she felt a bit unprepared with the lightweight pistol and non-lethal rounds. They were supposed to put a grown man down, but what if they didn't? She certainly had no experience with the weapon. It might be useless in a fight.

His hands rose above the barrels. They were small and he had a golden wedding band on his left hand. When he stood up, he looked odd. His face was puffy, his eyes red. It took her a moment to realize he had been crying.

"I'm sorry," he said, grunting a little as he stood up. "I'm sorry."

"You're under arrest for the murder of Jenna Frankle," Becky said. She felt a pang of sorrow for the man. He was clearly distraught. Yet she shoved that tiny bit of empathy away and reminded herself that Jenna had been sixteen years old and the man she was arresting had shoved her body into a narrow gap between freezing cold pipes of chemical coolants.

"I'm sorry," he said again.

"Save it for her father," Becky said. "Come out from the barrels. That's it, nice and slow. Keep your hands up, now turn around."

The most dangerous point of any arrest was detaining the suspect. There wasn't enough room to have him get down on the floor. He was facing away from her, with his hands in the air. To restrain him, she would have to holster her pistol and take hold of his arms. Like it or not, she was a woman. She was a strong, resourceful woman with training in a variety of combat styles, but all that couldn't overcome the fact that he was bigger and stronger than she was. Men had a higher bone density and more natural strength than women. If he fought her when she tried to restrain him, she would be vulnerable, especially in a confined space with no backup. That didn't stop her from doing her job.

She reached out with one hand and put it on his back. "Spread your legs!" she ordered in a firm voice. "Do you have anything in your pockets that might hurt me?"

He was wearing workman-style pants, work boots and a long-sleeved flannel shirt. The cuffs were rolled up to his elbows and his hair was messy as if he hadn't combed it that morning.

"No," he said.

She slipped her pistol into the holster and stepped closer to him. With one foot between his, she reached up and took hold of his left hand. He didn't resist. If he had, she would have driven her knee straight up into his crotch and pushed him away from her. But he had no fight left, and she felt a flood of relief as she slipped the plastic restraint over his left wrist and tightened it. After pulling his hand down and into the restraint, she patted him down. He had nothing in his pockets, no money, or drugs, or even a weapon. When she turned him around, there were tears on his face.

"I didn't..."

A sob caught in his throat. She tapped her cufflink and the recording that informed a detainee of their rights began to play from a tiny speaker. The administrators felt that a recorded message was better than trusting law enforcement officers to convey to a passenger their rights. Everything was familiar on the *Colossus*, but it was all slightly different, too. While the message on her cufflink continued, she tapped her comlink and reported.

"I have Henry Miller in custody," she said.

"Almost to your location," Logan Keys replied.

"Any signs of the son?" Flint asked from his deck nine office.

"Negative," Jeopardy said. "He's still in the wind."

"Alright, get the father up here. His attorney — I mean, his judicial advocate, is already waiting."

The recording on her cufflink ended. Becky looked at Henry Miller. He had a resigned look on his face. It was utter hopelessness.

Once more, she pushed the pang of empathy away and pressed the record button.

"Henry Miller, do you understand the rights that have just been explained to you?" she asked.

He nodded.

"I need you to say it out loud," she told him.

"I do... I understand my rights," he said in a tremulous voice.

She shut off the recording and took him by the arm. As she was leading him out of Waste Storage Room K, Logan arrived. Together, they escorted him to the nearest passenger elevators and up to deck nine.

CHAPTER 25

SERGEANT FLINT WAS NOT a big fan of lawyers, no matter what title they went by. In his opinion, nothing good ever came from having lawyers involved. Sven Hanson was no exception. He was tall, thin and clearly impatient. Flint watched him pace in the bullpen just outside his tiny office. It was impossible to tell if he was angry that his client had been caught or excited to have a real case. Either way, Flint didn't find the man any more likable.

He got to his feet and stepped to the door of his office. "My detectives have Henry Miller in custody," he said. "They'll be here soon."

"Good. I want to speak to him right away," Hanson said.

"I understand that, but we have an arrest warrant. I'm going to insist that he completes the booking process before you speak to him."

"Does that include questioning him?"

"No," Flint said. "Just the basics. We'll ensure he is who he says he is, and update his personnel file with the arrest. Once we're sure he doesn't have anything on him that he could use to hurt others or himself, we'll put him in a room and you can speak to him. I'll be glad to contact you when he's ready."

"No, no," Sven said. "I'll wait."

"Fine," Flint said. He closed the door and returned to his seat. He was no stranger to waiting himself. He had to wait to pursue the arrest of Johnny Miller, even though his instincts told him it was Johnny who had beaten Jenna Frankle. In fact, he had trouble not thinking about the facts he had learned concerning the case. It was troubling that Johnny Miller, popular and well cared for, had targeted Jenna Frankle, who was shy and had only one parent in her life. The poor girl was clearly struggling to find her place in the social scene of the *Colossus*. He knew that being a new student in school was tough. Perhaps with everyone being new, it should have been different, but it took less than two weeks for the cliques to form and the age-old cycles of bad behavior to take root.

Johnny Miller was a predator. Flint didn't use that term lightly, but he had studied enough cases to know what he was dealing with. Johnny had targeted a vulnerable member of his peer group and used his charisma to coerce her into a sexual relationship. At least, that was the picture that emerged from the private messages between them. Johnny's rage reaction to the news that Jenna was pregnant was not uncommon either. It was the way predators responded, almost as if they were just waiting for an excuse to unleash their vitriol in a physical way. If left to his own devices, there was just no telling how far down the dark path he was on he would have gotten.

The Special Investigation Unit's office space on deck nine was not the main processing center for law enforcement. But, they had all the necessary equipment to officially book a person into custody. Becky and Logan brought Henry Miller in. He was taken to a small room where he was ordered to take off his clothes. They were bagged and marked as evidence for testing. Then, when they were confident he had no weapons or possessions hidden on his person, he was dressed in a dark red jumpsuit. He also underwent a complete identity scan, which included finger and palm prints, facial recognition, retinal and vocal scans, as well as DNA testing. The ship already had what was considered vital identity information on every passenger and crew member. But getting all that information again, on the record, was a necessary step in the legality of the arrest.

It took only a few seconds for the computer to confirm that their prisoner was Henry Miller. They put him into the interrogation room opposite from where his wife was still waiting.

Becky was anxious to question him, but his lawyer insisted on time with his client first. Logan was sent back down to deck fifteen to help with the search while Becky and Flint waited for their chance to question Miller. In that time, Dave returned. He didn't look happy.

"Well," he said sadly, "that was about the worst thing ever."

"You took him to the med center to identify the body?"

"Yes, sir," Dave replied. "He had no idea about anything."

"Teenage girls don't often tell their fathers what they're up to," Becky said.

"Mr. Frankle takes classes six to seven hours a day, then serves on a janitorial crew," Dave explained. "He was accepted as a passenger due to his experience and willingness to work. He was putting in an eight-hour shift five days a week. He only got free time on the weekends. He was doing it all to give his daughter a better life and look at what's happened."

"He wasn't stoic then?" Becky asked.

"The big guy is a broken man," Dave said. "I can not imagine that kind of emotional pain."

"All we can do is ensure that the people responsible for his daughter's death are brought to justice."

They were all law enforcement professionals, so they knew that justice was a catchword that rarely meant what it portended. Justice didn't give a grieving father his daughter back and no amount of punishment for the guilty would ease his suffering. Society's concepts of justice were rarely in line with reality. All too often, the justice system was bound by the logistics of an overloaded penal system. How long a person served in prison was more in line with the amount of space that was available than with the heinous nature of their crimes. And prison was, in many cases, an alternate form of society.

Convicted felons in the penal system were given three meals a day, medical treatment, shelter, and a flawed but available sense of protection. Most had access to television, radio, libraries and the internet. Flint had arrested many criminals for whom prison life was a step up from their life on the outside. Not that any sane person would believe that life in a penitentiary was good. It was not good, but more of an ordered, structural hell. Bad food, bad living conditions and the constant threat of violence would break most people. But even as bad as it was, it did not meet the desire for justice.

An hour later, they were finally allowed to question their suspect. Becky took the lead while Dave stood at the door to the interrogation room. Flint watched from his office. The interview was recorded and Henry Miller's judicial advocate was present.

"Before we begin, please state your name for the record," Becky said.

"Henry Miller."

"I am Detective Becky Nash with the Special Investigation Unit. Also present is Detective David Bannon. With Mr. Miller is his advocate, Sven Hanson. Can you tell us what happened this morning, in your cabin on deck fifteen, Mr. Miller?"

"Go ahead," Sven said. "I've advised my client of his rights. He insists on making a full confession."

"The girl showed up, about seven thirty," Henry said in a quiet, remorseful tone.

"That is Jenna Frankle?" Becky asked.

"Yes, that's her," Miller said. "I didn't know her. Johnny hadn't introduced us before this morning."

He licked his lips nervously and looked down. "I was getting ready for work. I help the engineering team on Fifteen. It's not a big deal, really, just keeping tabs on the cooling system. But I..."

"You found out that Jenna Frankle was pregnant with your son's child," the lawyer prompted.

"That's right. It was a shock, as you might suppose," he said. "Johnny's just fifteen. We had... we had no idea he was... And she's talking about it like we should be excited for some reason. She was going to keep the baby and I... I flew into a rage... I really, I don't recall all the details."

He stopped, panting slightly, as if the story was difficult to speak about. Becky had no doubt the man was lying. For starters, he was remorseful, even as he talked about becoming enraged. Secondly, he wouldn't look at Becky. He stared instead at the table top and struggled to recall details as though he was trying to pull the details he had memorized from hidden files in the back of his mind. She had interviewed killers before, and their behavior was more pronounced, either aggressive or somehow excited by recalling their crimes.

"You flew into a rage and did what exactly?" Becky asked.

"Hit her," Miller said, his voice quivering. "I hit her again and again."

He was shaking his head as he said it, his eyes downcast. His lawyer reached over and put a comforting hand on the man's shoulder.

"I shouldn't have done it," he finally declared. It was the first thing he had said with any real conviction. "I know that. I'm sorry. I think I just went crazy for a minute."

"What happened after you hit her?" Becky said.

"I knew... I knew I had to... hide the body."

"She was dead?"

"She was vomiting blood. I sort of came back to my senses, see... and I... well, I knew I had done something wrong. So, I got her out of the apartment."

"She was still alive?"

"Yes," he said, breathing hard.

"Why not take her to a medical station?"

He licked his dry lips and spread his hands flat on the metal table. He had soft hands, almost delicate. There was no sign of bruising or scuffs on his knuckles.

"I didn't want to get into trouble," he said, once more shaking his head. "She wasn't going to make it. I knew that. She collapsed on the way to the work area. But I got her there and removed the panel on the big primary machine."

He described lifting and pushing her body into the cooling mechanism. Becky didn't interrupt, but she made a mental note that his recall of details was much more thorough at that point.

"I was on my way back when I saw the LEOs in the corridor," Henry Miller explained. "I knew I was in trouble and so I ran away. I removed my cufflink and tossed it into a compost bin, and then I hid."

Becky sighed. She knew at some point she would have to sift through the composting bins in search of Henry Miller's cufflink.

"What you're telling me is that you, and you alone, are responsible for Jenna Frankle's death?"

Henry nodded.

"I need you to say it out loud, Mr. Miller," Becky told him.

"I'm responsible," he said.

"You have my client's statement," Sven said. "I think he's been through enough for now."

"Not as much as Delmont Frankle," Dave said.

"Or the sixteen-year-old girl we pulled out of the engineering space who was frozen solid," Becky said.

But she stood up. "You'll have to wait here for now, Mr. Miller."

Dave opened the door and left the interrogation room. Becky followed, but Hanson stayed with Henry Miller. The two detectives walked through the bullpen to Sergeant Flint's office.

"He's lying," Becky said as she closed the door.

"Sure he is," Flint said. "Still trying to protect his kid."

"We aren't buying it, right?" she asked.

"We're going to find Johnny Miller and question him. The judge won't sign off on an arrest warrant until we've got more evidence on the son, but that shouldn't be a problem. We need more details to blow their story apart. Let's get to the nitty-gritty about the details of what happened in their cabin. We'll compare it with the wife's version. That should be enough to prompt our continued investigation into the boy."

"Any word on his whereabouts?" Dave asked.

"Not yet, but it's only a matter of time," Flint said. "There's no way off the ship. He can only run for so long."

The *Colossus* had a news service. It was run from one of the high-rise buildings on Topdeck with video footage and print stories running on the ship's information network. There were reporters who roamed the ship, looking for stories. And it didn't take them long to catch wind of the murder.

Becky and Dave had no sooner left his office than a woman with long, blonde hair, who looked more like a movie star than a field reporter, buzzed Flint's office. He glanced at the camera feed from outside. She was alone, but had a thick bag in one hand.

"Can I help you?" he said, utilizing the intercom.

"Sergeant Flint? You're head of the Special Investigation squad?"

"SIU," he said. "And you are?"

"Amber Fields," she replied. "Colossus News Network, I have some questions if you have a minute.

"We're pretty busy—"

"Investigating a murder?" Amber asked. She glanced at her cuff-link. "My sources tell me a teenage girl was found in the engineering bay. I'd like to get the facts, Sergeant."

"We can't share the details of an ongoing investigation."

"So, you're confirming that there was a murder."

"I'm not confirming or denying anything," Flint said. "I'm sorry to disappoint you, Ms. Fields. But I don't have time for an interview."

He felt pretty good about denying the reporter. He was a cop, not a politician. And in his experience, the press were prone to all kinds of exaggeration and speculation. There was no faster way to get into trouble than to talk to the press. Just as he was congratulating himself, his cufflink buzzed. He glanced at it. The message displayed was an order from the Commissioner's Office to report in immediately.

Flint sighed. There were downsides to being a boss, he decided. They were close to nailing down all the details of their case, but he couldn't put off the Commissioner. A few taps on his cuff link acknowledged his receipt of the order, and he stood up to put his jacket on. There was no time to go down to his berth and put on a clean shirt and tie. He was still in casual clothes since being called to the crime scene just an hour after he had gone to bed. He smoothed his hair back and left a quick message for Becky to continue the interrogations. Then he left his office.

His first surprise was finding the reporter, Amber Fields, waiting for him outside the SIU office.

"Sergeant Flint?" she asked.

He recognized her and was tempted to deny his own identity, but in his experience, lying never paid positive dividends. He had plenty of evidence after two failed marriages and their subsequent divorces.

"That's me," he said. "But I was clear, Ms. Fields. I can't give you an interview about an open case."

"Is that policy on the *Colossus* or just a holdover from your days with the police force back on Earth?"

"My personal policy," he said. "I'm sorry I can't help you."

He started for the elevators, and she hurried to stay beside him. "Okay, no interview. But you could share a few facts about the case. Or just confirm that what I have is accurate so that we don't run a story that isn't accurate."

"Nothing I say can be used on the record," he said as the elevator doors opened.

He got inside, and she followed.

"Off the record then," she pushed. "This is news... real news, Sergeant. Please, let me make my report. All I want is to get it straight."

"I'm on my way to Commissioner Forrest's office," Flint said. "After I speak to him, I'm sure he'll make time for you."

"You'll ask him to give me an interview?"

"Absolutely," Flint said.

The ride up to Topdeck only took a few moments. They caught a trolley that took them to the big city services building. Flint went straight up to the Law Enforcement offices. Commissioner Forrest had given the order to send Flint straight through. Amber Fields, however, was forced to wait in the outer reception room.

"Who was that with you?" Forrest asked as Flint stepped into the large office suite occupied by the Commissioner of Law Enforcement Services on the *Colossus*. Monty Forrest was on his feet, waiting in front of his desk. He extended a meaty hand and Flint shook it.

"A reporter," Flint said. "Amber Fields."

"Good grief," Forrest said. "They've got better intel gathering than we do."

"Maybe," Flint said.

"She knows about the murder?"

"She knows something, but doesn't have any facts."

"What did you tell her?"

"Nothing," Flint said. "Except that I would ask you to speak with her."

The commissioner grunted and looked down as he circled around his wide desk, but Flint caught the hint of a smile on the older man's face. "We'll see about that. What's the latest?"

"We have the father in custody," Flint said. "He made a full confession."

"Then it's done?"

"No, sir, his story doesn't hold air."

"What?"

"He's covering for his son."

"What does the son say?"

"We haven't located him. That's our priority at the moment."

"We have a suspect and a confession? Seems like that's the best case scenario."

"The father is trying to protect his son."

"You know that for a fact?" the Commissioner asked. "You have proof that the son committed the crime?"

"We have reason to believe he did," Flint said. "Look, sir, we've been doing this job a long time. Let us work the case."

"This isn't East Coast Metro, Sergeant," Monty Forrest said as he leaned back in his big executive chair and intertwined his fingers together over his stomach. "We have half a million people on this ship living in very close quarters. We have to do what's best for the well-being of the *Colossus*. And what people want to know is that the case is solved, not that the murderer is still running around free."

"Even if that means letting the real culprit get away?"

"No," he shook his head, "that's not what I'm saying. But it does make me a bit nervous that you're acting chummy with the pretty news girl and burying the lead on this case. Tell me you aren't pushing to keep it open because your people have nothing else to do."

"Sir, we would never do that," Flint said. "The evidence we have is circumstantial at the moment, but everything points to the son."

"Then find him. I'll buy you a few more hours, but you find the boy and get a full confession; otherwise, we accept the father's story and put the situation to bed."

Flint knew it would never be that easy. Even if they just accepted Henry Miller's confession, Johnny Miller and his mother wouldn't just go on with their lives. You couldn't just put a Band-Aid on a bullet wound. If the boy was prone to violence, especially in the face of extreme stress, how long would it be before he snapped again?

"A few more hours? Are we talking eight, twelve, twenty-four hours?"

"Three," Forrest said. "I'll put the pretty newsgirl off that long, but if you don't have more for me by then, I'll go on the record that we have made an arrest that includes a full confession."

Flint took a deep breath. Three hours wasn't long enough. They needed time to find Johnny Miller, and more time to finesse his confession. All he could do was light a fire under his people and pitch in to help them get their man.

CHAPTER 26

JD DIDN'T GET NERVOUS. Fear was something he had conquered on the streets. He had looked death in the eye on more than a few occasions and decided that he would rather be dead than a coward. He had seen his share of death, too, and was a firm believer that there was no afterlife. He had seen the light go out of a person's eyes. In his view, when a person died, they simply ceased to be, and that meant it was up to him to get everything he could, while he could, and enjoy it before he died.

His grandmother had been a religious woman, but her belief in God hadn't made her life, or his, any better. And JD had read some philosophy books that talked about morality being a construct intended to help build a civilized society. But to him, there was no moral code. In his experience, there was strength, daring, power and the striving of the masses. If a person didn't fight their way to the top of the heap and prove themselves of being capable to stay on top, they would just get swallowed up by the world. JD was determined not to let that happen to him.

Nor did he fear prison. The penitentiary was just a different playground. In his mind, it didn't matter if you were playing football or basketball; the goal was to win. And JD was a winner. He had won in his building and won on the streets. He had won in his neighborhood and he had won in contests over new ones. Yet he recognized that on Earth, the game was rigged. The rich and powerful had tilted the game in their favor and made it impossible for a man like JD to ever reach the halls of power. Not because of his skin color, or neighborhood, or education, but because of his bank account. Money was the path to power. If you had it, nothing would ever be denied to you. If you didn't have it, there was nothing you could do.

JD had money of a sort. Cash money had been transitioned out of society long before JD was born. Digital currency was better, at least for the powerful. It gave them complete control over a person. You might work to earn it, but you never owned it. Even while it was in your bank account, the bigwig money people had all kinds of strings attached to it. They knew everything you spent your money on. They had access to your funds with the click of a few computer keys. They could freeze that money or force you to only spend it on certain things. Digital money had become the cattle prod of humanity.

But there were two worlds. There was the surface world, where things were what they seemed and people followed the rules. Then there was the underworld, where people made their own rules. On the surface, everyone was a slave. They were chained with bills, debts and needs that forced them into certain behaviors. A man couldn't decide what he wanted to do with his life, not when he had bills to pay and people to take care of. Someone else told him what he would do with his life. Someone else determined when he would show up, when he could go home and how much his time was worth. Someone else said what he could do with the tiny bit of surplus he might have if he was lucky at the end of a month, on the surface world. Only a tiny fraction of one percent of all the people on Earth ever had enough money to break free and live as they saw fit.

But down under, on the shady side of the world, things were different. People weren't slaves, but they weren't free either. On the street, a man could decide what his fate would be, as long as he was

strong enough to forge it from the violence and temptations that were
so prevalent on the dark side of the world. If there was something you
wanted, you took it. Although if you weren't strong, someone else
would take it from you. Money was of little concern. A thing, or a
person, could be bought any number of ways, from bartering to pros-
titution. It was not civilized, and it certainly wasn't moral, but it was
real. On the streets, JD could see where the danger was coming from.
On the dark side of life, there was nothing that would be denied him.

JD longed for more. He longed to switch from the dark side of
things to the upper part of the world, where the really powerful
played their games of domination and control. He wanted to be at the
very top of the mountain, not just at the top of the neighborhood. So,
he had given up his life as a Ghetto King and taken passage on the
Colossus. But there wasn't anything or anyone on the colony ship that
JD feared. Especially not the man he had gone to meet.

They weren't on Topdeck, but rather in a service hallway on deck
fourteen. One level below him, the search for Johnny Miller continued, but on fourteen, a deal was being done. Vinnie Traymont was a
member of the ship's crew. He wore the light blue coveralls that
designated him as part of the engineering division, even though he
was not an engineer. He wasn't even a technician, but a laborer. His
title was Logistics Delivery Mate although, in truth, he was a gopher.
The *Colossus* was packed with useful items. Foodstuffs, utensils,
cleaning supplies, building supplies and parts for the ten million
things that needed attention on the huge ship. His job was to find
those things in the vast warehouses and deliver them to the people
who needed them. He was a gopher, but it was an important job. He
had spent days memorizing where things were stored. The huge
warehouse compartments were packed with huge shelves that were
loaded with all sorts of things. His job gave him access to all those
things, and many that were not needed on the ship, yet had been
brought along for the colonization effort on Secundo.

"These were the smallest I could find," Vinnie Traymont said,
opening a toolbox and removing the tray above the deeper section.

The top was loaded with screwdrivers and neatly organized socket heads. The larger lower section had a few tools too, but tucked between them were four small, semi-automatic pistols. "It's mostly rifles and shotguns in the colony supplies."

"Might could use a shotgun," JD said.

"No, these are the big, pump-action type," Vinnie said. "Long barrel, composite stock. It's not what you want."

"This punk thinks he knows what I want," JD said.

Slash leaned in close to the crew member. The big thug's arms flexed hard, the bare skin showing powerful muscles and frightening tattoos.

"No, no, I didn't mean it like that," Vinnie said.

JD pulled one of the guns from the toolbox. It was small. He preferred a larger weapon, but he understood the value of a small piece that could be more easily hidden. There was no way to smuggle weapons on the *Colossus*. Each passenger, their luggage and their carry-on bags were all searched multiple times. The ship officials used all sorts of scanners and machines looking for contraband. Word was, they even had a dog sniffing everyone's luggage. But since they were on board and the ship was underway, it was time for JD's crew to start packing heat. They might need it and there were a variety of ways to use a gun to get what a person wanted that didn't involve firing a single shot.

"You got ammo?"

"Two boxes," Vinnie said. "That's a hundred rounds. Each clip holds eight."

"Pay the man, Slash," JD ordered. "He came through."

"This way," Slash said.

They were in Slash's berth. It was small and of the same design as the Miller's cabin one floor below. Slash led Vinnie to the smaller room. A woman was waiting inside.

"Hello, honey," JD heard a feminine voice say just before the door shut.

Since drugs and gambling had been legalized, currency on the streets had been curtailed. Crank had hacked into the ship's financial system easily enough. JD could have ordered the computer genius to deposit whatever amount of money was necessary to purchase the guns into the crewman's account. That left a trail. Not one that led to JD, but still, it led to Vinnie, and it was better for everyone if there was no trail. Besides, every man had needs. JD had never struggled to find a willing partner when it came to his romantic proclivities, yet he knew some did struggle. That presented an opportunity that JD and his crew leveraged to the maximum.

JD handed one of the guns to Slash, who popped the magazine and checked the firing chamber.

"Seems okay," he said, running the top slide back and forth a few times. "Small though."

"Better to keep it hidden. We're respectable now. Gotta keep people thinking we're just like them."

"Till we ain't," Slash said.

"That time will come," JD assured him. "For now, you keep it out of sight."

They opened a box of bullets. They were small, golden rounds with hollow tips. They immediately began pressing them into the clip that came from the handle of the weapons.

"How's business?" JD asked.

"Slow," Slash said. "People up top just want to look. They ain't spending no money yet."

"They will," JD said. "They always do. Remember, we want names, job titles. Favors are worth more than anything. You getting the proof we need?"

"I got all my girls hooked up with the spy cameras Crank fixed up. Ain't no body getting a taste without us having proof of it."

"Including our pal Vinnie?"

"Especially, Vinnie. We own his skinny behind."

"That's what I'm talking about," JD said.

"What about them banking people?"

"Still working on that," JD said. "Getting close to 'em ain't as easy as I thought. I mean, we can get close, just can't get 'em alone. But it's only a matter of time ... and we got plenty of it."

The door to the little bedroom opened, and Vinnie came out. JD and Slash both turned and looked at him. He grinned.

"Same time tomorrow?"

"This earns you a pop every day for a week," Slash said.

"Yes!" Vinnie said with a sad little pump of his fist.

He gathered up his tool kit and left the berth. JD tucked his new pistol into the back of his pants and covered it with the tail of his shirt. Two more went into an attaché case, along with the rest of the bullets.

"That seemed fast," JD said.

"Was," Slash replied.

"See you in a few days," JD told his lieutenant. "Keep up the good work."

Slash nodded, tucked his own pistol into his pants and walked his boss to the door.

CHAPTER 27

JEOPARDY FELT FOR STU. The dog had a very difficult job. Following a scent through the crowded corridors with so many overlapping smells had to be difficult. But he surged forward and Jeopardy followed. She had the dog on a quick-release strap. It was little more than a narrow strap made of braided nylon. There was no loop at the end and she didn't wrap it around her hand. She held it loosely on the off chance that she would need to release the dog to stop a violent offender.

They got plenty of strange looks and more than a few passengers stuck their noses up or made a face as the dog passed. He was clean, but he was still an animal. Some stopped and pointed, a few even moved toward her. They were dog lovers and the absence of pets was difficult for some of the passengers. But Stu was not a pet. He was a member of the SIU team with a big responsibility on his sturdy shoulders. They had already proven the K-9's usefulness that day. Jeopardy had no doubts that their poor victim would have been hidden for months, maybe years, before the body was found. Certainly, long enough for the trail to go cold and the perpetrators to have a good chance of getting away with their crimes.

Ahead, Jeopardy spotted Logan. He was tall, lean, broad-shoul-dered with a shock of black hair and dark stubble on his prominent jaw line. Logan wasn't a pretty boy like most models and movie stars tended to be. He wasn't the sort of man who shaved his chest or had his nails done. He was rough, rugged, a hard-charging police officer who worked relentlessly. There was a very tangible air of danger about him. She knew letting herself give in to the infatuation that was developing for him was not a good idea. She probably understood him better than most, but that wouldn't insulate her from the pain when he chose the job over her. Or when his tendency to run toward danger cost him his life and left a hole in her heart.

"Any luck?" he asked as she and Stu drew near.

"Not yet, but Stu's onto something," she said.

She didn't stop or even slow the dog down. They surged past Logan and he followed behind.

"The father confessed," Jeopardy said.

"What?" Logan asked.

There were people around, and talking about a case in public was against regulations, but they were moving quickly past everyone else. It was late in the day. Shifts were ending and many passengers were wrapping up their day, planning their evening activities, moving slowly through the corridors.

"Said it was all him, that he killed the girl in a fit of rage."

"Do you believe him?" Logan asked.

"You tell me," she said. "Would a guy who hit a girl in the stom-ach, probably over and over again, have marks on his hands?"

Logan thought about it for a minute. "Depends, I guess. Someone who knows how to fight knows where to hit a person, maybe not. But only if every blow landed between the ribs and hips. One missed hit and there would be bruising. Depending on the person, if they weren't used to punching, there would be abrasions on the knuckles, too."

"That's what I thought," Jeopardy said. "The father's hands were clean."

Ahead of them, Stu stopped. He stood at an open doorway, growling low. It was barely audible, but Jeopardy heard it.

"What's in there?" Logan asked.

"Food prep area," Jeopardy replied. She had to raise her voice to be heard over the clash of pots and pans being moved around inside the room.

"You think he's just smelling food?"

Jeopardy shook her head. "He's a pro. He won't give up the hunt just to fill his belly."

"Then he's a better cop than most," Logan said.

Jeopardy shortened her leash. She couldn't let Stu get too far ahead of her. "Stu, *such!*"

It was the German word for *track*. Stu moved into the busy room.

"Hey! Come on!" a man with a beard net over the front of his face and a floppy chef's hat, shouted. "You can't bring that thing in here. We're preparing food in this space."

"Law enforcement," Logan said, holding up his badge. "Everyone, stay where you are."

Stu moved deeper into the room. There were ovens against one wall and along another were wash stations. The middle of the room held a series of stainless steel tables. There were over a dozen people working. They all wore white jumpsuits and aprons. Several doors led out of the food prep room. Stu worked his way around the outside of the table rows and toward a door. It was closed.

"What's in there?" Jeopardy asked.

"Storage is all," the man with the beard net said.

Jeopardy reached out and turned the handle. The heavy door swung open. Inside was a tall rack of canned goods. Stu surged in, growling. Jeopardy followed. They circled around the shelves of food and found Johnny Miller sitting in the corner. There were snack food wrappers on the floor, and empty bottles of soda. He was holding a tablet that was playing an action movie.

"What?" he asked as Jeopardy held Stu back.

"That's our guy," Logan said.

He moved around Jeopardy. Stu was still making his menacing growl, but she ordered him to heel and the dog didn't move from her side. She knew other cops who might feel like Logan was shoving her aside to make the big arrest. Even so, she didn't mind. She could have given the order for Stu to stay put and he would have. But she felt herself go hot all over when she saw Johnny Miller, surrounded by excess, watching a movie as if nothing had happened. She could remember seeing the frozen girl stuffed in between a row of pipes in the cooling unit. It made her furious to think that the boy responsible was seemingly nonplussed by his crime or by the cops who were clearly there to arrest him.

"On your feet!" Logan said, knocking the tablet aside and grabbing hold of Johnny's arm.

He pulled the teenager up in one fast tug, then pressed him against the wall.

"Hey! What the hell, man!" Johnny Miller shouted.

"Wait, wait," the man with the beard net said. "He's not hurting anything. I let him and some of his friends hang out in here sometimes. It's no big deal."

"Johnny Miller?" Logan asked.

"Yeah, that's right. And you're going to pay for that tablet, man."

"Sure, catch me when you get out of prison for murder," Logan told him.

"Murder?" the chef asked.

"Sir, please return to your station," Jeopardy said.

"I... I didn't know anything about a..."

"We know," Jeopardy said. "Just back up. Let us do our job."

"He... he killed somebody?"

"No, that's crazy!" Johnny shouted. "I didn't kill anyone."

Logan forced the teenager's hands behind his back and into the loops of the physical restraints. "Johnny Miller, you are being detained by law enforcement officials, in connection to the murder of Jenna Frankle."

"You're out of your mind," Johnny shouted angrily. "I didn't do anything. I didn't even know her."

Jeopardy wanted to point out all the physical evidence they had, but she remained quiet. There would be a moment to reveal what they already knew. But during the arrest wasn't the right time. A good interrogation would stack the evidence in front of him and result in a confession. That was every cop's goal. If she gave in to the temptation to refute his claims in the moment of his arrest, it would give him time to fabricate lies and excuses for why he couldn't have committed the crime. It was better to let the mountain of guilt fall on him, even if it was circumstantial, all at once.

"Let's go," Logan said.

"I want a lawyer," he shouted. "I'm not saying anything without my lawyer."

"You'll get one," Logan said as he moved past Jeopardy and Stu.

"Yeah, I know my rights, man. I know you can't question me without my lawyer. I don't have to talk to you."

Logan didn't reply. They weren't questioning Johnny, not yet. He would be played a recording of his rights. And as a minor, he would have a Judicial Advocate with him during questioning. He struggled at first, but Logan's iron grip on his arm settled the teenager down pretty quickly.

"Great job, detective," Logan said to Jeopardy. "Want to take him in? It's your collar."

She smiled. She had guessed that Logan wasn't the type to push her out of the way to make himself look good. It was a relief to see that she was right about him.

"No, we'll follow you," she said. "Besides, Stu did all the work."

"Yeah, that's right," Logan said. "We owe him a steak and a night on the town."

"He prefers the park," she said.

"The park it is," Logan said. "Alright, Johnny, let's go."

There had been looks as Stu led Jeopardy through the wide corridors of deck fifteen. But there were even more as Logan led Johnny Miller out and to the nearest elevator bank. Jeopardy called in their find.

"That's great," Flint told her. "Outstanding job, Detective Bass. I'll have a JA here and we'll question him right away."

She wondered if Sergeant Flint was always so eager when a suspect was detained. She had worked with all sorts of cops. From her days walking a beat to her time in the K-9 unit, she knew some police were hard-charging, especially when the goal was within sight. Others were cool, calculating, calm and, she might even say, reserved. Jeopardy Bess knew she was somewhere in the middle. Working K-9 drug cases was satisfying. Others did the legwork, and after her partner found the illicit contraband, they did all the follow-up. She and her K-9 partner didn't have to deal with the more frustrating aspects of an investigation. But she was in a specialized unit on the *Colossus* and it seemed that Sergeant Flint wanted her to be part of everything they did.

They took Johnny Miller to their offices on deck nine. He wasn't under arrest, not yet. They would need to question him and gather more evidence. They didn't book him or force him to change clothes. He was searched, but only had a wallet, a phone, and the tablet computer on him. His temperament was changing as he was put into the holding cell, which took place immediately after they had photographed his hands and run a medical scanner over them. His knuckles were red, the skin scuffed in places. His left hand was slightly swollen, with a dark bruise across the back of his hand.

"What do we know?" Becky asked once Johnny Miller was in the holding cell.

"Stu found him," Jeopardy said. "He was in a food storage room that was part of one of the prep areas."

"The chef was letting Miller and some of his friends in there to fool around," Logan said. "There were snack bags and empty soda bottles all over."

"He claims he didn't even know Jenna Frankle?" Jeopardy added.

"What did you tell him?" Becky asked.

"Nothing," Jeopardy said.

"Just that he was being detained for Jenna's murder," Logan said. "Was that too much?"

"Nah, let him sweat it," Becky said. "His Judicial Advocate is on the way down. I've already sent his mother home, but we have a good record of her testimony. The father is continuing to stick with his story, but there are some pretty big holes. I don't think they knew anything about Jenna until this morning."

A short time later, a judicial advocate named Penelope Parker arrived, and after they were given a few minutes together in the interrogation room, Becky and Jeopardy followed them in to begin questioning.

"I want it on the record that my client isn't under arrest," Parker said the moment the two detectives walked in.

"He isn't... yet," Becky said.

"And he has the right to remain silent," the lawyer pressed.

"You played him the recording of his rights, and he accepted them," Jeopardy pointed out. That much had been relayed to them by the ship's computer system, which was surprisingly fast and efficient.

"Alright, go ahead," the lawyer said.

Johnny had a defiant look about him. He was sitting pushed back as far as his metal folding chair would go from the table. His arms were crossed and his legs extended out in front of him. Despite everything, Jeopardy had to admit he was a handsome kid. His thick hair was styled to look as though he didn't care about it. He wore nice clothes that fit him well. He was thin, yet had the build of a young athlete. But the frown and angry expression across his face was almost too much. She felt certain they were a mask to hide the fear of a child.

Becky sat down and, once more, Jeopardy stayed by the door. She and Becky had been friends for a long time. There was no feeling of competition between the two female officers. Each had skills and Jeopardy recognized that Becky was a natural at many vital aspects of criminal investigation. She took her place in the room, but let Becky take the lead.

"Johnny Miller, my name is Becky Nash, I'm a detective in the Colossus Law Enforcement division. This interview is being recorded."

"Whatever," he mumbled.

His JA frowned, but didn't speak.

"Let me tell you why you are here," Becky said, setting a tablet on the table and propping it up where Johnny could see it. "This is security footage of Jenna Frankle. You said you didn't know her, but that's not true, is it? Here she is coming to your cabin. You let her inside."

Becky paused. They didn't expect the boy to respond, but they wanted him to realize he couldn't lie his way out of the trouble he was in.

"You knew her quite well," Becky continued. "We have overwhelming proof that you were engaged in a sexual relationship with her."

"That's not true," he snapped. "We weren't even friends. Ask anybody."

"You're saying you weren't sleeping with her?"

"No, of course not," he said. "Did she say that? It's not true. Maybe she had a crush on me or something, but I didn't sleep with her."

He made the last statement as if it were preposterous.

"Then why did you send these messages to her?" Becky said. She turned the tablet around and brought up the screenshots of their private communications. "'Let's meet at your place after school,' you said. 'Don't you have wrestling practice?' she asked. 'I'll skip it. I need you, baby. You're all I think about.' That's what you wrote to her. I can go on. It gets pretty graphic."

"You can't," he started to snap at Becky, but then turned to his

Judicial Advocate. "Why are you letting them invade my privacy. Those are private messages!"

"She can't help you," Becky said. "Your parents agreed to the terms of service on the *Colossus* information network, which keeps a record of every message you send or receive. As law enforcement officials, we have access to those records. That's the law on the ship, Johnny. We know about the love affair you two were having."

"It's not what you think," he said. "We were hanging out, sure, but that's all. We weren't doing anything."

"That's not what your messages say."

"Hey, I was trying, okay. I didn't ever think she would actually sleep with me, come on. That's all just kid stuff. I was joking around with her."

"It doesn't sound that way," Becky said.

"I swear it. I didn't sleep with her."

"She seems to think you did, and that you want to again. There are a lot of messages about it."

"It's just the hormones talking," Johnny replied. "I'm telling you the truth. I did not sleep with her."

"Odd," Becky said. "Because, according to the medical report, you got her pregnant."

That shut him up. His jaw clamped down hard and his face turned red. Becky leaned forward.

"We have the results of her medical scan that morning," Becky said. "She went to the nurse's station and complained that she was getting the flu, but the medical unit scanned her blood and discovered it was the pregnancy, not the flu."

"That's bullshit," he said, but his voice was low and tremulous.

"She left there, Johnny, and went straight to you. We have the messages, remember? We know she came to see you. The surveillance footage from outside your cabin proves it. You let her in, she told you about the baby and you lost it. You started hitting her."

"No," he said.

"Look at your hands, genius. We know what you did!" Becky said in a loud voice. "You hit her. You beat on a girl, Johnny. You hit her so hard she started bleeding on the inside."

"I think this has gone far enough," Parker said.

Johnny leaned forward, put his elbows on his knees and covered his face with both hands.

"You couldn't handle that your secret affair was about to get out, could you? It was all fun and games when no one knew. But the truth is, Johnny, everyone knew. Your friends told us about it. They saw through your flimsy charade."

"You're berating my client," Parker said. "I want the interview to stop."

Becky held up a hand to the woman. "I will stop. Just tell me the truth, Johnny. Why did you do it?"

"She lied!" he shouted, jumping from his chair and lunging at Becky, who slid her chair back from the table that was the only barrier between them.

Becky was calm and seemed unruffled. Parker screamed and Jeopardy rushed forward to help.

"She said she was protected! Then she shows up acting like she's excited to have my baby!"

Jeopardy grabbed Johnny Miller's wrist and twisted it behind his back. He bent forward over the table and she dropped her weight onto his back, but he was still reaching for Becky with his other hand.

"And what did you do, Johnny? Did you show her who's boss?" Becky asked.

"You're damn right I did. I beat her until she passed out and I'll beat you, too!"

"This is over!" Parker said. "I want out. Right now, let me out of here."

The door opened and the judicial advocate bolted. Logan came in and helped Jeopardy restrain Johnny. But the damage was done. He had confessed. It was legal and admissible. More evidence would be collected. Becky had been bluffing about the DNA results of the baby. For all she knew, the tiny fetus was too small to collect DNA from, but of course, Johnny didn't know that. He just knew he had done something wrong and he couldn't handle being called on the carpet.

"How'd you know?" Jeopardy asked her later. "How'd you know he would confess?"

"He flew into rage with Jenna. I figured he would do the same with me," Becky said. "Thanks for keeping him from reaching me."

"You played it pretty recklessly," Jeopardy said.

"I've faced some pretty scary individuals," Becky said. "Johnny Miller doesn't even rank in my top ten."

"Great job, team," Flint told the group as they gathered in the bullpen. "Judge St. Pierre just issued an official arrest warrant. We'll get him booked and moved downstairs with his father."

"What happens now?" Jeopardy asked.

"The Commissioner is taking a victory lap," Flint said. "We'll have some clean-up work to do, I'm sure. The prosecutor will send us a list of things he wants, but my guess is he'll offer the kid a plea deal."

"He doesn't deserve it," Dave replied. "Jenna Frankle didn't get a deal."

"That's true," Flint said. "Johnny will be in custody for the rest of the flight, that much is for sure."

"And what then? Are they going to let him loose on Secundo?" Becky asked.

"That isn't up to me. We did our part; others will see it to the goal line," Flint said. "Make your reports and take a little downtime. If you haven't eaten, get a meal inside you. There will be more work to do, but the danger is over. We got the people responsible. That's something worth celebrating. Just make sure you don't talk about it. We can't give these people any reason not to be held responsible for the damage they've done."

Flint returned to his office, and Jeopardy felt a sag of fatigue. She didn't even notice Logan, who had come up beside her, until he spoke.

"I'd say it's time to get Stu some park time," Logan said. "If you're up for it?"

"Sure," she said, smiling despite the resolve she had made. "He'll love that."

"Great," Logan said. "Dinner is on me."

CHAPTER 28

THE NEWS STORY hit and the entire ship was rocked by the news. A killer on the ship was enough to make everyone stop and think. They had grown apathetic to the stories of crime back on Earth. But it was much easier to downplay a horrific event if you didn't feel any connection to the people involved. There were over three hundred and fifty thousand passengers on the *Colossus*. The percentage of people who actually knew the Millers or the Frankles was minuscule, but the entire ship felt the effects of the murder. They were all fellow shipmates and, perhaps more importantly, none of them could escape. At times, the ship felt like an enormous city and, at other times, it felt confining and overcrowded.

The members of the SIU ignored it all. They gathered evidence from the sheets off Johnny and Jenna's beds, to affidavits from their classmates at their high school. They worked the case for three days until a deal was struck, mainly between the lawyers. Both Henry and Johnny Miller pled guilty to manslaughter, for which they would serve the maximum amount of time. Henry would be held in the ship's main detention center for the duration of the voyage. He would not be allowed to join the colonists, but would stay on the *Colossus* to work his way back to Earth, where he would serve another six years for his part in the crime.

Johnny Miller was still a minor, and so, he would spend the rest of the voyage in a special detention facility, but would be allowed to continue his schoolwork and have visitors twice a week. Upon reaching Secundo, he would be seventeen years old and have the option of working until his twenty-first birthday on a colony labor farm, or remaining in confinement on the Colossus for the return trip. He would be released upon turning twenty-one, no matter what option he selected.

Kathryn Miller was also charged with conspiracy, aiding in a criminal act and lying to law enforcement personnel. Her punishment was a form of house arrest. She was assigned to a work crew, but confined to deck fifteen for the duration of her flight. She was also charged for her passage, room, and board, which meant that she worked for next to nothing and would not be allowed to join the other passengers on Secundo.

It was, to Becky Nash's way of thinking, getting off easy for all three. They hadn't plotted to murder Jenna Frankle, but that's what they did in the end. Johnny beat her senseless in a fit of rage that left her with shattered ribs and ruptured internal organs. Still, if the Millers had taken her immediately for medical help, there was a slight chance she could have been saved. That meant they were guilty of killing her by their inaction. Henry Miller claimed that he intended to drop her off somewhere far from his cabin and that he didn't realize how bad off she was. Becky didn't believe that, yet it wasn't up to her.

The team settled back into more basic roles once the plea was reached. No more evidence was needed. Nothing significant happened for the next month. But it was not all that surprising when Kathryn Miller missed three shifts in a row and the Special Investigations unit was called in. Becky opened the door to cabin four-sixteen using her cufflink and law enforcement credentials. It was labeled a wellness check in the ship's computer system but she had known even before they arrived what they would find.

"Everything is clean," Dave said as the Miller's door slid open.

"There's the note," Becky said, pointing. There was, on an improvised stand set on the kitchen table, a handwritten note.

Dave went to the note while Becky checked the bedroom. Kathryn Miller lay in her bed, on the right-hand side, the covers smooth over her frail body. She appeared to be sleeping, but the odors wafting out of the enclosed space said otherwise.

"I've got a body," Becky said.

"You were right," Dave said, holding up the note. "Suicide."

A medical team was called in, and once more the Miller cabin was taped off. Becky made a visit to the main detention area. It was on deck seventeen and consisted of a row of double occupancy rooms with transparent doors and no walls between the recessed bunks and the toilet facilities. Likewise, the shower was made of see-through materials. There was no privacy at any time among the prisoners, of which Henry Miller was the first. His meals were brought to him and he was allowed a reader with preloaded books, but nothing else.

Visitation was once a month and consisted of prisoners on one side of a transparent booth, and visitors on the other side. Becky, being law enforcement, was allowed to see the prisoner. She was the one to break the news to Henry Miller about his wife.

"What now?" he asked, suspiciously as he sat down in the booth.

Becky smiled. "Just a courtesy visit with a bit of news."

Miller didn't speak, but he leaned forward and put a hand against the transparent material. There were tiny holes drilled through it to allow their voices to be heard. Becky showed no emotion. She wasn't cruel, but she knew that Henry Miller would feel a modicum of the pain he had caused others.

"Your wife committed suicide," she said.

"No," Henry said, squeezing his eyes shut tight.

"She blamed herself for Jenna's death. Her note didn't have kind things to say about you, but you'll have to wait until you're out of prison to read it."

Henry took a long, shuddering breath. "Please," he said. "Kathryn did nothing."

"That fact is well proven," Becky said. "It didn't make her innocent. Per her wishes, her remains are to be jettisoned from the ship. I thought you should know."

"You're a cruel woman," Henry growled.

"And you're a convicted murderer, who got off easy after killing an innocent child," Becky said. "Have a nice life, Mr. Miller."

She walked away without an ounce of regret.

Up on deck nine, Logan and Jeopardy were called out on a domestic case that evening. Bruno Wright, on deck four, had gotten drunk and put hands on his wife. They met her in the medical facility. She was dozing on one of the patient beds, her left arm in a heavy cast up to her shoulder, but the real damage was to her face. Patrol normally handled domestic disputes, but they weren't alerted to the scene until after Bruno had beaten his wife and left her alone in their cabin. Mrs. Lucilla Wright had crawled out and collapsed on the way to the nursing station. She had a broken nose, a ruptured left eye that would require surgery, and several missing teeth. Her face was so swollen by the time Logan and Jeopardy arrived, she couldn't see.

"Mrs. Wright, I'm Logan Keyes. This is Detective Bess. We're from the Special Investigations Unit. Can you tell us what happened to you?"

Lucilla groaned and reached out with her good hand. Logan took it and she gripped his hand hard. He looked over at Jeopardy, who gave him an encouraging nod.

"What happened to you, Lucilla?" Logan prompted.

She pulled him down toward her. Logan leaned over the hospital bed to hear her whispered response.

"Fell... down," she said, the words sliding out her split and swollen lips on a breathy exhale.

Logan could smell the alcohol on her breath.

"Mrs. Wright, with all due respect, no one has ever fallen down and gotten this hurt before."

"Was... dancing," she whispered. "On... kitchen... table."

Logan looked at Jeopardy. It wasn't their first domestic call, or the first time a battered woman had tried to play dumb, but it was frustrating just the same.

"I don't think that's true," Logan said.

"Your neighbors reported shouting from your cabin," Jeopardy added. "Sounds of fighting from inside."

Lucilla gave a small shake of her head, groaned in pain at the movement, then said, "Fell... down."

"Alright, but we need to speak to your husband," Logan said. "Where can we find him?"

"Don't... know..."

"Looks like we're doing this the hard way," Jeopardy said, turning away and starting to tap instructions into her cufflink.

"Mrs. Wright, we're going to find your husband. And if there's evidence that he hurt you, or even just left after you were hurt, we're going to arrest him."

"Nooooo...." the injured woman said, a tear welling up from her swollen eye slit. "Don't..."

"It's our job," Logan said. "According to ship's law, any violence inflicted on a person must be investigated and prosecuted."

"Nooooo," Lucilla cried in a weak, weepy voice.

"His locator is pinging on Topdeck," Jeopardy said. "Looks like he's at the Cosmic Cowboy Saloon."

"Let's bring him in," Logan said.

They left the medical ward, which was located on Deck four. Stu was lying calmly on his stomach, watching people walk by. He had a CLE patch on the body of his uniform right next to another patch that said DON'T PET, *work animal.*

"Stu, *Fuss,*" Jeopardy said as she came striding out of the medical center. She didn't slow down at all, but the dog bounded to his feet and walked right beside her. He had no issues keeping up with his handler.

"You don't need a leash?" Logan asked.

"Not unless we're tracking," she said. "Then I need a leash to keep up."

Logan chuckled, but it was true. Once the powerful German Shepherd fixed on a scent, the leash worked like a tether and it was especially useful in crowded spaces.

They took the nearest elevator up to Topdeck, then boarded the Tube to ride around the city to the depot closest to the Cosmic Cowboy. Once again, they got a lot of looks or Stu did. There were times when Jeopardy felt completely invisible next to the handsome work dog.

They walked the five blocks to the Cosmic Cowboy. It was more than a bar. Loud music was pumping from the speakers and people were dancing on a wooden floor in the middle of the saloon. There were long bars on both sides of the building, but no stools. Beer was flowing in abundance, but the *Colossus* had an exceedingly high tax on hard liquor. It was available, but it was five times as much as a soft drink and four times as much as beer.

Most of the patrons in the Cosmic Cowboy wore American western wear. Blue jeans, colorful shirts with snaps instead of buttons, boots and wide-brimmed hats were in abundance. Logan always felt a bit surprised to see the passengers in civilian clothes when most people below decks wore colored jumpsuits.

"Looks like a happening place," Jeopardy said.

"You like it?"

She shook her head. "Too loud. I don't hate Country music, but..."

"Same," he said. "Do you have a picture of this guy?"

Bruno Wright was listed as six feet, four inches tall. He was twenty-eight years old, a former bouncer, with an associate's degree in diesel mechanics and large machine maintenance. He wasn't hard to spot. He had short hair and a long beard that glistened with oil against his black button-up shirt.

Jeopardy showed her human partner the photo on her cufflink and they went into the saloon. There was a man at the door taking a five-credit cover charge. A big sign behind him said **2 Drink Minimum.** They showed the man their badges and he waved them through. He frowned at Stu, but didn't say anything about the dog.

The trio made their way through the crowds along the right side of the saloon. The walls were thick with insulation to keep the loud music from disturbing their neighbors. Space on Topdeck was at a premium. And inside the Cosmic Cowboy, the bodies were close together. Logan pushed his way through. They had traded their bifold badges for the larger kind on breakaway chains, which they wore around their necks. If things got heated and someone tried to use the chain to control Logan or Jeopardy, the device would simply snap off. The chains had been used for that purpose for a long, long time.

They had to get close to Bruno before calling him out. Partly because it was so loud in the bar and partly because it was taking time to work through the crowd. They needed to get into position before announcing themselves, although most everyone they passed took note that the LEOs were at the bar. Bruno was a big man, not just tall, but brawny. He had thick arms and broad shoulders. From a few paces away, Logan noticed the man had blood on the sleeves of his black, long-sleeved western shirt.

"Bruno Wright!" Logan shouted. "Sir, we need to speak with you."

Bruno turned from where he had been leaning against the bar. The woman working behind it was young, curvy and didn't mind showing it off. She had the tail of her own western shirt tied up high on her side so that at least four inches of midriff showed. The sleeves had been cut off, too, and she wore very short, tight, cut-off jeans. Her boots had bright designs on the side and she didn't mind flirting with the customers.

"Beat it," Bruno said. "I'm busy."

"Sir, I'm going to have to insist," Logan told him. "Your wife has been beaten pretty severely and we're going to need to talk to you about that."

"Well, I ain't got nothing to say to no cops," Bruno snarled. "Take your pansy ass right back out of here, before we do it for you."

Logan didn't flinch. Behind him, Jeopardy made a pass with Stu. She might not have been intimidating to the rough crowd, but the dog was. A small space opened around them until there was nothing between Logan and the dance floor. People were taking notice, pointing and watching. Bruno turned around and looked at Logan, then chuckled.

"You're a tough guy, huh?"

"Sir, I'm just doing my job. I have to insist that you come with us."

"Brought your dog with you," Bruno said. "You see this, Roy?"

"I do," another man with a thick mustache said.

Bruno turned the other way. "Trying to scare us, Jesse. You scared?"

"Nah, I ain't scared," a man in a tight shirt with bulging muscles said.

"Mr. Wright, if you resist, it's going to get ugly fast," Logan said. "I can't guarantee your safety, sir. Why don't you just come with us and avoid that sort of unpleasantness?"

Bruno laughed. "Howie, you hear this pig?" Bruno boomed, stepping away from the bar and rocking his head back and forth on his shoulders. "I think he just threatened me."

"I heard him," a man behind Logan said.

"You can take a cop off his home world, but you can't take the dirty out of the cop," another said. He was trying to be funny, but failed. Still, Logan counted at least five people, including Bruno, who were threatening him.

"Let me just say one thing before you do something stupid," Logan said. "Anyone who fights us will be going to jail tonight. You will be given restrictions on where you can go, what you can do and a fine on top of that. Is a bar brawl really worth all that?"

"Guess we'll just have to find out," Bruno said.

And then it was on.

CHAPTER 29

LOTS OF THINGS happened all at once. Bruno Wright rushed toward Logan, who moved backward. The music continued, but there were shouts of *Fight! Fight!* and the dancers scattered. Just as Logan reached the edge of the wooden dance floor, Bruno took his first swing. He threw a big-fisted haymaker from his right side straight toward Logan.

At the same time, someone grabbed Jeopardy from behind and flung her out across the polished wooden dance floor. She fell to her knees and then onto her side as she slid over the smooth surface. There was, among the roar of the crowded bar, the savage sounds of Stu attacking. There was a low growl that turned into the loud, high-pitched attack sound as the big German Shepherd latched onto the person who had flung Jeopardy aside. The dog's growl was followed by the scream of pain from the man who had attacked her.

"Stu! Halt! Heir!" Jeopardy shouted.

The screaming continued, but the growling did not. She saw a pair of men in dark blue denim shirts trying to grab Stu, but the dog was too fast. He nipped at the hand of one, then raced to Jeopardy and stood defiantly between her and the approaching figures.

Logan side-stepped the heavy punch and countered with a fast upper cut to Bruno's ribcage. The big man grunted, yet didn't slow down. He pivoted toward Logan and tried to grab the law enforcement officer, but Logan stepped back and, at the same time, kicked Bruno between his legs. The big man bent forward in pain and staggered backward, while two of his friends came from behind him straight toward Logan.

People were surging toward the dance floor, but stopping at the edges. They wanted to see the fight, but no one wanted to get caught up in it. Jeopardy got to her feet, drew her telescoping baton, and opened it with a flick of her wrist. It extended with a satisfying ~*Snap!*~, and she started toward Logan from behind him. One of the approaching figures moved sideways, planning to come at her from the side.

"Stu, *anzeigan*," she commanded, pointing at the man circling around the edges of the crowd. It was the German word for *alert*.

The dog gave another low growl, his teeth bared as he stared down the man.

"On your six," Jeopardy said as she turned with her back to Logan.

"You good?" He asked.

"Never better," Jeopardy replied.

It wasn't true. She was scared, but her adrenaline was pumping, and it overrode her fear. She raised the baton up and set her feet, just as another member of the rowdy crowd rushed toward her. Jeopardy felt Logan moving. Out of the corner of her eye, she saw the man circling. But there was no time to consider anything for more than a split second.

"*Fass!*" she shouted, as she and Stu launched themselves forward.

The dog was faster. It bounded forward, then jumped at the man circling around the edges of the crowd. He tried to hit the dog, but his clumsy punch missed the mark. He managed to bring his other hand up toward the dripping fangs that were flying toward his throat. Time seemed to slow to a crawl for the fighter. He felt hot breath and hard, wet points of very sharp teeth. Then the dog bit down hard. Those teeth punctured the skin and pierced the muscle in the man's hand before driving between the bones and tendons, where they stuck fast. The weight of the dog hit the man in the chest, knocking him off his feet. He fell backward, his head smacking hard into the wooden floor. At that point, the ship seemed to flip upside down, then spun around him in a wavy, surreal moment as the pain shot into his brain. Stu, who had landed on his feet, partly on the dance floor and partly on the man's body, shook his head. The sudden, powerful movement ripped bones and flesh as if they were wet paper. Blood flew out and the man on the ground wasn't the only person to scream.

Logan had his hands up near his face for protection, but open and ready to strike. The man stalking him down wasn't nearly so big as Bruno, but he set his feet and threw a hard jab straight at Logan's face. It was too fast to dodge or block. The man had combat training, perhaps a boxing background. Logan leaned back, but the punch caught his nose and smashed it. There wasn't a lot of damage, but Logan's eyes watered, and he immediately felt blood starting to flow. He countered with a left hook that the man stepped back to avoid. Logan let his punch's momentum turn his body. He twisted on his left foot, coiling his body as his right leg came up and then lashed out in a powerful kick to the man's chest. It landed and sent the man sprawling.

But just as Logan's kicking foot came back down to the floor, another assailant came rushing at him with a lowered shoulder. The impact knocked the wind out of Logan as the fighter slammed his shoulder straight into the law enforcement officer's abdomen. His head was to Logan's right side and, as they fell, Logan managed to turn in that direction. The fighter couldn't stop or even slow his momentum. He extended his hands to keep his face from smashing straight into the hardwood, but he hadn't expected Logan's weight to press down. The man's nose shattered as he hit the deck with all of Logan's momentum from the fall, crashing down on the back of his head. A tiny imperfection in the glossy polish ripped a shallow cut across the man's forehead. He let go of Logan and rolled away, his nose and the cut on his head gushing blood.

Jeopardy had no qualms about using the tools at her disposal. As a skinny man in a big, black hat came at her, she whipped the metal baton across his face. The metal hit his cheekbone, split the skin, and jerked his head sideways. He spun, his entire body going stiff, then dropped to the floor and didn't move.

A woman came screaming at Jeopardy from behind her. She spun around and drove the baton straight into the woman's stomach. She doubled over, retching, and then vomiting alcohol onto the dance floor. There was no time to even take note of the response, as Bruno lumbered toward Logan, who was on the ground. She started to intervene, but the woman she had just put down grabbed her foot.

"Stu!" Jeopardy shouted as she fell.

The K-9 came in a flash. It leaped over Jeopardy, who was falling onto her back, and crashed into the vomiting woman. That assailant was knocked back and Stu turned to charge down Bruno. Logan had gotten onto his hands and knees, even though it was clear that Bruno was going to drive a vicious kick into Logan's side. But he stopped and grabbed Stu as the dog leaped toward him. The big man's meaty hands caught in the fur on either side of Stu's neck, and he flung the dog to the side before it could harm him.

But in that second of time that Stu had bought Logan, the wily law enforcement scrapper twisted around and kicked out hard with one leg. His foot caught Bruno on the bend of his leg, and the big man came down hard on his knees. Still gasping for air, Logan threw himself at the bigger man. Their bodies crashed together in a violent collision and Logan pushed hard against the bigger man. Bruno hit the ground on his side and Logan landed on top of him. For a moment, they both scrambled for purchase, but it was Logan who got the superior position. He latched on to Bruno's wrist, pulling the big man's thick arm down between Logan's legs. Then, with all his strength, he kicked out. The heel of his shoe caught the big wife-beater in the jaw, breaking the big man's lower mandible, but Bruno was still trying to fight. Only Logan had all the leverage. With one foot across Bruno's throat, and the other across his chest, he leaned back and thrust his hips upward. The move fully extended Bruno's big arm. The fighter tried to resist, but Logan was too strong. There was a pop as the bones in the big man's forearm snapped right where they connected to the elbow.

Bruno screamed in pain, but the sudden break gave him enough leverage to grab Logan's shoe. He lifted the leg over his head and twisted around onto his knees. Even with a broken arm and a broken jaw, Bruno was still fighting. Logan raised his knees to ward the big man off, but that move pinned him in place. Someone from the crowd came running to help Bruno, but Jeopardy thrust out her baton between his feet,and the newcomer tripped.

Bruno raised his good hand to punch down on Logan, but at that same moment, Stu came rushing back into the fight. He bounded up from the floor, onto Bruno's back, and latched onto the big man's arm. His teeth snapped hard onto the big man's meaty forearm, breaking the skin and fixing tight. Stu's momentum carried him off Bruno's back, and tugged the big man off Logan at the same time.

It took Logan less than a second to scramble to his feet. Bruno was on his back, unable to use his other arm to fend Stu off. The dog was yanking at the big man's arm. Within seconds, it was drenched in blood. Logan stepped forward and put his foot on Bruno's thick neck.

"I got this, Stu," he said. "Thanks for the help."

The dog released Bruno, yet didn't back away. He stood over the fallen man, growling as blood dripped from his jowls. By that point, an alarm was sounding from outside the saloon and patrol officers were pushing their way through the crowd. Jeopardy got to her feet. There were several people on the ground, but no one else was ready to join in the brawl.

"Time to clean up the mess," she said.

"Looks that way," Logan said. "You okay?"

"Fine, but you're bleeding."

"Nothing broken," he said, swiping the blood off his upper lip.

"Stu, *zuriek... ruhe*," she said, ordering the dog to back up and quiet down. It obeyed, and they held up their badges as the patrol officers arrived on the scene.

"Better call in medical," Logan said. "We've got some suspects with injuries."

The patrol officers made the call and began restraining the fighters who weren't bleeding profusely or suffering from broken bones. The Topdeck had several medical response crew stations. They had hoverskiffs with medical supplies and gurneys. Bruno and his fellow brawlers were hauled away, while Logan, and Jeopardy gave verbal accounts to the responding officers. There would be reports to write up and evidence to gather. The club, like most of the establishments on Topdeck, had surveillance cameras. The entire fight had been caught on video and recorded - and there was no shortage of witnesses. Some accused the trio of SIU officers of inciting the fight, but others were more honest in their testimony. That, added to the fact that it didn't make any sense for two people to take on an entire crowd full of drunken cowboys, cemented their case.

Everyone was charged with assault of a law enforcement officer, disturbing the peace,and resisting arrest. Those whose blood tests came back over the limit were also charged with drunk & disorderly. Most importantly, Bruno Wright was charged with spousal abuse and attempted homicide. The prosecutor on the case told the SIU team it would most likely be knocked down to felony assault unless Lucinda Wright changed her mind and testified against her husband. It was as close to justice as the law enforcement squad could hope for.

The following day, Flint found himself giving a report of the incident to Commander Lova Koll. She was the ship's officer who was directly in charge of the passengers. So, while she was not part of the law enforcement hierarchy directly, she did have authority over what they did. Part of that was getting detailed reports on the cases being worked.

"A brawl that put four people in the med bay is not what we're striving for, Sergeant," she said.

"Yes, ma'am, I understand that."

"Good ... and your people are okay?"

"They're fine, Commander."

"Consider yourself sternly warned to do better, Sergeant," she said with a dazzling smile. She was a stereotypical Scandinavian, tall, blonde and beautiful. But she worked hard to overcome the assumptions that her looks alone produced. Including wearing a uniform that didn't hide, but didn't accentuate, her figure. Nor did she wear much make-up, which she didn't need. She had beautiful skin, large, icy blue eyes, and although her hair was cut short, it was a bright blonde color.

"Now, for the real reason I'm here," she said, glancing over her shoulder to ensure the door to his little office was closed. "I apologize for being forward, but most people who serve with me feel they can't move toward a romantic relationship. I don't want to pressure you, Sergeant, so if you aren't interested—"

"I am," he said. "And I'm glad you brought it up."

"Because?" she asked.

"Because I would love nothing more than to take you to dinner," Flint said. "If that's not against the rules."

"I'm free tonight," she said. "And I've heard good things about Le Feu."

"Can I pick you up?"

She chuckled at that. "I imagine if you tried hard, you could. But why don't we meet at Tube Depot Alpha and we go from there? Say 1900 hours?"

"I'll be there," Flint said.

"I look forward to it, Sergeant."

She left and Flint had to sit down. He hadn't been asked out on a date in a long time and never by anyone as incredibly beautiful as Commander Koll. But dating one's superior was always tricky. The rest of the day, he waffled back and forth between feeling lucky and worried.

That night, he shaved for the second time that day and put on his best suit. Flint was not a dapper man, but he did his best to look nice for his date.

He went early and paced at Tube Depot Alpha until Lova Koll arrived. When she did, she took his breath away. She was wearing a short, black dress that came to just above her knees. It was elegant, but modest, which he respected.

"Wow, you look amazing," he said.

"It's good to get out of a uniform," she said.

He gave her his arm and she took hold of it. Then they walked together along the wide street that led toward the city in the center of Topdeck. The road ran beside one of the four green areas. It was amazing to see grass and trees. The big, hard lights were off, and there were lampposts in the park that looked magical underneath the transparent dome that showed thousands of stars overhead.

"It's easy to forget how wonderful this vessel truly is," she said.

"That's so true," he agreed. "I've been up here plenty, but always on a task or errand. I've never stopped to just soak in the beauty."

"It's an auspicious start to what could be a beautiful evening."

"Agreed," he said.

They strolled for a good while, then caught a trolley through the town. They got off at a small but busy restaurant called La Feu. He had called ahead and set a reservation, so they were immediately shown to their table.

There were thousands of crew members on the *Colossus*, but most were part of divisions that had nothing to do with sailing the spaceship. Those who recognized the Commander were few and far between. To most people, she was just a beauty queen and he was the lucky SOB who had caught her eye. He certainly felt that way. Under different circumstances, he would have assumed he was either being pranked by his friends or set up by his enemies. On earth, women like Lova Koll had little interest in a cop.

"How did you become part of the crew?" he asked her.

"I was nominated by my country's navy," she said. "I was a Captain. We have a very good navy, you know. The North Sea is difficult to sail in, but we make it look easy."

"I know you make it look good," Flint said.

"You flatter me," she said. "I went through the protocols and was offered the post of commander. It was a step down, perhaps, but still progressive. Plus, it gives me the opportunity to go to Secundo when I retire."

"That's your plan?" he asked.

"It is. I will stay on the *Colossus* for at least four trips. After that, I will return and live on the new world."

"Sounds like you've worked things out."

"I like to plan ahead," she said. "And you? How did you get this post?"

"You know about the first team," he said.

"Yes, a tragedy," she replied.

"Well, the truth is I was the right guy at the right time. They needed someone who could drop everything and leave their life behind at a moment's notice."

"And you could do that?"

"I was in transition when I was approached," he said.

"Transition?"

"I had just completed my divorce."

"Ah, you are an interesting man," she said. "I must know all about this marriage. You had time for it?"

"No," he said, "not really."

"But you loved her?"

"I did. She broke my heart. But I'm partially to blame. I shouldn't have asked her to marry me. But at that time, I knew she would leave me if I didn't. And then, once we were married, I couldn't give her what she wanted. Eventually, she stepped out on me."

"And you divorced her?"

"No," he said. "She filed. I don't know. It wasn't working, but I don't give up on things very easily."

"That is a good trait," Lova said. "I like that."

Their conversation was good. There was plenty to talk about. They both had interesting jobs and the food was good at Le Feu. It wasn't until they were finished and Lova had gone to powder her nose, that Flint was approached.

"Dining alone, Sergeant?" Harmonia Lukid said as she approached his table.

Flint got to his feet. "No, actually, I'm on a date."

"Oh," Harmonia said. "I am jealous."

She was every bit as beautiful as Lova Koll, but the exact opposite. Harmonia's skin was a deep bronze color. She had emerald green eyes and black hair that was long and flowed down over her bare shoulders. She wore a tight red dress that accentuated her figure and four-inch designer heels, yet she wasn't as tall as Flint.

"You have great taste. This is an excellent restaurant. The chef is classically trained, but not close-minded to new ideas. You have to be creative to be good in the kitchen. New flavors, new cooking techniques, it's always changing."

"That's interesting," Flint said. "You really know your stuff."

"I'd love to show you. Can we get together sometime soon? I want to cook for you, Sergeant."

"I'd like that, but I'm pretty busy."

"Never too busy to eat, though," she said. "Have dinner with me. I promise, you will not regret it."

"Alright, how should I contact you?"

"You know where I live. Use your investigative powers to track me down."

The look she gave him as she said it made him feel weak suddenly, like his knees might buckle beneath him. He stood there at his table and watched her walk away.

Normally, Flint was aware of his surroundings. But his head was still spinning as Lova approached.

"Who was that?" she asked.

"Ah, a passenger that I escorted to her cabin when she first arrived."

"She's lovely."

"Yes, she's a chef and a food scientist. I don't really know what it means."

"Oh, she's Harmonia Lukid," Lova said. "Yes, I know who she is. We had a cabin designed especially for her. She will be important on Secundo, I think. Shall we go?"

"Yes," Flint said.

They walked back through the park and then parted ways. Flint had never felt so thrilled by a first date and yet he couldn't deny that he also felt a very real spark for Harmonia Lukid. As he rode the elevator back down to his dreary cabin on deck eighteen, his mind was spinning with thoughts of the two beautiful women. But his excitement didn't last long. Just two days later, they had much bigger concerns to deal with.

CHAPTER 30

IT WAS an odd bit of chance that both the assassin Filo and the gangster JD decided to make their move on Everett Goddard the same day.

For Filo, every circumstance had been considered. He had been watching the bank executive for over a month. Every working day, the president of the *Colossus* Bank took an elevator from deck two. From there, he rode the trolley into the city to where the bank tower was located. Just outside the tall building, he purchased himself a large, black coffee from a street vendor, sometimes adding a breakfast sandwich to his order. He then took his beverage, and sometimes food, to the executive elevator. Yet it was the ride on the trolley when he was the most vulnerable in Filo's mind. He considered poisoning the coffee, but he didn't know what the hot beverage's temperature would do to a toxic compound. If he didn't drink it all, the effort might fail. It was better to make certain of the outcome.

For JD, the time had come to make himself known to the bank president. Jerome Donald had become Julius Descarte with a business degree from the Wharton School of Business and a master's degree from Yale. He was, at least on the ship's personnel files, an expert in supply chain creation/management and logistics. In reality, his education had come via books and hard-earned experience. But he had taken the Ghetto Kings from a group of street toughs who slung illegal smack to the homeless and street junkies who needed more than the government fix could provide them, to being masters of their domain, with interests in all sorts of criminal enterprises. The GKs had cooked their own dope, branched out into organ theft, human trafficking and a wide variety of government scams. But it wasn't the crime that made him great; rather, it was his resourcefulness in discovering ways to clean their illicit funds and the development of the black market bartering system that really set him apart.

His goal since going on board the *Colossus* had been to get close to Everett Goddard. While he had allowed the great man to see him on a variety of occasions, they had never spoken. JD had finally decided that he needed to change. His plan was to be on the trolley when Everett boarded, then, in what would seem like a random moment of chance, he would strike up a conversation. Crank could do all the behind-the-scenes work to make JD and his lieutenants appear to be upstanding men of good moral character, even pillars of the community. But the real test would be if JD could fool the banker into thinking they were business leaders from the same background and with the same goals.

Eventually, JD would find a way to facilitate an illegal and scandalous moment for Goddard. It would have no direct ties to JD or the Ghetto Kings, but they would have undeniable proof that would be used to leverage themselves into positions of great power on the new world. It was, in many ways, a very simple plan. The devil was in the details and those had to be handled very carefully.

JD was completely unaware of Filo's plans. The assassin had no way of knowing that the gangster was planning to make contact with Everett on the same day that Filo planned to kill him. The hitman would have said it didn't matter who Everett met or what he did before the hit. But while Everett was from old money and very accustomed to a sense of being above the huddled masses around him, JD was always on the lookout for danger. It was just part of life in the neighborhood he had grown up in. The more success a street hustler had, the bigger a target he became. There were always fools thinking they could take him down. He had been shot three times and stabbed once. Another time, he was sliced open from his left shoulder to the right side of his rib cage. And another time, he had almost been poisoned. In every case, he survived and had gotten a little wiser.

Everett Goddard worked to ignore what was happening around him when he wasn't in his office on the top floor of the banking tower. He had no love for the little people and no concern for others. What they did held no interest to him. Even if they were working for him. The man who drove his private hovercraft was of no more interest to him than the man who operated the trolley on the *Colossus* Topdeck. They might not be complete strangers to him, but they might as well have been.

And so it was that Everett Goddard got off the trolley and started toward the coffee stand with no idea that a hardened assassin was matching him stride for stride just a few paces behind him.

JD had already ordered his coffee and was pretending to wait for it, but in reality, he was waiting for Everett. He turned, thinking that he was merely going to watch the banking mogul approach the stand for his own cup of coffee. But when JD turned, he noticed the man behind Everett. He was unassuming in every way— not too tall, not flashy, not handsome but dressed in decent clothes that were clean and pressed. Nothing about the man stood out and, in a crowd, no one would take note of him. But JD recognized an intensity in the man's gaze that was fixed on the back of Everett's head. It wasn't natural. There was maybe a hint of hatred there and almost certainly the look of a predator was in the man's stare. He was a hunter who had fixed his attention completely on his prey.

JD was walking toward them without even realizing it. In truth, he cared nothing for Everett Goddard. The man was merely a means to an end for JD. But he wasn't about to sit back and let another player take his man off the board. If that became necessary, JD would see to it. He had never lost a moment's sleep over killing a person, be it a man, woman, or child. Even when he killed, it was always on purpose and there was always a reason for it.

He glanced down at the hands of the man following Everett. It was another reaction to hard-lived experience. And it was no surprise to see the small device slip down from the man's sleeve and into his hand. It wasn't a blade, but it was more than a needle, yet it would serve the same purpose. It was like an ice pick, but with a toxin that would ensure the death of whoever was stabbed by it. The killer, which was what JD recognized the unassuming man to be, was waiting for his moment. JD quickened his pace.

Filo never saw JD coming. They met at a moment of convergence in the crowd. It was Filo's moment to act. When Everett slowed, he sped up. He was planning to stab the bank president with one swift plunge of his loaded shiv. His hand came up and JD's did the same. The thrust was made, but instead of puncturing the bank executive, the tool stabbed through JD's hand.

There was a shout of pain, people turned and Filo fled. He blended into the shocked crowd, his body moving away from the cry, just like those closest to JD did. In seconds, he was gone. JD would have tracked him. Under different circumstances, he would have fought the assassin man-to-man. The shock of the stabbing and the fear of knowing what the weapon was really used for shifted his focus.

Surprisingly, the shiv stabbed directly through his hand, missing the bones and ligaments that should have triggered the poison. Instead, it went in through his palm and out the back of his hand before the poison was released. And it was so close to Everett Goddard that the toxin squirted into the back of his suit jacket.

"Take it off," JD shouted at him. "Your jacket. Get it off! There's poison on it."

JD went down to one knee. He was angry, but also alarmed. Sticking his hand out had been a stupid move. He had meant to deflect the assassin, but instead, he had moved directly into the killer's path. JD didn't fear death, but he didn't want to die. Yet in that moment, knowing what he knew, he thought he was already a dead man. He stayed on his knee, his elbow on his other leg as he gripped his wrist tight, foolishly hoping he might be able to strangle his hand hard enough to stop the poison from entering his bloodstream.

He was so determined that if he'd had access to a knife, he would have cut off his own hand. Instead, all he could do was kneel in the street and wait to die.

"What happened?" Everett said as he pulled off his suit jacket.

"That man's been stabbed," another person said.

"Look at his hand," someone exclaimed.

"What is that?" another person asked.

JD knew what it was. And he knew what it was used for. His people made them from the big needles used to inject turkeys with seasoning before they were deep-fried. He had a contact in a restaurant supply company who got them for his people when the need arose. Only the one sticking through his hand wasn't a makeshift device. It was clearly created for the purpose. The back side didn't have a plunger, but a small, rubber device that, when squeezed or smashed, would push air through the thick stabbing needle and deliver whatever substance had been stored there.

"Who are you?" Everett asked, putting a hand on JD's shoulder.

"Julius," he answered, proud that he could stay in character right until the end. If crime was a career, he was a consummate professional.

"Someone, call for help," Everett said. "Quick, this man needs medical attention."

"Already on it," someone said.

"Help is on the way, mister," a woman close to JD said.

"Who saw what happened?" Everett asked, looking at the back of his expensive suit jacket. It was stained with a pale white liquid.

"I saw some guy try to stab you," a man in a flannel shirt and baggy pants said. "This dude stopped him."

"Not how I meant to," JD said through clenched teeth.

The pain was like fire in his hand, but that was nothing compared to the expectation of whatever toxin had been in the device would do. JD didn't know why he couldn't feel it burning through his veins, but he expected to at any moment.

"Good God, are you saying someone tried to stab me?" Everett said.

"That's right," JD told him. "I saw the guy move up behind you. Saw the shiv in his hand. Next thing I know, he's thrusting it toward your back."

"I saw that," the flannel-clad man said. "That's what happened."

"But..." Everett was suddenly feeling weak.

It was one thing to be close to a violent incident, although it was something else to realize you were the intended target of violence.

"Why?" he asked. "Why me?"

People were shrugging and looking confused. The police arrived before more could be discussed. A medical services team was right on their heels. The suit jacket was bagged. The medical team used a portable scanner that was powerful enough to register foreign antibodies in a person's bloodstream. When that came back clear, they wrapped his hand in gauze, then bagged it. The toxin would have to be identified and neutralized before the device was removed from his hand.

The crowd had dispersed, and JD was starting to think he had somehow dodged a bullet, when a man with salt and pepper hair, wearing a suit that screamed police, arrived. With him was a woman wearing jeans, a white tee-shirt and a black jacket that covered the pistol she wore on her hip. JD clocked the piece, but also the fact that the woman was attractive. Unfortunately, she was sent to talk to Everett, while the older man approached JD.

"Sorry for what happened to you, sir. My name is Sergeant Sawyer Flint with the Colossus Law Enforcement Special Investigations Unit. Can you tell me your name?"

JD knew that everyone already knew his name. The patrolmen

and the med team had both scanned his cufflink. And JD had no reason to believe the cover that Crank had established for him wouldn't hold up. Many players from deep in the big cities of Earth took pride in speaking differently from regular folks. For a while, JD had done that too. But in his quest to rise above the level of street hood, he had put away the vernacular of the street.

"My name is Julius Descarte," he said. "But I go by JD."

"JD, got it. Thank you for that. I know a lot of people are asking a lot of questions."

"It's fine."

"Are you in much pain?"

"They gave me a little something to take the edge off," JD said. "I'll be fine as long as they don't poison me getting it out."

"That's a strange weapon," Flint said. "How did you know what it was?"

"I didn't," JD said. "I thought it was a knife. I meant to hit the guy's hand, but I missed."

He did his best to seem embarrassed, even though he was burning with fury. He still planned to carry out his scheme and had even considered that the incident might help him pull it off. But he was not the kind of person who took a physical assault in stride. He wanted revenge. He was anxious to get back to his homies and start plotting it in earnest.

"You saw that he was stalking Mister Goddard?"

"No," JD lied. "I just looked up as I was passing him, saw the knife and reacted. It was really more instinct than anything. I wouldn't have done it if I had a moment to think about things. I don't like getting involved in things like this."

"No one does, I'm afraid," Flint said. "But at least you can rest knowing you saved a man's life."

"Just so long as it doesn't cost me mine," JD said.

"Sergeant, we need to transport the patient to the medical facilities," one of the medical technicians said. "I'm sorry, you can come with us. I'm sure the doctors will let you continue your interview once they get a plan of action for his hand."

"That's okay," Flint said. "Good luck, Mr. Descarte. I'll be by to see you later today."

"Yeah, okay," JD said.

The tech strapped JD in place, then activated the hovercart. They zoomed away from the scene of the crime and Filo watched from the top of a nearby building. He had a new target and his time was running out. Sooner or later, if he didn't take out Goddard, the powers behind the hitman would activate their second option. Filo was certain he didn't want to be around if that happened.

CHAPTER 31

DAVE ARRIVED at the scene with a tablet with access to the ship surveillance files.

"It's not much," he said. "The suspect was a pro."

"As in a professional hit man?" Becky asked as she and Flint moved close to Dave in order to see the video feed. "On this ship?"

"Hard to believe," Flint said. "But anything is possible."

They knew the lottery system wasn't perfect. Just like any large-scale government operation, it was rife for enterprising criminals to take advantage of. But a hit man on a ship with no way to escape seemed almost ridiculous.

"Who would take a job like that?" Becky persisted.

"Someone desperate, maybe," Flint said. "Someone with problems back home."

"Here it is," Dave said, bringing the right footage up on the tablet. "Best angle we've got."

It was from across the street. People were walking past, dozens, maybe even hundreds. It was difficult to focus on any one person. The people were moving in different directions and at different speeds.

"There's our vic," said Dave, pointing with his free hand.

"The good Samaritan is there," Becky said, as JD appeared from behind the coffee kiosk.

"Julius," Flint said. "That guy should be a professional gambler."

"How so?" Dave asked.

"He won the lottery just to be on board," Flint explained. "Now, he somehow stops the assassin and manages not to be killed by the toxin in the weapon."

"Some people are lucky," Becky said.

But none of them really believed in luck. They had been on the job too long and seen too many scams. Flint's comment made their internal alarms go off.

"What do we know about him?" Dave asked, pausing the video feed.

"Just what's in the file," Flint said, referring to the ship's digital personnel listing as if it were an old-fashioned paper file in a cabinet somewhere. "Business guy, logistics specialist. He was recruited. Has a berth down on deck three."

"Fancy," Becky said. "Must have a family."

"He'll be at med for a bit. We'll go and check back in, once they clear him."

"Where's the hit man?"

"You can't see him until right before he strikes," Dave said, letting the footage roll again. "He stays in the crowd."

"Almost as if he knows where the cameras are," Becky said.

Just as the video shows JD passing Everett Goddard, a man steps closer and thrusts his hand toward the banker. The video doesn't have a good angle on the actual strike. They see the thrust of the would-be killer's shoulders, but JD's body is blocking what is happening. Then JD goes down on one knee and people begin to bunch up. The assassin seemingly gets caught up in the crowd as people turn and start to bunch up around JD.

"That's it?" Flint asked.

"Best footage of the actual deed," Dave said. "I've run all the angles. I've checked the back footage. Our man rode the same trolley as Goddard, but managed to stay buried in the crowd. I can't get a decent look at him. Definitely not enough for facial recognition."

"What's that leave us with?" Flint said. "Did you run the cufflink data?"

"Sure, but there were three dozen people on the trolley. Only eight of them were women. That leaves twenty-seven suspects."

"Get me a list," Flint said, as Logan and Jeopardy arrived with Stu in tow.

"Alright, we've got a hit, people," Flint continued. "A good old-fashioned assassination attempt. Dave is scrubbing the ship's data for clues about our hit man. I'm going up to have a conversation with Goddard. What do we know about him?"

"He's the mastermind behind the financial system on the ship," Becky said. "Rich, recently divorced, only thirty-eight years old, no children and he divested from all his business interests back on Earth. He'll be establishing the monetary systems on Secundo."

"What's to establish?" Logan asked. "It's all digital, right?"

Flint answered the question. "Eventually, they will revert to all digital, but with Secundo being a new colony, it was decided to revert to a physical currency."

"So, he's important," Jeopardy said. "Maybe someone wants the colony to fail."

"We'll worry about that after we find the suspect," Flint said. "Dave, get us a short list of names. I don't want anyone going after this guy alone. When we start knocking on doors, we do it in pairs. Jeopardy, go find out what that toxin was. They're running it through the chem lab on deck twelve."

"Roger that," she said.

"Logan, I want you at the medical center. Let's make sure no one is trying to tie up loose ends. Keep Julius Descarte there until I arrive."

"Got it," Logan said as he and Jeopardy left.

"Becky, you're with me. We'll interview Goddard. Dave, get back to HQ and coordinate. The higher-ups will want to know what's happening. Give them everything."

Speed was what they needed, but there was nothing speedy about an investigation. The strange substance that came from the plunger, as Flint thought of the weapon, had been sent to a lab for identification, but who knew how long that would take. They needed to do a cursory look into twenty-seven passengers, then follow up with the most viable suspects, in the hopes that they could identify the assassin. But the truth was, unless more evidence came to light, they were shooting in the dark.

Goddard was already in his office on the top floor of the bank tower. Flint and Becky found him sitting on a tufted leather sofa, not at his desk, swirling a tumbler filled with scotch on the rocks. He didn't get up when they were shown in.

"How are you, Mr. Goddard?" Flint asked.

"Who are you?" he asked them.

"Sergeant Flint, Detective Nash, we're with the Special Investigation Unit," Flint told him. "Were you hurt in the assault?"

"No," he said. "Lost my suit jacket, but I wasn't hurt."

"Is it a good idea for you to be drinking right now?" Becky asked. It was only a little past nine in the morning by ship reckoning.

"Oh, this," he said, looking down at the tumbler. "I don't normally imbibe this early, but I've never been almost killed either."

"Any idea who might want you dead, Mr. Goddard?"

"Call me Everett. Do either of you want anything? My assistant can get whatever you like."

"We're fine, thank you," Becky said as she wandered around the large office.

Flint sat down directly across from Goddard. "Who might want to kill you, Everett?"

"Oh, I'm sure you could make a list," the banker said. "Former lovers, past business partners, crazy yahoos who think that fiscal policy makers are working to keep them poor. I really have no idea."

"Well, let's start with your ex-wife," Flint said. "Would she want you dead?"

"For the sheer pleasure of watching me die," he replied. "There is no other benefit to her. We had a prenup. She got fifty million and nothing more. The divorce is final. To be honest, if she wanted to kill me, she should have done it sooner."

"You mentioned lovers?"

"Sure," Goddard said. "I've had several. Some people call it a vice, but I just can't seem to help myself."

"Any crazy enough to want to see you dead?"

"Oh, I prefer the crazy ones," he said with a sigh. "Look, when you have as much money as I have, trust becomes a difficult thing. It's easier to find people who can give you what you need in the moment and put off the ties that bind, so to speak."

"Like prostitutes?" Becky said from across the room, where she was examining the knickknacks that were neatly arranged on his shelves.

"Not professionals," Goddard said. "But I suppose they fit the technical details. Beautiful women who want to be with a man who can give them all the expensive baubles they've dreamed of. Which, by the way, I'm happy to do just to make them happy. When it ends, it is rarely pleasant. Many feel betrayed, but it isn't personal. I have only made the mistake of making a commitment to one woman, who was my wife. Our relationship ended, much like all the others, and in the end, what she really wanted was money. Perhaps if I found a woman who cared more about me than my money, I could be faithful, but I have yet to find that kind of love."

"Maybe you're looking in the wrong places," Becky said.

Flint felt the interview was veering off track and quickly regained control. "Everett, we have reason to believe that the person who attacked you was hired to do it. Now, I'm getting the impression that most of the people in your love life lack the means to hire a hit man and get them on board the *Colossus*."

"That would be an accurate assessment," he said, taking a sip and making a face as the old liquor scalded its way down his throat.

"What about sabotaging the colony? How would killing you do that?"

"Well, that's a complex answer. I'll be in charge of fiscal oversight for at least the first ten years. That involves all sorts of things, but the most basic is managing the money supply. We'll be printing money and, in almost every circumstance, that process has led to disaster. We have to be careful and we have to sell the colonists on the concept. In other words, every person will have to agree that what we produce is valuable and that it is of the same value. Without that, things could devolve on Secundo very fast."

"Bartering won't work?"

"It can, but typically it leads to hoarding and then violence. Let's say you're a farmer. You've grown a fantastic crop of potatoes. But your child is sick and needs medicine. What if the people who produce medicine want half your crop of potatoes for what amounts to a shot of penicillin? Or what if they don't like potatoes at all? That leaves you in a very precarious position."

"Can't they trade the potatoes for something else?" Becky asked.

"They could, and should, but that's extra work for the medicine makers. And there aren't very many of them. What if they force you to trade your potatoes for bread, then that bread for the medicine? At some point, people will get anxious enough to simply force the medicine makers to hand over the needed pharmaceuticals and, in the process, people will be killed. Are you following that train of thought?"

"We are," Flint said. "So, your job will be to create the money and make sure that it is equally available to all people, and holds its value, and so on."

"Correct."

"What happens if you die?"

"Someone else will have to do it. Someone with less experience than me. Maybe someone with more to gain from having that control."

Flint realized that the list of suspects was enormous. There were countless groups on Earth who wanted to see the colonies fail. They were mostly anarchists and terrorists, but still, they might try to sabotage the colony in order to put more pressure on Earth's governments to give in to the demands of the fringe groups. Or, it could be someone on the ship who, as Everett had explained, wanted his job. That made nearly every person on the ship a suspect. They didn't all have to be in line for Everett's role on the new world. All they needed to do was have a way to get the next guy in line to favor them in some way.

But if Dave and Becky were right about the hit man being a professional, then the odds were good the person who hired him wasn't on the ship. Or, at the very least, weren't part of the lottery system. It could be one of the VIP's who had bought passage on the *Colossus*. That still left thousands of possibilities. The only way they could hope to find out for certain was by catching the suspect.

"I'm going to recommend that you have a security escort for a while," Flint said. "Mainly for travel around the ship, just until we catch the person responsible and get to the bottom of things."

"Fine by me," Everett said.

"For the next few days, I'd prefer it if you just went to work and then back to your berth."

"I have no problem with that," he said, taking another sip of his whiskey.

"Are there people you interact with on a regular basis outside of work?"

"Just the cleaning crew," he said. "I have a day maid."

"Are you seeing anyone right now?"

"Not at this moment," Everett said. "Harmonia Lukid and I have a past. We might have a future. She is supposed to be cooking me dinner this evening, but we're just friends at the moment."

Flint balked for a moment. He had a connection to Harmony, and it felt like more than friendship, although he hadn't pursued it as ardently as he could have. Fortunately, their relationship wasn't enough to make Flint feel the need to hand the case off to someone else.

"Alright," Flint said. "I'm going to have my K-9 officer go through your cabin. Detective Bess and Keys will be assigned to you from the time you leave the office until you get back to it."

"Thank you," Everett said. "I really do appreciate all that you're doing. I'm rattled, I know that. But I've always supported the police and I'll do whatever I need to do."

"As will we," Flint said. "We'll get to the bottom of things, Mr. Goddard. Can you stay put? Maybe have lunch brought in?"

"We often do. That won't be a problem."

"Good. Look for my people this afternoon."

They shook hands, then the LEOs left.

"What do you think?" Flint said as they stepped onto the elevator.

Becky shrugged. "He's a rich guy. They're always targets for one reason or another."

"He's a rich, important guy," Flint corrected. "We need to dig into him. I'm sure he was vetted, but people with money can get away with things most people can't."

"And you think he's dirty?"

"I think that's a very good possibility."

"Not much we can do from here," she said.

"I don't want to arrest him. But I want to know who his enemies really are."

Twenty minutes later, they entered the medical facility on deck four. Flint was expecting to see his officers or a doctor. Instead, it was Commander Koll who met them as they walked into the facility.

"Sergeant, I'm glad to find you here," she said, as if it was an accident.

Flint knew that every person on board could be tracked via their cufflink. She must have known he was on his way to the medical facility.

"Detective Nash, can you get me an update on Julius Descarte?" he asked, before turning toward Commander Lova Koll. "Let me fill you in on what's happened."

"Thank you," she said.

He made his report brief. Commander Koll listened. "And the assailant?" she asked.

"We're trying to identify him. But the weapon suggests a professional. If that's the case, there's a good chance his identity is fake. He might even have a secondary identity he can assume, which would make our jobs much harder."

"That's impossible," the executive officer said. "We have very strict protocols for the cufflinks. Each one is assigned to a single passenger. The identities we have on file were entered into our computer system before the passengers were ever allowed on board."

"Doesn't mean they can't be hacked," Flint said.

It wasn't pessimism, but realism learned from years of seeing devious felons devise all sorts of ways to break the law. Computers were a major source of crime. Governments and businesses spent huge sums of money trying to fend off cyber criminals, but the bad guys always found a way to break through.

"Not our system," she said.

Flint frowned, but didn't argue the point. "Whatever he's doing, we'll find him," he assured her.

"Good," she said. "The captain has heard about the attack."

"As he should have," Flint said. "Goddard is an important part of the colony's future government. If we lose him, things could get hairy on Secundo."

"What can we do to help?"

"For now, nothing," Flint said. "We're already tracking down the assailant. I'm hopeful that Julius Descarte will pull through. Do you know him?" Lova shook her head. "He's some sort of logistical expert. He saved Goddard's life, you know."

"I do, the Captain will want to see him. We'll have some sort of award for him. It's rubbish really, but his heroics should be recognized."

"Keep me in the loop," Flint said.

"I will," she said. "Maybe we can have dinner again. I know things have been a bit mad around here, but at least we can steal a few hours... alone."

Flint wasn't afraid of taking things with Lova Koll to the next level. She was smart, beautiful and very interesting. But he also had a connection with Harmony Lukid. To make things even more complicated, Flint hadn't decided if he would join the colonists or return to Earth and work the next shuttle. There would be work for him on Secundo, and he knew he wanted to retire to that world, yet he wasn't sure if he was ready. They still had over a year and a half just to reach the system. And shuttling down the passengers would take months. There was plenty of time for him to make up his mind.

But if he chose to date Commander Lova Koll, he would either have to end things when he left the ship or stay on. If he dated Harmony Lukid, it would be the same choice in reverse. Which meant the person he chose to get close to would have a big impact on his future and he wanted to be careful.

"I would like that," he said. "I need to be up front about something."

"You're seeing someone else?"

"Not in any official way. But I did agree to a date."

"That's fine," Lova said, although Flint didn't think she meant it. "I know I'm busy."

"We both are," he said. "And we've got time."

"Are you staying for the return voyage?"

"I don't know yet," Flint admitted. "I didn't think I needed to decide any time soon."

"You don't," Lova said quickly. "It's just something I think about. The return voyage would be very different."

"No passengers," he said.

"A skeleton crew. Most of the ship will be shut down. There will be much more free time. Think about it. I will be in touch very soon. Please cc me on all your reports pertaining to this matter."

"I will do so, Commander," Flint said

She nodded and walked away. He watched her. It was hard to imagine why someone as stunning as Commander Koll would have any interest in him, but he wasn't complaining.

"You done flirting, Sarge?" Becky asked.

"I was giving an update to the ship's executive officer, Detective Nash. Not flirting."

"Sure," Becky said with a grin. "Doc wants to see you."

"Lead the way."

CHAPTER 32

"IT'S A PARALYTIC," the doctor said. "Very rare. An injection of it would cause a person to fatigue quickly, within, say, ninety seconds. And then complete heart failure by the three-minute mark. It's also painless. No burning sensation as it gets into the bloodstream and it doesn't cause seizures or hemorrhaging."

"In other words, it kills without drawing attention," Becky said.

Flint nodded. Poisons were rare. They were effective if utilized the right way, but they left traces behind. Everyone but Dave Bannon was in the small exam room where Dr. Issac Takami was explaining about the chemical that was found on the assassin's shiv.

"Wouldn't it be discovered in the autopsy?" Flint asked.

"It can be, but this toxin has a very short life. It dissolves quickly and looks like lactic acid unless it's collected and sent to a lab for samples. In most cases, a person dies, all indications are that something happened to his heart, a medical examiner would do a blood test, but the results would just show elevated levels of lactic acid, which aren't unusual when a person has a heart attack."

"But if he was stabbed," Flint said. "Surely, no one would be fooled by it."

"You're assuming the victim would know he had been stabbed, and that is doubtful. May I?" he asked, turning Flint around.

Becky was grinning. She liked it when her superior was the example. Beside them, Stu gave a low growl.

"Stu," Jeopardy said. "Ruhe."

The dog quieted down, and Dr. Takami continued explaining.

"If a person gets stabbed in the back, there is a lot of pain," he said, jamming a thumb into Flint's kidney. "Lots of organs up here. The chest might be better, but the rib cage can thwart a blade or, as in this case, a pointed object."

"What are you saying, doctor?"

"I'm saying, if you stab here," he poked Flint in his rear, "it is much less noticeable. A person might hop a few steps and even turn around, but they won't be expecting that they were stabbed. Most people are very modest and would say nothing. Three minutes later, they would be dead."

"Wouldn't a shiv of that size leave a mark?" Becky asked.

"It is bigger than a needle. It would leave a small scab. But there are many reasons for such epidermal lesions, especially on a person's gluteus maximus region. I doubt it would be noticed as a link to the death."

"What about our good Samaritan?" Flint asked, turning around. "Was he affected by the toxin?"

"Impossible to say for certain," Dr. Takami said. "What we do know is that he is no longer in danger. The object has been removed from his hand, which should heal perfectly. He was very lucky. The puncture did not hit a bone or snag on a tendon. It was, in many ways, a clean cut. We've put him on antibiotics and given him a tetanus shot, just as a precaution."

"Can we see him?" Becky asked.

"Yes, of course," the doctor said with a slight bow.

"Thanks for the information, doctor. It was very helpful. Alright, I'll see Mr. Descarte. The rest of you check in with Dave. He should have a list of suspects now. You put eyes on each of them. If they match the physical characteristics, you pin down their alibi. If this guy is a pro, he won't be an easy catch. Make sure we cross every T and dot every I. And remember, no one does anything alone. We're searching for a murderer. If he tried to kill one person, he won't hesitate to kill you if he's got the chance. Don't give it to him."

Becky didn't mind not seeing Julius Descarte, or JD, or whatever handle he went by. Questioning witnesses was a vital part of any investigation. Without witnesses, crimes could rarely be proven beyond a reasonable doubt. But questioning witnesses wasn't nearly as exciting as questioning suspects. While the odds were against her finding the actual hit man were slim, she preferred that task than talking to the man who had saved Goddard.

The medical center was five levels above their offices, but in the same exact location on the ship. All the group needed to do was catch the nearest elevator. They were in the bullpen with Dave Bannon three minutes after walking out of the med center doors.

"I've narrowed it down to ten people," Dave explained. "The others have physical characteristics that don't fit. Four are too tall, three are bald, the rest have different colored hair, or they're too heavy. I've watched the footage several times. Our guy isn't pudgy."

"Wow, Dave," Jeopardy said. "I never thought you were *that* guy."

"What?" Dave asked.

"You work with somebody, and think you know them," Becky said, nodding at Jeopardy.

"Hey, he can't help it," Logan said, slapping Dave on the shoulder. "Compared to a physical specimen like him, we're all pudgy."

"Oh, ha, ha," Dave said. "You're teasing me for fat shaming. I get it. Very funny."

"It's you and me," Becky told him. "Give those three half the list."

Dave hit a few buttons on his computer, and their cufflinks buzzed with the new information.

"You're both armed?" Logan asked.

It wasn't a dumb question. They were tracking a killer. But it was unnecessary, as regulations required them to have their sidearms on their person during work hours.

"Yeah, we've got our pop guns," Becky said. "I miss my old firearm."

"These aren't properly firearms," Dave said. "They're railguns."

"It wouldn't hurt to arm up," Logan said.

"We go trouncing through the ship with rifles and people will freak out," Jeopardy said.

"Better than one of us getting hurt," Logan said.

He was a protector and Becky knew he would always put himself between the team and danger. But if they split up, he couldn't do that.

"We're just questioning," Becky said. "Unless someone confesses, we're just gathering data."

"Watch your six just the same," Jeopardy said.

They took their lists and headed out. Becky and Dave's first stop was at the cabin of one Raul Garcia. He wasn't home. The crime wasn't yet serious enough, at least on paper, to justify their overriding the security and entering Garcia's private abode. However, they did put a notification alert on the security panel. When the resident returned home, or if anyone opened the door to that particular berth, they would get an alert on their cufflink.

The next name on the list was Reggie Smith. He was home. It was his day off and he had been in the city exploring. After getting questioned by law enforcement, he decided to go back to his berth, which he shared with another passenger on deck fourteen. It might have seemed like they should start at the top of the ship and work their way down, but moving up and down between levels was easy, while moving through the ship was a much longer process.

Reggie wasn't their man. He fit the physical characteristics, but he was much too nervous around the law enforcement officers. He was either a great actor, or it was impossible that he could be a cold-blooded assassin. Becky and Dave had done the job long enough to trust their instincts about people. Reggie was an open book. He had gotten into some trouble as a teenager, although nothing serious. Still, that experience had left an indelible impression on him.

The third visit was to a Filo Manns on deck fifteen. He wasn't home, but his roommate was. A woman of Asian ethnicity stood in the doorway. She wore baggy pants that hung low on her skinny hips. A sweatshirt with sleeves rolled up and cut off along the bottom so that a strip of skin showed. Becky noticed a tattoo on the woman's right hip, but couldn't make it out.

"Hello," Dave said. "I'm Detective David Bannon and this is my partner, Detective Becky Nash. We're with the Special Investigation Unit."

"Far out," the woman said, leaning against the door jamb. "Are you here to investigate me?"

The way she spoke was oddly suggestive. Out of the corner of her eye, Becky watched Dave, who didn't seem like he was accustomed to being the center of a woman's attention.

"Actually," Dave said with a goofy grin on his face. "We're looking for Filo Manns. Is he here?"

"Nope," the woman replied. "It's just me. You can come in if you want?"

Dave shook his head, but Becky interjected. "That would be great, thank you."

"Cool," the woman said.

The room was small, like most berths, just enough room for a pair of individuals to live in, although Becky had never heard of mixed gender roommates. She knew she wouldn't feel comfortable if she had been assigned to a room with a strange man. Becky didn't think of herself as prudish or insecure, but she wasn't the type to flaunt herself about, either. Even with a female roommate, she got dressed in the bathroom and didn't leave her undergarments just lying about.

"How long have you known Filo?" Becky asked, taking charge of the questioning.

"I don't know. How long have we been on the ship?" the woman asked.

"You weren't partners before coming on board?"

The woman shook her head.

"What's your name?" Becky asked as she nosed around the room. Some law enforcement officers felt hesitant to be nosy in a person's private space. Becky had no such qualms. She felt she could learn a lot about a person by the way they live. The occupants of room seven-twenty-one on deck fifteen were either exceedingly private or hiding something. The room was neat. There were almost no personal possessions in sight. Both bunks were empty, yet the beds were made. Everett Goddard had a day maid, but Becky would have bet a year's salary that Filo Manns and his Asian roommate didn't.

"Evie," the woman said as she sat on the lower bunk and leaned back, letting her sweatshirt ride up her stomach and reveal more skin. Her eyes never left Dave Bannon, who stood just inside the door. "You can sit down. Here, sit," she said, patting the mattress beside her.

"What do you know about Filo Manns?" Becky asked, ignoring the invitation to her partner.

"Not much," she said. "Works a lot. He's neat."

"And you aren't lovers?"

"Is that a crime? You must be the love police."

"Your roommate is a person of interest in a serious crime," Becky said. "What can you tell us about him?"

"He's neat," Evie said. "Not bad looking, but probably average. Doesn't talk much. Snores sometimes. He watches Anime in his bunk when he's not sleeping."

"Have you ever heard him mention Everett Goddard?"

"No."

"Does he talk about money or banking?"

"He talks about boring stuff. I don't really pay much attention," Evie said, then pointed at Dave. "But I bet you could tell some stories."

Becky felt like there was more going on than she could put her finger on in the cabin. A glance in the bathroom revealed nothing and she didn't have a reason to override the locks on Filo's personal lockers or the drawer beneath his bunk.

"When will he be back?" Becky asked.

"Hard to say," Evie replied. "Like I said, he works a lot. I don't keep tabs on his schedule." She focused on Dave again, "But if you give me your contact info, I'll message you when he's around."

"That's not necessary," Becky said. "We'll either find him at work or come back."

"Sure... suit yourself," Evie said.

Dave was the first through the door. Becky didn't know him well enough to be certain, but she thought he seemed relieved and wondered if it was because Evie made him uncomfortable or if her suggestive behavior tempted him. The woman was attractive. She had straight black hair that hung down just above her shoulders, one of which was visible through the big collar in her sweatshirt. She was thin, with symmetrical facial features and light brown skin. Becky didn't know if Dave had a type, but he could do a lot worse than the eager woman. But she also thought Evie's attitude was a cover. For what, she couldn't be sure. Was it possible that the assassin had a partner?

"Thank you for your time," Becky told the woman.

"Yes," Dave said. "We appreciate your cooperation."

"For you, I would cooperate anytime."

She stood in the open doorway, once more leaning against the door frame. The pair of detectives headed for the nearby elevator. When they reached it and pushed the button to call it to their floor, Becky glanced back. Evie was still watching them.

"Any chance you saw an Asian woman in the video footage?" Becky asked.

"No," Dave said softly. He was looking down at his shoes. "And no one with her name was on the Trolley."

"Interesting though," Becky said as the elevator dinged and the doors opened. "She put on quite a show."

"I haven't been that embarrassed in a long time," Dave said.

"You didn't seem embarrassed," Becky said.

"Please, don't start."

"What?"

"Just tell me what you got from the place?"

"Nothing," Becky said. "It was sterile."

"Strange," Dave said.

"Yes, it was. I want to know if the ship assigned mixed gender berths to passengers."

"I'll do a search for that information," Dave said, pulling his tablet from a wide pocket in his trousers. "Who's next?"

"Patrick Savage, deck eight."

CHAPTER 33

JEOPARDY, Stu, and Logan returned to the bullpen before Becky and Dave.

"Anything?" Flint asked as he came striding from his office.

"No," Logan said.

Jeopardy picked up Stu's water dish and refilled it.

"How many suspects did you clear?" Flint asked.

"Three with solid alibis," Jeopardy said. "They didn't get off the trolley when Mr. Goddard did. Surveillance shows them getting off the public transit farther down the line."

"And the other three?" Flint asked.

"Two weren't home. The other fits our criteria, but didn't raise any red flags."

"The medical team got DNA hits on the shiv," Flint said. "They're running it now. They'll have to see what matches are from Descarte and the med teams, but it might lead back to our guy."

Jeopardy dropped into her desk chair and leaned back. She was still working through the tension when Becky and Dave returned.

"Anything?" Flint asked.

"Maybe," Becky said. "We found something odd."

"Show us," Flint said.

Dave pecked away on his tablet, and then on the big display screen built into the wall, a face appeared. It was a very plain face, short brown hair, poorly cut, pale white skin and brown eyes.

"Who's this?" Logan asked.

"Filo Manns," Becky said. "He wasn't home, but his roommate was."

Another picture went up on the wall. Evie Norada had on bright lipstick and heavy eyeshadow in her picture. Her hair was pulled back into a ponytail with short bangs. In many ways, she looked completely different from the woman in room seven-twenty-one.

"This is Evie Norada," Dave explained. "Korean birth parents. They moved to Seattle just before Evie was born. They were very involved in the liberal movement that swept through the city. Our records don't have access, but they lived on the streets for a period of time. And there's some indications that Evie was involved in criminal activity. All that was expunged when she turned eighteen and, since then, she's had no run-ins with law enforcement."

Becky picked up the story. "She joined the Marines and was immediately recruited for intelligence operations."

"Which means we know nothing about this woman," Flint said.

"It's all classified," Becky said. "If the assassin had been a woman, my money would be on Evie."

"But the video shows a man," Dave went on. "Which brings us back to Filo Manns. He is a lottery passenger, as is Evie. He has experience in the food service industry. But dig a little deeper and you discover he was a sharpshooter in the military. Served six years, honorably discharged and, since then, he's bounced around. Officially, he's worked as a restaurant consultant."

"And we've got no way to confirm any of that," Flint said. "Dollars to donuts if we could trace the places he's consulted, they would be close to unsolved murders in both location and timing."

"Maybe," Becky said. "There's one more wrinkle in all this. His roommate claims they didn't know each other before coming on board."

"Is that unusual?" Jeopardy asked. "I didn't know mine, either."

"Ship policy is not to mix genders in the two-person cabins," Dave explained, "unless they had a prior relationship and requested to room together."

"Which means what?" Logan asked.

"My gut is telling me that they hacked the system, or someone did," Becky said. "They weren't lottery winners. Someone slipped them in and put them in the same room. Maybe they're working together or, at least, they won't rat the other out. Otherwise, they wouldn't both have been assigned to that room."

"Now all we need is some proof tying them to the murder attempt," Flint said.

"We still need to talk to Filo," Becky said. "I want to get a read on him."

"What are you waiting for?" Flint asked.

"Looking for him on the cufflink locator," Dave said. "He was on the grid when we tried earlier."

"What about the other suspects?" Jeopardy asked.

"Nothing about them raised any red flags," Becky said. "They were either eyewitnesses or had alibis. We'll check them out, but first we want to find and speak to Filo Manns."

"You go," Flint said. "Jeopardy and Logan will go to their berth and get DNA. If they can hack the computer on the ship, they could change their DNA profile. I want to nail this guy before someone gets killed."

"You got it," Becky said

"Come on, Stu, back to work," Jeopardy said.

The four law enforcement officers went to the same bank of elevators, and Dave warned Logan about Evie.

"Watch yourself," he said. "Evie Norada is pretty hard to handle."

"Got it," Logan said. "Thanks for the warning."

Becky and Dave were headed up to Topdeck. Jeopardy, Stu and Logan were going down to deck fifteen. They took separate elevators. After disembarking, they pulled hoverboards from the locked containers between the elevator doors. Jeopardy had become adept at riding on the very back edge and giving her K-9 partner room between her and the handlebars. Stu was calm. He let his tongue hang and turned his face forward as they zoomed down the wide corridors until they came to berth seven-twenty-one.

After buzzing the intercom twice with no answer, they called Sergeant Flint.

"No one is answering, sir," Jeopardy said.

"But her cufflink is pinging at that location," he said. "She might be in distress. Override the door lock."

"Copy that," Jeopardy said.

Logan waved his arm at the control panel, then tapped the icons on his cufflink to force the doors open. The door was only wide enough for one person to pass through at a time. It slid open sideways and the interior lights that were off came slowly to life.

"Looks empty," Logan said.

"Stu, *suchen!*" Jeopardy said, giving the dog the command to search.

He went in, his head rising and falling as he sniffed the air. There was no movement inside. Jeopardy did a quick glance to make sure no one was waiting to ambush them between the recessed beds and doorway. The table was folded up.

"Odd," Logan said as he followed Jeopardy inside. "Their drawers are open."

Jeopardy glanced over and found both drawers open and empty. She went immediately back to the lockers. They were open and empty, too. The only thing that remained was Evie's cufflink. It hung on a hook inside the locker, still powered on.

"They've fled," Jeopardy said.

"I'll call it in," Logan replied.

Before he could, Stu barked. The dog was in the bathroom. They had come for DNA, which could be gathered from a hair comb or tooth brush. But there was none to be found. What was found looked to Jeopardy like ashes. It was a powdery black substance in the dry shower stall.

"Smell that?" Jeopardy asked as Logan stuck his head in the bathroom doorway.

"Yeah, like something burned."

"They must have burned some evidence in here. It's gone. There's nothing but a few ashes and soot."

"Take photos," Logan said. "I'm stepping out to call it in."

He made the call up to their offices, where Flint was waiting.

"That's it," Flint said. "That's exigent circumstances. You three get to Topdeck immediately. We've got to back up Becky and Dave. I'll meet you there."

"Time to go," Logan said.

"Yeah, I heard," Becky said. She and Stu were still in the bathroom. She turned toward the door and saw Logan coming toward her. But something about him was different. He looked sad. "What?"

He didn't speak, but blood suddenly bubbled up on his lips, like a baby cooing. He went down hard on his hands and knees and behind him was a thin woman in all black compression clothing. In her left hand was a short, slightly curved knife that glistened with Logan's blood. She raised that arm and threw the knife with alarming precision. Time seemed to slow down for Jeopardy. The spinning blade was like a hypnotist's pendulum watch. She was drawing her pistol, but she knew she wasn't fast enough. The blade was coming for her, spinning its way through time and space with one certain location, her heart. In that millionth of a second, her entire life flashed before her eyes. Her sad childhood being passed between her parents, always an afterthought. Her years in boarding school, avoiding the bullies, biding her time. The liberation of turning eighteen years old and getting her first real job. Being accepted to the police academy. Walking a beat as a young patrol officer. Discovering that she could work with animals and get paid to do it. Becky's call about joining the

SIU team on the *Colossus*. There were happy memories and sad ones. They flashed through her mind clearly, yet so fast, and she could still see the knife spinning toward her. The pistol seemed too high on her hip. Her jacket was in the way. She felt clumsy and frightened.

Then a heavy weight slammed into her from the side, and everything sped back up to normal speed. The knife flew past her shoulder, cutting the sleeve of her jacket with the razor-sharp edge, then smashed into the mirror behind her. At the same moment, Stu went darting out. Jeopardy saw the assassin's eyes open wide in surprise, then she set her feet. There was something about the way the woman looked that told Jeopardy that they were in real danger. She jerked her pistol free and started to raise it just as Stu jumped toward the woman.

The assassin twisted, her right hand coming up fast and hitting Stu on the side of his head. Her momentum and strength pushed the dog away from her and into the wall. Stu hit with a bone-jarring crash, yelped, then collapsed on the floor. The assassin was turning back toward Jeopardy and drawing another slightly curved knife from a hidden sheath on her black clothing.

Jeopardy didn't hesitate. She pulled the trigger. The plunger on the gun slammed forward, and the bullet shot out. It hit Evie in the left shoulder, spun her around and caused her to stagger backward. The knife came flying so fast Jeopardy didn't even see it. She felt a bump on her leg, then she fired again. Her second shot hit the assassin in her forehead. It whipped backward then forward, her eyes rolling up in their sockets until only the whites showed and then she dropped onto her back.

"Logan!" Jeopardy shouted.

He groaned in response. Jeopardy started toward him; her leg gave out under her. It was only as she fell that she realized the knife was stuck in her thigh. It had caught the outer edge, piercing her quadriceps. Blood was flowing from the wound, soaking her pant leg as the pain roared up into her brain like a pillar of fire.

"Stu!" she cried.

The dog didn't move or respond. Jeopardy's hands were shaking. She was leaning against the door jamb to the bathroom. Her wounded leg stuck out to the side. She put her pistol down and tapped the Law Enforcement folder on her cufflink. A series of icons appeared on the screen. One said *Emergency Response Requested*. She tapped it. The rest of the screen went blank, and it asked if she was sure. She tapped the *yes,* and it asked her to hold her finger on the icon for three seconds. They felt like an eternity. She was weak, shaking, shock was setting in fast, but she held her finger on the icon until it beeped. A second later, a voice came through her comlink.

"Jeopardy? What's going on?" Flint asked.

Her mind was receding, and a memory from her academy days kicked in. "Officers down," she said in a husky voice. "Send medical help."

It was all she could do. The cabin started spinning around her. She leaned over and vomited onto the bathroom floor. Everything was going dark. And in the split second before she passed out, she wondered if the assassin's knives had been tainted with a killer toxin. Maybe she was dying. That didn't seem so bad at the moment. A warm, comforting darkness was rising up all around her, whisking her away from the pain and danger. She might never come back, but in that moment, she was okay with it and let herself go.

CHAPTER 34

BECKY AND DAVE didn't get the emergency call. Only supervisors and medical personnel were informed. The two detectives had tracked Filo's signal to a gap in the grid. It was a dark alley between two tall buildings, sealed off with a metal gate that had been painted with a mural, so that it seemed like a work of art, rather than a restricted area. But the lock on the gate was open and the two detectives followed their suspect into the darkness between the buildings.

It was dark because of the deep shadows and lack of lighting, but also because the building blocked the wireless network signals. And so, as they entered the alley, they missed Logan's distress call and warning that Filo was the assassin. Not that it would have made them turn back, but they would have been more cautious.

In the alley were several large heating units. The *Colossus* had plenty of heat from the engines and power plant, but the warm air had to be circulated. The big air movers hummed and vibrated, blocking out the noise from the city around the dark alley. It was close to everything, yet completely secluded. Even if a person noticed the big gate was unlocked, one glance down the dark alley would scare off most people. They were used to dirty, dingy alleyways where trash collected and the homeless hid from police. The alley on the *Colossus* wasn't dirty. There was no trash piled up, no stinking metal bins overflowing with garbage. But it was dark and loud, and uninviting.

"Looks like a good place to lay low," Dave said, pulling a hand-held flashlight from his pocket.

Becky had one too, a small, metal-shrouded flashlight that could come in handy in a fight. It could also be snapped onto the rail on top of her sidearm. She clicked it on and followed Dave into the darkness.

"Why would someone come here except to hide?" she asked as she drew her pistol and snapped the flashlight onto the sidearm.

"This could be the guy," Dave said. "Either way, this joker is up to no good."

Becky saw a shadow move ahead. She followed it with her light, but couldn't find the source of the movement. What she found, however, sent chills down her spine.

"Dave, don't move," she said, having to speak loudly just to be heard over the roar of the air movers.

"What?" he asked.

She pointed the beam of her flashlight low, and across the alley at the narrow point between two of the big humming machines, was a glimmer of a filament. She had no idea what it was, but it was pulled tight and low, maybe six inches off the ground. She followed the filament with her flashlight. Affixed to one of the machines was a small, round grenade. The string was tied to the pin. She played her light back across the line and found another grenade on the opposite side from the first.

"Moses sandals," Dave said. "Those are grenades."

"Yeah, how do you suppose those got on board?"

"This is bad. We should call for backup?"

"No signal," Becky said. "What do you want to do?"

"What's at the other end of this alley?"

"Another gate," Becky said.

"Can't get around to it before he could slip away," Dave said, thinking through their options. "Why don't you go back and call for help. I'll see if I can flush him out."

"No," Becky said. "We stay together."

Dave gave a low chuckle. "I won't pretend I'm upset to hear you say that."

"Yeah, I know what you mean."

She reached to the back of her belt, pulled out a pair of old-fashioned, metal handcuffs. They were still standard issue for new patrol officers. And while most law enforcement organizations were using plastic restraints, she liked having the cuffs just in case. She pulled them out and laid the cuffs on the ground, then slid them under the filament with her foot.

"To remind us where it's at," she said.

"Good thinking," Dave said.

He stepped over the line first. His focus was on the ground and their immediate surroundings. Becky had to keep watching for their target. She was pretty sure he was in the alley. Why else booby trap it? Her heart was beating hard. She had been just a few steps away from getting killed and that realization was like a vice grip on her mind, pinching down, narrowing her focus. There was just the alley, Dave, and the shadowy suspect. Those three things had become her entire world.

Guns weren't allowed on the *Colossus*, at least not in the passenger areas. There were a wide variety of guns in the storage compartments among the cargo for Secundo. Filo had tried to get a gun, but hadn't been successful. What he had instead was a set of small, curved fighting knives. They were held by the handle and had a ring at the pommel for a person's index finger. The blades came out from the bottom of one's fist and curved slightly forward. They were razor sharp on the inside curve and pointed to a hardened tip.

As Dave came around the next big air mover, Filo rushed him. Becky was well-trained and good at her job. Inside the alley, she easily identified the danger areas. As Dave went wide around the air mover ahead of her, she watched the gap. As the assassin flashed through her beam of light, she fired. The bullet was made of rubber and relied on the transfer of kinetic energy to take down a target. Her shot was online and on time, but the bullet was traveling at sub-sonic speed. It glanced off the assassin's left shoulder with only enough force to make him stagger slightly. Although it did give Dave a split second to jump backward, so that the assassins' first swipe with the deadly knife cut nothing but air.

Most people hesitate in a high-stress moment. They freeze up, unsure what to do. It is a natural reaction. Becky had trained herself to do the opposite. When her first shot didn't take the assassin down, she turned, following his movement and also dashing toward him. Her second shot coincided with his second slash. The knife blade ripped across the back of Dave's left hand. He shouted in pain just as Becky fired. The second bullet hit her target, center mass. It didn't break his sternum, yet it left a nasty bruise and sent him falling backward. He hit the ground hard, his legs flying up, but used their momentum and his hardened core muscles to fling his legs over and rolled into an upright position.

Becky was still coming at him and fired a third shot. There was no echoing report from the pistol, not even the muffled pop of most small-caliber guns. Instead, it made a dull ~Thwock!~ sound. The third bullet hit the assassin on the front of his left shoulder and he dove for cover behind the big machine he had come out from behind. It left his arm numb and he dropped the knife that was in that hand.

"Dave?" Becky shouted.

"I'm okay," he called back. "On your six."

He followed her around the air mover. The assassin was gone. She moved her light back and forth, then up the big machine.

"No, down," Dave said.

She instantly lowered his pistol and light followed. On the ground at the back of the big machine was a slow-moving puddle of blood. Becky would have called for medical immediately, but she knew she had no signal and the threat wasn't over. She moved against the building on the same side of the alley as the air mover. There was about a foot and a half clearance behind the big machine. The assassin lay there, a massive gash on his inner thigh was pumping out blood.

For the next ten minutes, the pair of LEOs did everything they could to save the assassin, but he bled to death. And when they were finally out of the alley, they were covered in his blood.

"I made the call," Dave said. "Medical is on the way."

"Good, you need to have that hand looked at."

"I will," Dave said softly. "But Becky, there's news."

In policing, danger was a constant. One learned to live with it. And death seemed to be always lurking. She had just failed to save a man who committed suicide rather than surrender. It was awful, but seeing a stranger die didn't compare with losing a fellow police officer. They were like family and the only people who really understood what the job was like. It didn't just get hard when she clocked in; the difficulties of policing stayed with a person. They haunted a LEO's dreams and hounded their relationships. They made everything harder, even what a person was capable of believing about God.

And in Dave's voice was the note of news no police officer ever wants to hear.

"What?" she asked.

"Jeopardy's been stabbed, but she's okay. Evie attacked them. Stabbed her leg. Lost a lot of blood, but she'll recover."

"And!"

"And Logan is in surgery. He was stabbed, too, in the back. He's touch and go."

"Oh, God," Becky said, covering her mouth with a trembling, blood-stained hand.

CHAPTER 35

"HEY THERE," Becky said, coming into the room. "Someone wants to see you."

Jeopardy was tired. Everything was difficult. Even shifting her eyes to look at her best friend was wearisome. It had been that way since she woke up. They told it was partly from the blood loss and partly from the morphine. They were weaning her off the strong narcotic, but it wasn't making her feel stronger.

"Stu," she said as the black German Shepherd came into the room.

Becky followed. The big dog bounded up onto a chair beside the patient's bed and bent down to lick Jeopardy's hand, which had only made it as far as the bed railing before she ran out of strength.

"We're so glad you're okay," Becky said, tears streaming down her cheeks.

"Logan?"

"He made it," Becky said. "We just got word. He's still critical, but he's out of surgery and stable. The doctor says he'll make it."

Jeopardy smiled. That was the only news she wanted. Stu was

okay, Logan would be okay and she let the fatigue sweep her away into the darkness again.

Flint stuck his head in the door. "How is she?"

"Sleeping, I think," Becky said, wiping her cheeks.

It had been a long twenty-four hours. Much work had to be done. Reports made and bodies removed. Becky, having fired her gun, had been forced to turn it in and undergo questioning by her superiors. It was standard policing. The *Colossus* didn't have an Internal Affairs Bureau, but Lieutenant Janson had done as thorough a job as any review board Becky had sat under.

No evidence, beyond the actions of the assassins themselves, was recovered. Weapons, yes, including the grenades in the alley. But no correspondence, papers or plans were found. Something had been burned in the bathroom of berth seven-twenty-one on deck fifteen, but it had been incinerated so completely that it was impossible to know what it might have been. There was no luggage, no personal item or even clothing to suggest who the killers really were.

Surveillance footage showed Filo on the trolley with Everett Goddard. The man knew where the cameras were. He always managed to sit where the camera couldn't see his face. But he was there. What was more disturbing was the fact that his cufflink locator didn't always show him on the trolley, when the surveillance footage did. The incident was setting off a total review of the ship's security protocols and passengers. It wasn't even a third of the way into its voyage, and already it was becoming clear that there were real safety concerns.

"That's good," Flint said. "She needs rest to heal. When was the last time you got some rest?"

Becky had taken the time to shower after her long interview. She scrubbed her skin almost raw in an effort to get all of the assassin's blood off. Every time she thought she was done, she found a bit more. It was exhausting, both mentally and physically.

"It's been a while," Becky said.

"Head back to your berth," Flint said. "I'll stay. If anything changes while you're gone, I'll notify you. I promise."

"What about this guy?" Becky said.

Stu was still on the chair, but had his paw on the foot of the bed, and his head was laid across one of Jeopardy's feet.

"I think he's fine right where he's at," Flint said.

Becky nodded. It was true, she was exhausted. She left the hospital room and was making her way through the hall when a voice called to her.

"Officer Nash," JD said.

He was in a nice-looking robe and sitting in a chair in his own room. There was a bandage over one hand. Becky stopped and looked at him.

"I heard about your friends," he said. "I'm sorry."

"Me too," Becky said. "I'm surprised you're still here."

"They wanted to keep me overnight for observation."

"Well, it's morning," Becky said. "You'll get to go back to your cabin soon."

"I was hoping that I might see you again," he said. "Would you let me take you out to dinner?"

Suddenly, Becky felt as flustered as Dave had looked when Evie had flirted with him. She had done it to scare him off, but Becky didn't think that was what Julius Descarte had in mind. In fact, she got the impression he wanted the opposite. It didn't help that he was a handsome man. Tall, with short, neat hair and a beard. He was fit, with broad shoulders and a slender waist. If they had been anywhere else, she would have labeled him as a player and brushed off his invitation. But she found that harder to do at the moment. Maybe it was because she was so tired, but she felt a tingle in her stomach when she looked at him.

"I don't think that's a good idea," she managed to say.

"Why not?" he pressed. "I'm a good guy. And we all have to eat, right? Let me buy you a meal and thank you for what you did for us."

"Us?"

"The ship," he said. "We all owe you a debt we can't repay. But this is a start."

"So, you're not coming on to me?" she asked.

Of course, she knew he was. But she wanted to turn the tables.

"Oh, I definitely am," he said with a charming grin. "You're a beautiful woman. Capable, strong, smart, those are rare qualities to find in one package."

"You are too much," she said.

"Ain't no such thing when it comes to someone like you," he said. "Never too much."

She smiled. It felt good to be wanted. She stepped into his room and looked at him. He looked good even though he was in pajamas and a robe.

"Give me your number," she said. "When all this mess is over, I'll take you up on that dinner."

"Promise?" he asked.

"I promise," she said.

He laughed and gave her his contact information, which she put into her cufflink. Then she left the medical center and made the long journey back down to her berth on deck eighteen. But JD's laugh followed her. It echoed in her mind all the way.

EPILOGUE

TITUS WAS ALONE in a small berth meant for two. It was slightly larger than those occupied by the SIU team. And on the table were a wide array of gadgets that were in various states of disassembly. He was removing the parts he needed and throwing the rest away. His berth had a small mini-kitchen. Soon, he would begin cooking the needed ingredients to make the explosive paste that he would stuff into glass bottles. The explosion didn't have to be big to take down the ship's engines.

On the big entertainment screen was the ship's live information feed. Throughout the day and into the night, announcements ran, along with commercials for the various businesses on Topdeck. At set times, a live news show aired. And, Titus was rewatching the press conference held outside the bank tower on Topdeck. It showed the ship Captain, the Commissioner of Law Enforcement Services, and the man in charge of the investigation squad. Titus kept the unit muted until Sergeant Sawyer Flint stepped toward the podium.

"As you've heard, we stopped an attempt on the life of Banking President, Everett Goddard. It was a team effort, and did not come without a cost. I'm happy to report that all three members of the

Special Investigations Unit who were injured during the investigation are doing well and recovering. In the meantime, we will continue to work, ensuring the safety of the passengers and crew of the *Colossus*. Thank you."

Titus muted the entertainment unit. He didn't need to hear the names of the assassins. He knew them. Evie had been a special friend. Her death was shocking and unexpected. But Titus wasn't building his explosive device to avenge her. Rather, he was fulfilling the contract for which he had been hired. There were powerful people who didn't want to see the colony on Secundo succeed. They had paid a lot of money to ensure that if Filo Manns failed in his mission, that no one from the *Colossus* would ever reach Secundo alive.

"There's no hurry," he said out loud. "No hurry. There is plenty of time."

And time was what he needed. Time to gather the final pieces of the puzzle he was building. Time to plan his delivery of the device... and time to make his peace before he joined his friends in blessed oblivion.

AFTERWORD

Thanks for reading *Colossus*. As an author who writes a lot of stories, I'm always anxious to take a stab at something new. This book stretched me, but I also had a real blast diving into this new world. I love the idea of a contained space, but one so big it is both confining and yet has tons of hidden spaces.

My plan as of this writing is to continue the story. I'm not sure how much of a series the SIU will be, but there are plenty of loose threads to tie up and the door of more adventures is always open.

Please take a moment and leave a review on Amazon or Goodreads. It's a huge help to any author, and I appreciate every single one. Look for book two in the SIU series early in 2026.

12.21.25

ALSO BY TOBY NEIGHBORS

End Times

The Four Horsemen

Surviving Wormwood

Wizard Rising

Magic Awakening

Hidden Fire

Crying Havoc

Fierce Loyalty

Evil Tide

Wizard Falling

Chaos Descending

Into Chaos

Chaos Reigning

Chaos Raging

Controlling Chaos

Killing Chaos

Elder Wizard

Lorik

Lorik the Protector

Lorik the Defender

We Are The Wolf

Welcome To The Wolfpack

Embracing Oblivion

Joined In Battle

The Abyss Of Savagery

The Vault Of Mysteries

Lords Of Ascension

The Elusive Executioner

Gryphon Warriors

Regulators Revealed

Avondale

Draggah

Balestone

Arcanius

Avondale V

Third Prince

Royal Destiny

The Other Side

The New World

Luck Holds

Zompocalypse

Spartan Company

Spartan Valor

Spartan Guile

Dragon Team Seven

Uncommon Loyalty

Total Allegiance

Kestrel Class

Jump Point

Gravity Flux

Modulus Echo

Zero Friction

Planet Fall

Charter

Jack & Roxie

My Lady Sorceress

The Man With No Hands

ARC Angel

Battle ARC

Broken Crucible

Hidden Kingdom

War INC

Carthage Prime

Cronus Team

Skandia Seven

Mercurial

Magnificus Prime

Incursio

Merlin Appears

Runners

Survivors

Infiltrators

Resistance

Conquest

Occupation

Extraction

The Signal

Battle Orders

Base Of Fire

Hard Site

Recall

Evade

Assault

Space Fever

Staying Alive

Fractal Cut

Blast Zone

Action Zone

Covert Infil

Armor Brigade

Havoc Squad

Thunderbird

Ghost Tactics

Quantum Combat

Infinite Threat

Shadow Threat

Evolving Threat

Lingering Threat

Latent Prowess

Gravity Masters

Gravity Storm

Daughter of the Night

Supernova

Artifact

Blood Moon

Renegade

Juggernaut

Retribution

Independence

Sons of Perdition

Iron Man

Brutal Planet

Hell Flyers

Foray

Conspire

Siege

With Pete Garcia

Apocalypse One Percenters

www.ingramcontent.com/pod-product-compliance
Lightning Source LLC
Chambersburg PA
CBHW031556240626
47153CB00002B/531

* 9 7 8 1 9 6 8 1 8 9 1 8 1 *